THEODORE

ELENA M. REYES

SUMMARY

I AM DARKNESS.
I AM SIN.
I AM YOURS.

A truth imprinted onto my skin—its sharp vines digging into my flesh as our bond strengthens with each shallow intake of breath my love takes. Her life is intertwined with the devil, a man who hungers for depravity and death, and yet, I bend my knee for her.

Only her. Always her.

She is mine, and I will kill to protect. Kill to own her.

Gabriella Moore will never leave me. Not by choice or circumstance.

Check out the Spotify Playlist for LITTLE LIES.
Each song has been my faithful companion while I write
this dark and delicious romance.

LITTLE
LIES
playlist

ACKNOWLEDGMENTS

This one's for the girls that love their books dark, crazy AF,
and the heroes a little dirty.

HAPPY READING, MY BEAUTIFUL BABES!!!

Also, a huge THANK YOU to my team.
Seriously, I couldn't do this without you.

Michelle Myers, Ana Rita, K.I. Lynn, C.M. Steele, Marti Lynch, &
Mary B. Moore; you guys keep me going when I lose track of my
goals. You push me to be better, to not second guess myself when I
think I lost my flow. This book was finished because each of you
never let me quit or let my fears of entering a new genre stop me.

I love you all so much and I'm thankful to have you in my life.

XOXO

CONTENTS

TRIGGER WARNINGS

This book contains dark elements that some readers might find triggering. This man is brutal and unapologetic, please read at your own discretion.

Explicit Violence/Death Scenes (Gore)
Large Snakes & Feedings
Explicit Sex
Stalking
Mating Bite
PNR Elements
Blood
Some Primal Play

KING

The act of sleeping has always been special to me. The naivete that even the vilest creatures adapt while their bodies succumb to exhaustion is an intriguing thing.

You have no choice. You're not aware of your surroundings or the danger that lurks around each corner, and it's at that time of day when even the strongest become prey. Weak. Where vulnerability and fear rule as king while those without a moral compass, who thirst for blood more than they do breathing, roam freely and without remorse.

Because at night, there are no rules or societal demands for complacency. No masks to hide behind as I slice a throat clear across from one side to the other and watch my victims bleed. Moreover, in that moment, they see me. All of me—the evil that most ignore while walking down a sidewalk and cross my path—it's all clear to them then, and their expressions always make me smile.

Confusion.

Terror.

Acceptance.

I yearn for those moments. To hear that last gurgle of blood as it rises and escapes the wound, tempting me to cut deeper, to prolong the inevitable fate for those dumb enough to believe good looks and an affluential status in a city as large as Seattle only belong to those who are honest and hardworking.

I'm not a good man. Will never claim to be.

I watch. I hunt. I take.

And right now, I'm reveling at the thrashing sight before me. She's my obsession.

Has always been mine.

Perspiration beads across Gabriella's temples and down her neck, pooling at the base while a whimper passes through full, berry lips. She's the sweetest there. So tempting. So pure *for now*.

"Blood. So much blood," the little beauty whispers in her sleep, her tiny fingers gripping the carelessly thrown sheet across her abdomen and hip, exposing the lovely pair of purple bikini panties covering her mound.

It showcases just enough to tease and taunt as the tight fabric molds over her clit and labia. *She'll fit perfectly in my palm.* Her warmth will soothe the beast residing within who needs a queen.

I push off from my perch against the painting she skillfully made of my home down to the smallest detail and stop beside her bed. With each step closer, my cock throbs. It's hard for her. I'm near the point of praying at her temple for a taste, but not yet.

Today is about her. About celebrating what drew me in the day she crossed my dark path.

With the tips of two fingers, I caress her left leg with gentle sweeps up and down until reaching her knee. She's soft, and her flesh so pliant beneath my touch. It's a heady feeling knowing that I could break her without exerting much force, but it's just as humbling to know that I'll never harm her physically.

Mentally, though, I'll revel as she crumbles into madness. A broken doll.

Because this pretty girl knows me. Our paths have crossed more than once, but where she has failed to remember me, forgetting her is impossible. Will never happen no matter what life we're reincarnated to.

The day Gabriella Moore stepped foot inside my home, asking for help, I found my angel. My perfect prey.

I trace her kneecap and then farther up, pausing where the heat between her thighs kisses my flesh. Even without cupping her pussy, with the tips of my digits just a few inches to the left, it burns me. This need is near maddening and so is the rise of goose bumps across her flesh, showing me without words how much she will always enjoy my touch.

A hard shiver runs through her frame, and I lower my face so our lips hover, not touching as I breathe her in. Tasting her sweetness in the air around us. Pushing myself past rationality, my will is stronger because I know the reward is worth the brief denial.

"Always cherries with a hint of vanilla." Her nose twitches at my words, but she doesn't wake up. If anything, she settles and sighs. Such a lovely sound.

For a few minutes we remain this way, my hand on her skin and her breathing even beneath me while I watch and re-memorize every freckle and luscious red curl on her head. A true ginger, the tone is luminous and one of the first things I noticed about her, the second being her delicate height at only five-foot-one; she's short with an indecent amount of curves for someone so petite.

Soon, I mouth and move down, stopping at the area just above her clit. There, I inhale deeply, and my mouth waters at the heady scent she emits from between her thighs.

It'd be so easy to taste her. To force her will to become one with mine.

"Not motherfucking yet," I hiss out from between clenched teeth and get off the bed, retracing my steps until I'm once again beside the painting. I've tempted her fate enough for one night and need to leave before the fragile tether holding my desires hostage snaps and I bloody her bed.

I survey the room a final time before pausing at her door where a soft scratching sound catches my attention. It's low and the whine accompanying it pulls a low chuckle from me.

That dog hates me, while I find its loyalty admirable.

He's of use to me. I know his weakness, and he will submit.

Looking at her a final time, I bite my lip. "Goodbye for now, pretty girl." And when I walk to the door and open it slowly, revealing myself to her pet, the way he lowers his head and averts his eyes gets a nod of approval from me. I step out, and he shivers. I close the door and he knows his place, following behind me without another sound as I make my way to her studio.

My little artist.

Canvas after canvas fills every inch of wall space, pictures full of color and celebrating life while others depict death and a morbid curiosity. The latter are my favorite.

Blacks and reds and the emotion of grief reach across the finished pieces, and I finger one in particular of a man in shadow. No face can be seen and he's tall, his build muscular as his exposed torso is the focal point.

Not the blood dripping from his hand.

Not the small body on the ground or the other three strewn about in different sections of the dilapidated road where he stands staring at the destruction left behind.

I want this one.

I know how to get it.

"I'll see you soon."

Gabriella

"**G**oodbye for now, pretty girl."

I awake with a start.

Chest heaving. Palms sweaty. With this all-consuming feeling—fear—gripping me in its stinging bonds while refusing to let go.

Because all I see is red. Red everywhere.

Everything.

It's all one shade, and yet depending on the lighting, the tone changes its hue to an eerie reminiscence of blood. This blasphemous and disturbing tint that slides down each corner and object I see, destroying any hint of purity within the four walls my mind is trapped within—where breathing is a struggle and my chest aches from the terrifying memory that feels real.

"Pretty girl."

Inside that room—the same cursed room—and the voice that I've dreamed of every night for the past year as if my mind refuses to escape its dreariness while demanding that I remember each detail vividly. To catalog the representation of death. To embrace its mockery of my sanity.

And I do. Even while lying in bed, fully awake, I'm held inside my mind in an inescapable trap.

With each shaky inhale, I still see the antique furniture with intricate carvings in a black mahogany wood that shouldn't be seen unless under direct sunlight, and yet, in the dead of night as I visit this room, the symbols glare at me. They dare me to ignore the circular carvings with a hidden meaning that I've yet to uncover.

You're awake. Focus, Gabriella. And yet, I can't.

No matter what books I look into while awake. No matter what internet searches I perform, dating back to a time where each house held a crest that symbolized their status, I fail.

No amount of searching or digging provides answers to the questions destroying my mind like a horror-filled movie reel. No matter the days lost behind a screen or sitting cross-legged between shelves in the back corner of a library, stacks of books burying me within their information; I've done it all, but still come up blank.

"Pretty girl."

Taking in another deep breath, I focus on the rise and fall of my chest while ignoring the male voice. I'm begging my lungs to cooperate and my mind to fight this suffocating hold those words have on me when spoken by the rich and gravelly tone. *In and out. Slowly, Gabriella.* However, my body feels as though a heavy weight sits atop my chest, slowly suffocating me.

I'm scared, but curious. Idiotically so.

"I am safe." *Christ,* those three words are hard to say. Each one tastes of lies, and it's a feeling I'm unable to shake.

Glancing at my bedside alarm, I grimace at the glaring numbers blaring across its screen: *3:15 a.m.* Tonight I slept longer than the last five days, but there's no relief for my tired form.

Months reliving this same dream.

Months fighting to shake off this gripping unease that makes no sense, and yet, I know my response holds merit. Something is wrong.

Another deep breath. Another twitch of my fingers as a soft breeze infiltrates the room, and I'm almost grateful for the distraction. Almost. Because next to the flowy white curtains moving over my half-opened window is a painting I've come to loathe even though I'm its creator.

However, today it snaps me back to the present with an invisible snap so hard I gasp.

It's across the bed from me. The first thing I see each day when I open my eyes.

With each stroke of my brush, I added every last detail down to the shade of red split in half with a contrast portraying day and night. Moreover, the opulent decor is full of teasing mockery that pulls me in.

I study it each day after waking up. Cling to this obsession.

Because that's what this is.

An obsession. A need. A compulsion I can't control.

"Why are you haunting me?" No answer, not that I expect one. Instead, I let my eyes skim across the painting, and I do my customary intake of items, placements, and lastly the haunting shade. Yet this time, I don't finish as I pause on a white piece of paper taped to the right bottom corner.

It's small and folded, and my anxiety rises with its presence. The choppy breaths I've fought hard to calm are now a choking sound as air fails to enter my airways and a seductive scent makes its presence known.

It's manly. Earthy. Nothing of mine smells like this, and I'm once again confused. "Am I still dreaming?"

Then there's the note, and it's never appeared in my nightly visits. Which leaves me asking myself *how*; it wasn't there when I fell asleep after popping an over-the-counter sleeping aid. Furthermore, it causes my heart to palpitate with a speed that frightens me.

I'm shaking slightly, and the air in the room seems to have dropped to near freezing.

The blood in my veins turns to ice.

The sight in front of me shifts in and out of focus, only coming back to attention when glass breaks in the hallway outside my bedroom door.

From one extreme to the other, I'm suddenly pushed into a manic *fight or flight*. I become a spectator—watching—while within a disconnected state of mind I scramble off the bed and open the bedside drawer to my left. My gun is there, loaded, and I don't hesitate to pick it up and remove the safety.

The audible click seems loud inside the room, but the harsh breaths escaping my chest drown it out. "It's nothing. Probably Mr. Pickles wandering around."

As if on cue, my dog barks but it's not outside my door. No, his small little warrior growl comes from down the hall inside my home studio where he likes to burrow in an oversized chair that I kept from my one year of college before quitting.

He yips and I'm rushing out the door, ignoring the broken shards I'm walking over. A few cut the soles of my feet, leaving behind a small trail of blood across my wooden floor as I run toward the sound of his fear.

It takes me seconds to enter the eclectic room, my eyes darting around every inch of space, and find nothing. No intruder. No monster.

Instead, I make out Mr. Pickles's huddled form just beneath my easel and stool, paws covering his face while pitiful sounds escape his muzzle. He's shivering—afraid—and my heart clenches at the sight.

Walking across the room, I pause just beside him, bending at the waist to pick up my all-black Frenchie after placing my gun down. His tiny body seeks out my comfort once within my arms, rubbing his face against my chest while I lay a tiny kiss between his ears.

"You okay, buddy?" His answer to my coo is a huffing/grunting sound that any other day would make me smile. Not today, though. I'm spooked; the remnants of my dream, the broken glass, and that note... "Lord, what is happening to me?"

Small dark eyes watch me with worry. Mr. Pickles is trying to convey something, but all I can do is hold him a little tighter and soothe him with light scratches at the nape of his furry neck. It takes him a few minutes to calm, for the shivering to stop, but eventually he does and my breaths now match his.

Quiet surrounds us, a stillness that both soothes and creates a false sense of safety I'm not quick to trust. I do, however, turn around and walk us out of the room, ignoring my bleeding soles while heading back toward my room.

The hall is dark, the only source of illumination coming from a night-light right beside an accent table near the center. Before I'd gone to bed, there was a lovely lamp I'd bought from a second-hand shop and a pictureless frame on the table. Both were made in India; vibrant colors, woods, and glass that stood out against the white backdrop of my walls. Two beautiful pieces that now lie broken, shattered beyond repair across the wooden floor.

"Did you do this?" I ask Mr. Pickles, but the cutie's eyes are closed. "He must've bumped into it and got scared."

It's the only plausible explanation I'm willing to accept. *Then why didn't I hear him hit it? Why didn't he yelp near my door?*

Ignoring the sting of the crunching glass beneath my feet as another piece slices my flesh, I pause outside my bedroom door. The room is brighter now, no longer that low, dimmed light I keep on during my sleep hours because the thought of total darkness creeps me out.

No. Now, it's lit up, and the pitter-patter of rain hitting the windowpane is loud. Eerie.

"Get yourself together and read the note. I probably hit the switch in my rush." *Maybe I also forgot and put it there myself. Maybe I've started sleepwalking, a possible side effect?* "That has to be it, due to my irregular sleeping patterns and new when-needed medication."

My low muttering doesn't wake up the now passed-out Frenchie in my arms, and I place him down on my bed before walking toward the large painting. I can't look away from the neatly folded note. I almost trip in my determined state to reach it, and when I do, a near knee-buckling sensation overthrows my senses when I read the message within, written in a perfect penmanship that is familiar yet foreign.

Everything around me shakes. Or maybe it's me.

And at this point, I don't know.

All I know, beyond the hard pounding inside my chest and the sudden bout of dread, are those four words...

Happy Birthday, Pretty Girl.

Gabriella

Every single muscle in my body tenses, my breathing becoming erratic as I struggle to see anything past those words: *pretty girl*. Because immediately it's *his* voice I hear in my head crooning it, that gravelly timbre that accompanies me every night. It swirls around me, chokes me, and I swallow hard —bite back the screams that want to escape but don't.

Instead, I wheeze. It's the only sound that comes out as reality merges with my dream. For a few seconds, I'm there again and watching the stillness—how the objects glimmer in the darkness, beckoning me to stay.

The blood sings. It also calls to me.

And more than anything, that scares me. Those two words cause my heart to clench while my body betrays me, and I sway as my fingers tighten on the piece of paper. Where I squeeze, it crumbles, which causes my finger to move and expose the two extra letters I'd missed in my freak out.

L. Y.

Pretty girly.

Happy birthday, pretty girly.

Jesus, I'm a mess. And a bit crazy.

Batshit.

Flipping the paper over, I see the familiar stationery and a small laugh slips through my parted lips. It's not in amusement, but concern. *How did I miss her being here?* But more importantly, how did she get in?

"It was just Elise." This causes a different case of unease to settle in the pit of my stomach. That's not the norm for her. Not for someone who needs acknowledgement over her every deed. Moreover, for as much as she annoys me with her pushy need to micromanage and I-know-better-because-I'm-older-by eight-years mentality—trying to make my career hers—she's the only person in Seattle I consider a friend. "Crap! The key. I gave her a key for emergency situations, and she must've used it to surprise me."

I don't know how to feel about that, but breathing becomes easier. Everything does within a few minutes, and after tossing her birthday wishes aside, I crawl up the bed to lie beside Mr. Pickles while ignoring the cuts on my feet. I ignore the blood more than likely staining my sheets while his small body snuggles closer, his cold nose rubbing against my arm.

"Momma's being paranoid again, buddy." He doesn't answer, but he does lick my forearm. "I know. I know." A small headbutt comes next. "A good night's sleep would do me wonders." This earns me a grunt. "Double my dose, you say?"

His silence is response enough, and I half turn, blindly opening the bedside drawer where a bottle of Melatonin and the meds my doctor prescribed sit.

Both are for sleeping. Both will knock me out, but the one I pop the top of will leave me shaky tomorrow. Will make me nauseous, but I dry-swallow two and flip the consequences off.

I'll deal with it whenever I wake up.

"Calm your breathing and empty your thoughts," I whisper to the silent room and close my eyes, forcing myself to ignore the painting and the dream I'll more than likely fall right back into. "One sheep. Two sheep. Three..."

The more I count, the more I begin to settle deeper into my sheets, welcoming the warmth as the minutes tick by and my conscious mind finally begins to rest. One minute I'm awake, and the next I'm sitting inside a mindless abyss where nothing happens.

No dreams. No voices.

Just rest.

———

AN OBNOXIOUS SOUND pulls me from my sleep. It's close and chirpy and stops after a few minutes, leaving me in that half-awake, half-asleep state where it can go either way. But then the damn thing starts again, and I groan, knowing the owner of the ringtone she set for herself won't stop bothering me.

"What?" I say, eyes closed after blindly answering. There's a lot of noise in the background, people having multiple conversations and all centered around one thing: coffee. Not that it surprises me in Seattle where we are all addicted slaves to the roasted bean.

"You're late." Elise's voice comes through as annoyed and I'm not comprehending the why. "Seriously, Gabriella. How could you forget the meeting I set up with the gallery owner on Pioneer Square?"

"Easy. I didn't approve of it." Her snarky tone rubs me wrong, especially after her coming into my home without permission. That key was for emergencies only, not trespassing as she pleases. "Now, I'll be going back to sleep, and I expect an apology next time we see each other. Quit pushing me."

"I'm sorry." It comes out low and meek, something my friend is not. "Pissing you off wasn't my intention, but I know you like his space and wanted to show there. They have an opening coming up,

Gabby, and I want to help you book it before we start the birthday celebrations."

A harsh breath escapes me and I rub a hand down my face, sitting up now that the last dredges of sleep have evaporated. "Okay."

"Okay?" The hopefulness in her tone makes me feel a bit guilty. "Because I'll stall to buy you some time if—"

"The usual place?" I cut her off before quickly pulling my phone away to see the time. It's a little after ten in the morning. *I haven't had six hours of continuous sleep in so long.* "Or the brunch place, Tilikum?"

"Tilikum." She's giddy. Way too bubbly this morning, and I'm wondering how many mimosas she's downed. "I'm craving Eggs Benedict."

"Got it." Without conscious thought, my eyes flick to the painting and skim across it; I'm calm while doing so. Today, right this second, there's no accelerated breathing or sweaty palms. No full-body chills. *Was everything just a lack of sleep?*

"Gabby, you there?"

"Yeah, I'll be there in thirty. Keep whoever comes from the gallery busy until I arrive."

"You're the best!" she squeals, and I can't stop the laugh from bursting through on my end. Hers is excitement, while mine is relief. "Thank you, babes. I know you put up with my annoying habits and humor me with all the shows, but you really are my best friend. I'm like this because I love and believe in you."

"I know. It's why I haven't fired you from this fake position yet." Mr. Pickles chooses that moment to stretch, an annoyed grunt escaping his small body before jumping from the bed and going to lay in a plush doggy bed I keep in here for him. "Which reminds me...we need to talk."

"Uh oh."

"You could say that." Placing the cell phone on the nightstand, I press the speakerphone option and stretch. My muscles feel tight, more than likely from staying in one position for the last few hours, but after a bit they give way to a delicious burn. "But it can wait until after the meeting. See you soon."

"Okay, but—" Elise is cut off by the ending of the call.

"Now, what to wear when you don't feel like schmoozing someone and don't want it to show?" I muse out loud, padding over to my walk-in closet, and then pause because sitting atop the catch-all chair I keep near the door is a gift bag. This also keeps me from checking the cuts on my feet that feel dry, burn a bit from the stretching of skin, but are no longer bleeding, thank God. *There's enough I need to clean before leaving.* But instead of doing that, my focus is on the bag with black and gold polka dots with a large bow in a velvet-like material. "What the hell?" *Elise. That sneaky little pain in my butt.*

My annoyance with her is still there, but I can't deny that I'm smiling at the gesture. I have no living family. No siblings that I know of. No one to celebrate the small and big moments.

No one but her, and I'm enjoying the feeling of being cared for too much at the moment.

In the light of day and after a few hours of solid sleep, I'm beginning to see the gesture for what it is: my friend is celebrating something that I've always ignored in my own loneliness.

"I'm a jerk." The guilt is hitting me now, too. Her pushiness and no-boundary personality isn't coming from a malicious place, and I need to remember this. Be thankful for it. "Wonder what she got me..."

My legs carry me over to the bag and I pry off the bow with care, wanting to keep it. It's pretty, delicate, and the all-black tone shimmers in the soft-white lighting.

Then, I pry apart the tape and pull out what feels like clothes wrapped in tissue paper the same colors as the bag. They're thin and very lightweight. Feels like something I'd normally never wear, but I find myself wanting to today.

It feels right. This garment makes me giggle, and I've yet to see it. *Since when do I giggle?*

Tearing the tissue off, I gasp at the pretty little number in my hands. It's blood-red, leaning a bit more toward a wine color, and in lace with spaghetti straps—a slip dress, and will easily fall to mid-thigh. This type of attire is so far removed from my day-to-day look —almost scarily so—yet I'm nodding as I finger the bottom edge detail where the material is cut to follow the pattern and not a straight line around.

This gives it dimension. Makes it stand out as flirty and fun.

Moreover, I find myself not finding a reason to chuck it toward the back of my closet. I *want* to put it on.

And as I place it atop my bed and walk toward the bathroom, I envision a finished, put-together look. See a different side of me that I've never embraced before. The words also slip through my consciousness without a second thought or hint of fear.

I'm going to be a pretty girl in the crowd.

I TAKE an Uber to the Tilikum Café, not wanting to walk or drive after cleaning my cuts, which were smaller than I originally thought. There was no real damage somehow, and after placing a bandage on the larger one and sweeping up the broken shards, I fed Mr. Pickles and walked out the door. I'm not far from the cafe, but I sit back just the same and take in the scenery around Prospect Street near the Facebook building and acknowledge just how much my life has changed in the last two years.

This area is quaint; it's a beautiful little bite of Seattle that's close enough to the downtown area that I don't miss the hustle and bustle of city life as the water sits nearby and seeing the Space Needle is nothing but a short walk to Volunteer Park. I'm a car ride away from bars, shopping, and killer food—a vast difference from the way I grew up being a ward of the state.

Thank you, Uncle Moore, for leaving me your house and enough money to pursue my dreams.

Never met the man, but I'm grateful for his generous donation. He could've given it away and ignored me as he did all his life, but the gift is appreciated nonetheless.

I couldn't afford to live here or chase the artist dream without it.

"We're here, Miss," the driver says suddenly, pulling me away from my thoughts. "Are you okay?"

Am I? Right now, I feel like I am.

"Sorry." Meeting his eyes through the rearview mirror, I give him a sheepish grin. "Just got lost in my thoughts for a minute."

"No worries."

"Thank you." The phone in my hand vibrates then with the total and tip option on the screen; I accept after rounding out the fare to twenty from a twelve-dollar flat rate, and open the door. "Have a good day."

"You're welcome, and have a pleasant day yourself, Miss."

"I will, after I have some coffee." His chuckle greets my ears before the door closes and he drives off, causing me to smile. Ever since opening that birthday gift, I've felt lighter than I have since the first night I dreamt of that room. *Don't think of that. Enjoy the day and no weirdness.*

A light summer breeze greets me, pulls me closer to the building while it swirls around me, flirting with the lace edge of my dress as it sways across my thighs. Each step toward the door brings a nervousness I'm not accustomed to. I feel as though something important is inside, and it has to be the art gallery offering me a show.

It's not my first anonymous show and won't be my last, but this particular building appeals to me with its three large showrooms and floor-to-ceiling windows with exposed beams. The place is industrial-meets-gothic chic and has a cult following of celebrity clientele that could give me the boost I need to expand to other cities.

Maybe I should officially hire Elise as my manager? The thought disappears just as soon as it comes as a hand shoots out and grips the door handle in front of me. This hand belongs to a man, a well-dressed one with a Piguet watch on his wrist and the decadent scent of cedarwood with a hint of citrus emanating from his larger frame.

He overshadows me. His fingers skim my knuckles right before I look back, and a gasp escapes my lips.

This man is the walking embodiment of trouble.

Gabriella

"Ladies first, Miss...." His voice is close to my ear seconds after I turn to face the door. But more importantly, I'm trying to avoid making a fool out of myself after the surprised noise that escaped at the mere sight of him.

Tall, dark, and handsome on a level I've never encountered before with jet black hair and amber eyes. There's also something about how he towers over me, making me feel dainty when my five-foot-one frame has never been so on display. This man, who has a warm smile and who's wearing a tailored suit—whose skin grazed mine for a second and left tiny sparks behind—easily stands a foot over my head while watching me with interest.

I feel those eyes boring into the back of my head.

I also don't miss the fishing for my name, but I'm lost in concentration on an on-purpose basis. It's a chosen distraction—the need to take a moment and compose myself—yet I'm spellbound by his hand.

On his knuckles, to be precise.

On the tight grip he has on the handle.

How they're white from exertion, and I'm piqued by the elegance in his hold. They look strong, yet his skin isn't rough like someone who works with his hands. However, there's this aura of dominant power that prickles my flesh from the sight.

From his nearness. From a scent that feels familiar for some reason.

His hand flexes, a gentle open and close as he exhales roughly behind me. The warm breath caresses the shell of my ear, and curiosity is a dangerous thing, because for a brief second, I close my eyes and imagine a single finger running down the volume of my neck, pausing near the neckline of my dress.

"Oh!" Another embarrassing sound as a warm hand grips my elbow, and a shiver rushes down my spine. This reaction isn't subtle as every single cell in my body thrums to life and my breathing accelerates. My nipples throb and stiffen, pushing against the thin fabric keeping me from a public indecency charge. *What the hell is wrong with me?* "I'm sorry, did you say something?"

Why is he affecting me so much? No man has before.

I'm finding myself curious about those hands skimming places no one but me has touched and pleased before.

"I did." The hint of amusement in his tone makes me blush, but I don't look back. Instead, I acknowledge him with a tilt of my head and a wave of the hand. I've hit my quota for embarrassing myself today, handsome stranger or not. "Can you take a step back for me, please? You'll get hit with the door otherwise."

"Of course." My reply is breathy as I follow his request, moving slightly back and against a strong chest. There's a small rumble, this low groan that comes from his throat, and I fight back another shiver. This sudden need to whimper for a man I don't know is unnerving and I swallow hard, forcing myself to create space between us. "I'm sorry, did I step on you?"

Not that I'd be able to tell. I can't think past that sound. How good that small moment—his nearness—felt.

Maybe Elise is right and I should start dating. Look at my behavior toward this stranger; it screams needy. How embarrassing.

"Not at all, beautiful."

"What?" Surprise colors my tone and my head turns, meeting his eyes. *Christ,* you created this man to tempt and destroy. He's the literal definition of lust. A weakness I'm all too eager to indulge in.

Striking amber eyes meet my green ones, and my knees grow weak. "Are you okay?"

"Yes." A lie. They tremble and my hand shoots out, gripping onto the lapels of his black suit jacket to steady myself. "I must've stepped on a crack."

"Then let me help you inside." His own hand comes around my waist and steadies me, holding me tucked against him for a second before walking me inside. I feel flushed, the hand now on my back causing goose bumps to rise across my flesh. I'm attuned to his movements, to the ease in which he touches me and guides me through the packed dining room where Elise sits near the back and center at a round table.

For some reason, being here in this moment feels right, a sensation I've been weak to fight against since opening Elise's gift, and more so after slipping on the delicate dress. Moreover, while I'm tempted to wave at her—to get her attention because nervousness seems to be the predominant emotion waging war against me—I don't. Instead, I follow his lead without questioning the end destination.

Maybe he wants to have brunch with me. Maybe he just wants to make sure I don't stumble again and—

"There you are, Mr. Astor!" Elise stands from the table, giving him a wide smile that makes me frown. *How do they know each other?* But more importantly, I don't like the tightness around her eyes when she sees he's with me. She walks toward us, hips swaying from side to side while flicking her blonde hair over her right shoulder. Her smile is for him, though. Her body language screams *look at me.* "You've kept me waiting long enough, don't you think?"

"My apologies." At his words, I move to step aside, but his hand on my back grips my dress. "I lost track of time rescuing a damsel in distress."

"Did you, now?" Her tone is sugary sweet, but there's that tightness again. The tick of her right eye. "What did my girl do?"

"I'm standing right here." If there's one thing I hate, it's people talking about me as though I'm not in the room. It's rude and disrespectful, more so when I didn't ask to spend my birthday talking business or having someone set up plans without my permission. "Now, introductions please."

Both turn to look at me; one with amusement, and the other with a sour expression. I meet her hard stare head on and raise a challenging brow. I may be a softie at times, choosing my battles, but stubbornness is a trait I inherited from someone—they had to have been a master class teacher on the subject.

Elise giggles after a few seconds and reaches for my hand, pulling me to her side where she throws her arm casually over my shoulder. "This little girlish gem you helped out is the painter I've been talking to you about, Theodore. Meet Gabriella Moore."

The urge to roll my eyes is strong, but I bite the inside of my cheek instead while looking away. *Christ, that introduction made me sound like someone's little sister and not the professional artist I am. I take back my interest in hiring her.*

"I know who she is, Miss Scott. You did send her bio and picture with a few samples of her work to my assistant last week." His tone isn't as friendly as it'd been a few minutes ago when we'd been outside, and my brows furrow. I flick my eyes to Theodore and while I find an annoyed expression, the second our stares connect, his eyes soften at the corners and lips tug upward into a small smile. "It's been an absolute pleasure to bump into you today, Gabriella."

"Likewise." And I find myself grinning back while holding up a hand with my fingers extended. "Definitely a top five in my first impression file, Mr. Astor."

"Theodore, please." But then his brow arches, and I find the action sexy. *I truly need Jesus today.* "Is that so? Just top five."

I nod nonchalantly. "You're sitting at a solid three."

"Maybe by the end of today I can slide into the top position?"

"Once we sign that contract, I'm sure she'll be more than happy I set this up."

At Elise's words, I frown and turn to look at her. "Are you okay?"

"Yeah, why?" she asks, but her attention is on Theodore. Her body language is flirtatious, twirling a piece of blonde hair around her finger while cocking a hip out. I'm reminded of the halls of my high school and every time a girl crushing hard stood near her obsession. *And she's older than me.* "But let's all sit down and order. We have much to discuss."

"Lead the way." Theodore waits for her to turn around and then winks at me before tilting his head in her direction, silently asking that I walk ahead of him. The simple act makes my cheeks feel warm and I quickly follow Elise, trying to calm down my blushing before taking a seat to her left. Not that it lasts long because Mr. Astor takes his place beside me while leaving two empty chairs between himself and Elise, something that makes my friend frown. "My assistant, Tero, will also be joining us this morning. He'll be here shortly."

His explanation doesn't appease her, but she keeps that smile bright. "Of course. Should we wait, or—"

"I'm here." All eyes turn toward a younger man, more in my age range than theirs, that takes one of the empty seats while placing a portfolio bag atop the other beside him. He's pale with nearly-white blond hair, but it's the eyes that are striking in a shade reminiscent of pastel blue. So clear. So expressive. "My apologies for the delay. I was stuck behind a small fender bender that forced the two-lane road to become a total standstill."

"No worries. We were all running a bit behind schedule," I answer while picking up my menu, perusing the choices even though my eyes keep coming back to their *fry up,* which I've had more than once. It's just what I need after the rough night and...

That's when I notice that for once, I'm not nauseous after taking the prescribed sleeping aid. I have no stomachache or a migraine. No dry mouth with a sensitivity to light.

Did I confuse the Melatonin for the harsher stuff? Normally food would be the last thing on my mind after waking from a deep sleep like that.

"...isn't that right, Gabriella?"

"Run that by me again, please."

Elise's nose flares a bit. "That we are interested in taking the opening night for the summer series the Astor Gallery hosts every year. It's going to be your first public appearance, and what better way than to come out—"

The blood in my veins pulses with ire. "No."

"Were you not aware of her request?"

I ignore Theodore's question and instead narrow my eyes at Elise, who has the audacity to seem taken aback. "Bathroom, now."

"Gabriella, let's—"

"Elise, I will not repeat myself. You have two minutes." Turning my attention to Theodore, I give him a forced smile. "I apologize, but it seems my friend has given you the impression that I will be attending the show, and that is not feasible. I am anonymous for a reason and will stay that way. If that isn't something you're interested in, please let me know and I'll apologize ahead of time for wasting your time."

"No apologies needed. I thought ahead and just have a standard contract with me today. But once we agree on the terms, I'll have it ready for your signature in less than twenty-four hours."

"Smart man." At my words, his lips quirk up at the right corner into a devilish smirk that both comforts and simmers the anger within. Without conscious thought, I find myself leaning over and placing a hand on his forearm, and his muscles tense beneath. They flex and my chest rises and falls rapidly, his scent pulling me in closer by an invisible thread that dominates my senses and bends my will. "Your rank just moved to number two."

"Would you believe I was a Boy Scout?"

"Not really." Theodore just doesn't seem the type to go camping and work toward badges while following directions. The aura surrounding this man is confusing: good and bad. Holy and evil. "Unless you were the one giving orders."

"Very astute of you." His long pointer finger traces across the top of my hand and then around the underside of my wrist, lingering on my pulse point. "I've always been authoritative—a prepared man—but more so when it comes to something I want to acquire. To keep."

"Should I be afraid?" Amber eyes settle on my green ones and hold me captive.

"Of me? Never."

THEODORE

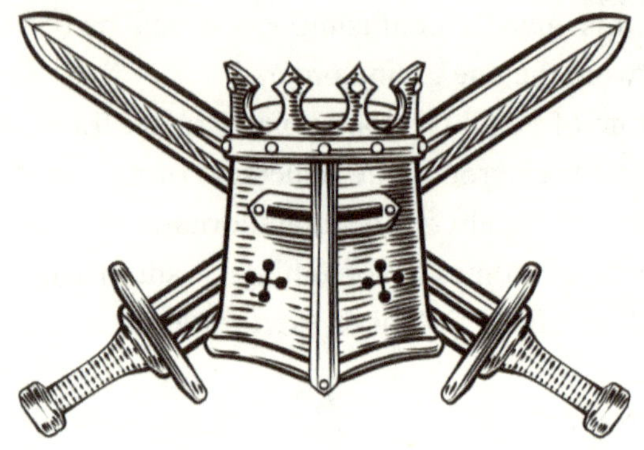

Gabriella is simply stunning.

Breathtakingly so.

She has the kind of beauty that's natural—dripping with a hidden sweetness meant to entice even those devoting their lives to sainthood. It's there in each fiery strand of red hair and the gem-colored eyes that are currently glaring at her manager, or at least who presented herself to my office as this unique talent's representative. The same woman who now refuses to go have a word with Gabriella and instead chooses to study the menu with in-depth concentration.

It's all fake, and I'm not the only one who sees this.

"Can you please answer my earlier question, Mr. Astor?" Gabriella's features relax when she looks over, her blood-red painted nails tapping twice on the tabletop. "Tell me what you need from me."

"Please remind me, Miss Moore." I won't deny nor apologize for finding her beautiful. I'm neither blind nor a monk, and more than one man inside this room has taken notice of her as well. It's there in the curves I had the pleasure of holding against my body, her heat searing my skin through layers of clothing, and yet, I felt her as if skin on skin.

So warm. So soft.

But then again, I've imagined her just like this for a while. More so after her photo landed on my desk, connecting the dots between her and the anonymous artist quickly gaining a following and the possibility to work together. However, the portfolio sent over didn't do her or her artwork any justice. Because I know all about her pieces, own a few from showings she's done over the last year at smaller galleries downtown, and what was sent to me isn't her.

No. They actually looked nothing like what I know she's capable of.

Gabriella's work is provocative and edgy, not basic or unimaginative. She's not flowers with the silhouette of a woman forcing femininity into a sexual box. She's more hard strokes and deep colors, reds with black and a touch of gold—abstract or symbolisms are her area of expertise.

It fits her.

Wild. Free. Dark.

"So will you humor me?" I ask just as the server comes over with a carafe and a questioning glance around the table. No one answers, waiting for Gabriella to decide, and her nod makes me smile. The young lady serves everyone a cup silently and when done, I signal to my menu to say I'm still looking. She walks away and I look at Elise first, taking in her over-bleached hair and see the intentions in her eyes clear as day before returning my attention where it belongs. I've met people like her before, and crooked intentions never stay hidden for long. "Thank you."

"None needed. I'm thankful for the opportunity to discuss the possibility of working together." Her cheeks warm up a bit, and she fingers the neckline of her dress, a subconscious act that makes her more attractive. "But I'll still need a minute with Miss Scott, if you don't mind. We won't be gone for long."

"Of course."

"Gabby, we can discuss this later. No bad vibes on your birthday." Elise's interjection doesn't come off good-naturedly, and Gabriella notices this. After taking a single sip, she places her coffee mug down with a bit of force, and the people to the left of us look over.

There's a furrow between her brows now that I want to smooth over with the tip of a finger, and then trace the contour of her cheek before cupping her chin and kissing the swollen lips the ripe color of berries that have been tempting me since our encounter outside. Her green eyes are blazing, her body language clearly upset, yet she breathes in deeply and waves over the waitress who's been hovering nearby.

"Are you ready to order?"

"Yes." Gabriella hands the young woman the menu. "I want the fry up, while she'll have the Eggs Benedict."

"Perfect." The waitress's attention turns to my assistant with a blush. "And you?"

"Same. Fry up will do."

"Okay."

"Nothing for me. I've already eaten."

"Would you like me to get you some fresh coffee instead, or something else?"

Mine has gone untouched so I nod, pushing the ceramic cup toward the center of the table. "An orange juice will suffice."

"I'll go put those in and be right back with your drink."

Once the waitress is gone, Gabriella turns to look at me. And I love it. Her attention. "We could wait if you want, and go through the contract first?"

"Very thoughtful, Miss Moore, but what kind of man would I be if I made you starve on your birthday?"

There's that hint of a blush again. So pretty. So innocent.

"To be honest, not a very nice one." At her response, I chuckle. *Beautiful and sassy.* "But I also understand that you are a busy man and this isn't your only stop for the day."

"It isn't."

"All the more reason to—"

"Let me buy you breakfast and kick off your birthday celebrations."

She nods and then takes a sip of coffee. "You only turn twenty-one once."

"Happy Birthday, Miss Moore," Tero says from beside me, holding his own cup up in salute. "I hope it brings you joy, love, and *peace*."

"Thank you."

"Add to that a showing at such a prestigious gallery, and Gabby has the kind of life most would kill for."

"Indeed." It takes everything in me not to glare at her friend. Something isn't right with her, the backhanded comments showing her jealousy—the desperation to be the center of attention. "But Gabriella isn't getting a handout from me, Elise. On the contrary; I've seen her work and have heard the admiration some of the most respected in the community have for her, especially her lack of need for constant validation from her peers or art enthusiasts. That shows maturity and confidence in her pieces. Miss Moore knows her worth."

"That's very kind of you to say..." Elise pauses, but I shake my head before she continues digging herself a bigger hole.

"It's not. I'm merely stating a fact." Holding a hand out toward Tero, I wait for him to place a file in my palm, and a few seconds later when he does, I put it next to Gabriella's coffee mug. "My plans for the exposition are big, Miss Moore, and I will be demanding, but I believe that this business relationship can be more than beneficial for the two of us. You can go ahead and go through the file, or as much as you can while we wait for your meal."

"I can read the files, but I'd much prefer to hear your thoughts and what you'd need from me." With two dainty fingers, she traces the top of the manila folder and levels me with a serious stare. No playfulness, and I find her business face quite adorable. "What part of my soul are you looking to uncover?"

"Spoken like a true—"

"Mr. Astor doesn't have time to detail a plan out, Gabriella. Read the files and sign." Elise huffs out while I grit my teeth at her blatant disrespect and bite back the retort that sits on the tip of my tongue while she's giving me what she thinks is an apologetic expression and Gabriella watches us with uncertainty. Moreover, had the little beauty not been sitting right beside me, I would've put Elise in her place long before now. I have no patience for the kind of woman I know she is. "Don't play into the poster-child syndrome of a temperamental artist when he's doing *you* the favor."

"I'm going to ask that you either remain silent or leave, Miss Scott, as you have no stake in this matter. You are neither employed by my employer nor Gabriella, and are hindering this meeting." Tero's voice comes across as a low hiss, his posture a little imposing, and I shake my head. This is neither the time nor place to lose our cool, even if Elise is becoming rather obnoxious in her pursuit of importance. "Please let them speak, as at the end of the day, those are the two names that matter in the contract."

"How dare you—"

"Enough." It leaves me on a low growl and all three at the table pause, not a sound or movement from any of them. My glare settles on my assistant and Elise, but I can't help but soften my expression when my eyes meet hers. She looks a bit scared and a lot embarrassed and to me, that is unacceptable. "Please accept my apologies, Miss Moore. It seems hunger has made those at the table a bit pushy."

"Apology accepted." Her voice is a bit shaky, but I'm proud of the way she squares her shoulders and meets my stare head on. No hiding. "We'll leave it at nothing more than a weird morning meeting."

"Thank you." Our server chooses that moment to drop off my juice and I smile, shaking my head before she has the chance to ask if we need anything. "And as for your question, I want it all. The beautiful and ugly. The smiles and tears. Your blood on each canvas."

"That's a bit grandiose while being vague, Mr. Astor. I'll need more than that." If she's surprised by the request or my wording, Gabriella lets neither show. Instead, she takes a sip of coffee while eyeing me over the rim with the smallest hint of amusement dancing in her eyes.

Tero chuckles beside me at her quick wit, while I fight back my own amusement. "My vision for this season is the jungle of sin, with a macabre theme. I want to highlight the seven deadly sins through your eyes as the main attraction, Miss Moore." She's intrigued, her smile widening, and those pearly whites bite softly into the plump bottom lip. *So beautiful.* "You will have the top floor with the glass dome as a roof and our lighting department at your disposal. The exposition will be held in the dark with those walking the show following each piece by the faint light highlighting each."

"A dark maze?'

"More like a black hole." I can almost see the wheels turning in her head; it's there in the drumming of her fingers and the purse of those damn lips that are driving me insane. *Just one bite. That's all I want.* "Now, tell me, Gabriella. Is this something that intrigues you?"

"You could say that." Shifting in her seat so she's fully facing me with her knees touching my chair, she giggles and the sound is enchanting. Distracting. "I have the worst obsession with serial killer documentaries and cult mass executions. They're morbid, I know, but my mind can't help but draw my own conclusions on each crimi-nal...human nature, I guess, but it's fascinating to hear the stories from their mouths or those who were present at the time."

Our server chooses that moment to deliver their food, placing down each hot plate and then refreshing the coffees that are either lukewarm or empty. Without talking, she makes sure they have what they need and then walks away, smiling down at Gabriella who's the only one that thanks her.

Elise huffs once the woman is out of earshot, stabbing her fork while sliding her knife through the yolk of her poached egg. "That's sick. I just don't know how you can watch—"

"The same way you can spend hours at the mall while buying crap you don't need." Gabriella's grin is saccharine sweet while holding her fork toward her friend. "You just do and enjoy the time without judgement from me, so equate it to that."

"Spoken like a true artist." Tero nods his approval at her response before digging into his meal. And while they eat in silence, I open the file and place the first page in her direct line of sight, blocking it from view from Elise behind the carafe of water left by the waitress.

Our contract wouldn't need endless pages of information with hidden clauses to protect myself or my business, the one of many. No. Not with her. I'm leaving it open for her without a single noose tying her to my gallery unless she wants to be, but the money is detailed and fair with a timeline I require as non-negotiable.

Seven paintings.
Two months.
An entire summer at my disposal.

Gabriella

S*even paintings.*
    Two months.
    An entire summer at my disposal.

As my eyes skim down the few and detailed lines of the contract, I can't help but ask myself why? Why is he offering me a five-figure advance with another hefty sum after opening night?

Then, there's the timeline and the limited number of hours I'll have. I'm not someone who does well with deadlines; I like to fly by the seat of my pants and paint as the creativity hits. I've never done a show in this fashion with such a limited amount of time between signing the contract and delivering each piece.

Can I do this? My eyes go to the advance and it's tempting—too lucrative to deny when most in my position don't get the chance to show for the Astor galleries, much less have the owner personally offer the exclusivity of the top floor with its glass ceiling and their private clientele who attends these functions.

The notoriety alone gives me goose bumps. Anonymous or not,

the Astor name is one of wealth and affluence—it opens the kind of doors I've dreamed of in the past but never had the opportunity to walk through. He owns and oversees each of his galleries worldwide and is known to broker deals for politicians and those with obscene amounts of money looking to add an original piece from some of the greatest minds to pick up a brush.

"What are you thinking about?" Theodore's voice cuts through my mental giddiness, bringing me back to the present where all eyes are on me. Heat rises to my cheeks just as my palms begin to sweat. "What do you need to make this happen? Name your price."

"Three months," I blurt out instead, and he merely raises an amused brow. Clearing my throat, I will my breathing to remain calm and stray my eyes toward the paper once again. "What I am trying to say is that for the amount of pieces you require and all of them being new, I'll need the extra thirty days. There's a concept already forming in my head, but I'm also realistic, and while excitement is a heady motivator, I'll need more time."

"Done." At Theodore's quick response, I snap my eyes to his and find them watching me intently. "We aren't due to show this exposition until mid-August so it won't affect us really, but we will need your help with the lighting setup. We will just use mock pieces until yours arrive...is that something you can agree to?" My nod is his answer, and those smoldering amber eyes look toward Tero who's taken the folder and is busy amending it by hand. "Anything else?"

"You do understand that I will attend opening night, but not as the artist. My name—my legal name—is never to be leaked at any point, or I will sue."

"Gabriella!" Elise hisses out, her tone low but full of a fury I ignore. "You can't—"

Theodore's glare is enough to silence her rant before it begins. "If you interrupt us again, I will ask you to leave, Miss Scott. Understood?"

"Yes." Low. Meek. Yet, the hold she has on her fork displays the fury simmering beneath the surface. "It won't happen again."

"Good." Grabbing the papers from Tero who's finished, Theodore places the sheet once again in my line of sight. And damn them, I almost laugh out loud at what greets me because in large and bold letters it states: ***Gabriella Moore will remain anonymous and will stay that way or the owner will fine himself. Stipulation is non-negotiable.*** "Does that appease you? If you say yes, I will have the contract re-typed and sent over via courier to your home or your place of choosing for signature tomorrow morning."

"It does." My poker face is strong, but inside I'm squealing like a prepubescent tween at a boy-band concert. *This is really happening.* "And you have yourself an artist for the show."

"I never thought otherwise." Removing the file from the table, he passes it back to a waiting Tero while nodding toward my plate. "Now eat. Everything else can wait until tomorrow."

"Thank you." And then silence falls on the table as we eat, eyes staying on the plates even though I know Elise is pissed. Her posture is stiff, the skin around her eyes and mouth taut.

"Well, that most certainly hit the spot this morning," Tero says when I push my plate away, having eaten every last bite, which isn't the norm for me. To be honest, this is the best meal I've had in months, and I feel great. No nausea or discomfort of any kind. *Is there such a thing as birthday luck?* "Thank you for allowing us to eat with you this morning, Miss Moore."

"Please don't. I should be thanking you."

"You should be," Elise says under her breath, and by the way the man beside me tenses, Theodore heard her. "Now, if that's the end of this meeting, I'd like to steal the lucky girl away for a mani/pedi and some much-needed shopping."

"Then we won't hold you." Theodore stands first, extending a hand out toward Elise who eagerly shakes it, leaning toward him while slyly adjusting her top—exposing a little more skin. He doesn't look, but Tero does and his expression is one of disgust until he notices I'm watching and schools his features. *The only two men I've ever met that are immune to her charms.* Mr. Astor pulls his hand back and then holds it out to me, waiting for me to take it and I do so after a second, letting him tug me gently to my feet.

We are close. So close that his warm breath skims across my forehead and I take a step back, creating the space needed so I don't embarrass myself. Because this man smells good. He feels good this close, and that makes me nervous.

More than.

Taking in a deep breath, I hold it for a second and then offer him a smile. An honest one. "Thank you so much for everything today. This opportunity means the world to me, and I promise to not disappoint or be difficult. If you have any questions or doubts or just need to see the progress, please don't hesitate to call me."

"The pleasure is all mine, Miss Moore." Theodore brings my hand to his lips and kisses the middle knuckle, lingering there for a second while his chest expands once quickly. Then, he lets go and I feel a coldness sweep across every limb and settle on my chest. *The hell is that?* Moreover, I'm so lost in that thought that I almost miss what he says. "...need that phone number to contact you later today regarding the contract."

"You can always call me."

Once more he ignores Elise, this time holding his hand out. "Your phone, please."

"Of course," I say instead of telling him a business card would be fine, handing over the device that's almost always on silent. Especially when working. Then there's the tiny spark I feel when our fingers touch, this sensation that crawls up my arms and to my chest, settling into a warm buzz. *What is that?* A question I swallow back, turning my attention to Tero for a second who has a smug look on his face. *This is getting weirder by the second.*

The device pings in his hand before he passes it to me. "Expect a call around nine tomorrow, Gabriella. We'll meet where it's convenient for you."

"No need to go out of your way. I can meet you tomorrow at the gallery—"

"No more business talk on your birthday. Tomorrow, we'll agree and sign...sound good?"

I'm nodding before he's done talking. "Thank you for the opportunity."

"Remember what I said, Miss Moore. Pleasure is always mine." With that, he steps back and at once, I miss the feel of him close. And more embarrassing is the smile on his handsome face, as if he somehow knows my thoughts that are inappropriate and confusing and dangerous for my psyche. He's a danger to my tranquility. "Please enjoy your day in that pretty dress. The color suits you perfectly."

Theodore nods at Tero, who drops a few bills on the table that more than takes care of brunch, and walks away without another glance while I'm left blushing. I finger the lace edge, and there's an urge in me to thank Elise for the dress but I don't.

Something is telling me to remain quiet. To wait.

Neither man addresses Elise before leaving nor has she been included in any future plans, something I'm sure she'll complain of soon enough.

Moreover, she does the moment they step through the cafe's door after coming to my side, her grip on my arm tight. "How could you ruin this for me? After everything I've done for you."

"What have you done for me?" I ask, because my mind is reeling and her reactions today don't make sense. Yes, she's my friend, but I've never asked for anything. I've never used her. Instead, Elise has used my name and inserted herself in my career without asking.

Pushy. Judgmental. Yet, I've taken her as is and never once made her feel anything less than my best friend.

"Who set this meeting up?" Her tone is acerbic, her face pinched tight. "Who did the homework and flirted with his staff for insider information—"

My head turns to her as I pull my arm from her grasp. "Did I ask you to?"

"You'd never get into a place like this without my help."

"That's not the answer to the question I asked, Elise." The table near us looks over, but I ignore the curious looks and maintain a neutral expression. "Because we both know I didn't. We both know I'm not a person who flaunts or likes to attract attention—"

"Could've fooled me with what you're wearing." Those seven words make me freeze as the blood in my veins turns ice cold. "Since when do you wear lacy dresses and show off skin? You knew who was coming and tried to show me up. How could..."

The rush of happiness is gone sooner than it came, and I'm left repeating her words over and over again. Not because I'm upset over her accusation or the embarrassing behavior I'll deal with later, but because the garment I'm wearing—the lacy gift left inside my home, in my room—didn't come from her.

Then who? Who was in my room?

"I have to go," I say and rush out, leaving her to her rant while my feet carry me out the cafe's door and down the block before I register what's happening. I'm walking aimlessly, without direction, but the tears rushing down my cheeks I feel. The tremor in my limbs makes this real. "No one else has a key. It's impossible—"

"Miss Moore, what's wrong?" a male voice calls out before a hand grips my elbow, pausing me in my tracks. The hold isn't tight or painful, but I can't help the terrified scream that rips from my throat as my breathing accelerates. All the calm from before the meeting is gone. All the hours of rest have amounted to nothing as my body sways and knees falter. "Hey. Hey. Please, look at me, Gabriella." My eyes close instead, head shaking as this unadulterated fear sets in deep. "It's me, Tero. Theodore's assistant."

"Theodore?" I manage to choke out, stumbling and falling a bit into him. For some reason I can't explain nor have the capacity to question at the moment, I trust Theodore Astor and take in a deep breath. *I've gone insane.* "Where is he?"

Tero helps me stand upright, but stands close enough to catch me if I lose my balance again. "Can you look at me, please? I need to make sure you're okay." It takes me a minute, but I manage to meet his stare and force out a smile he isn't buying. Tero's near pastel-blue eyes watch me with concern. He waits until I nod to answer my earlier question. "He left for a meeting across town while I stayed back to pick up pastries from a bakery a few shops down."

"I'm sorry to keep you. Please—"

"Hush, now." Pulling his phone from his satchel, he slides a finger across the screen and then types out a quick message. The device pings a few seconds later and for a brief moment, I catch a sudden tilt of his head and the flaring of his nose while those unique eyes slide across the street and then down to the opposite end. "You're safe. Understood?"

Had this been any other time, I would've thought the action was sweet, but my concern is ever present. Someone had been inside my room. Someone could've hurt me.

"I'll be fine in a minute."

"Liars never enter the kingdom of Heaven." He raises a brow, expression a bit mocking but not in a disrespectful way—more like he's trying to make me laugh, and he succeeds as a giggle slips through at the absurdity of it. "That's more like it. No freaking out on me."

"Sorry."

"What scared you, Gabriella? Do you need help with something?"

"I think God will forgive me this one time," is my answer instead. I'm deflecting, and we both know it.

"Would you rather I call Theodore?"

"No."

"Then?" Another ping, and this time he shows me the message.

Get extra and bring her with you. ~Astor

"What is that supposed to mean? I'm not—"

"It means *you* are going to come with me and pick out an obscene amount of bakery treats and then take a ride with me across town. We have much to discuss, Miss Moore. Your fear being one of them."

"And if I say no?" This is crazy. I'm even crazier for considering tagging along, especially with the butterflies that took flight at the text message his boss sent. "Then what?"

"Then I'll let your blonde friend know you are with me. She's just stepped out of the restaurant and is looking—"

"Deal."

"How do you pick?" I mutter under my breath, my eyes traveling from one edge of the glass display that holds my one true weakness: chocolate. In every style and degree of sweetness, this place is like the mecca for cocoa worshippers, and I'm left standing with parted lips. To some, it might seem a little obscene. I am near panting, but if you love this decadent food like I do, you get it. "There are just too many. I'm—"

"You don't, Gabriella." Tero is standing at another case to my right, this one holding nothing but fruit tarts and macarons. He eyes each, simply pointing at the ones he wants while an older lady boxes up the purchase with a smile. So far she's put together three boxes of his chosen treats, the embossing glinting in gold after it's closed. "Get what you want. No regrets."

"No regrets?"

"No regrets. Go nuts."

"If Mr. Astor gets mad, this is on you." In front of me there's another woman, a bit younger and just as excited to help. "I want one of everything in this case and the entire Millionaire's Cake you have on the other stand."

"I'll get those packed, and I have a little something extra for you. It's new and not on the shelf, but I think you'll really enjoy it," she says and gets back to work, diligently filling my order while customers wait behind us. The place is pretty full, all tables occupied except the booth at the back with people munching and sipping their coffees, while we're in and out in minutes.

I also find myself following Tero to a black Audi parked not far from Hortencia's Delights. "Give me one second," he says, walking toward the back driver's side door and after pressing a key on his fob, opens it and places our packages on the seat. My six to his three, and he didn't bat a single eyelash at the price, nor was I allowed to pay for my purchases. Once he's done, like a gentleman he comes to the door I'm standing in front of and opens it for me, ushering me inside. "We have a bit of a drive, and Mr. Astor is waiting on us."

"Don't I get a say in this?"

"Convince me once I'm behind the wheel." He winks at me before coming to the driver's side and slipping inside, and it doesn't come across creepy or lecherous. On the contrary, there's something about him that puts me at complete ease. "Now, you have until we reach the end of this street before I have to make a turn to change my mind about dragging you out to a location my boss is looking to buy."

"One, that sounds incredibly boring." I tick off and then count the next before he can counter my honest answer. "And two, it's my birthday, and I would rather be lazy and eat the chocolate in the back. Honestly, Tero. Let a girl live through the cocoa bean diet while Netflix and chilling."

"Okay," he chokes with a laugh, covering it quickly behind a cough, "that was compelling and even somewhat on a soul-moving level. Very solid arguments."

"And?" I wave my hand in the air, no patience in me whatsoever after the weird morning I've had. Not to mention I'm also needing to change my locks before the day is through. "Do I win?"

"You do, but don't make a habit of getting me in trouble."

"I'd never." The side eye he gives me lets me know he's not buying the mock outrage, but it's the sudden serious expression that makes me apprehensive. "What?"

"What scared you back there?" His voice is low, and yet to my ears, it's as if someone shot a cannon. My reaction is automatic, and I shrink back, leaning heavily on the passenger side door while avoiding his gaze. The buildings in my line of sight begin to blur a bit after a minute of silence and the car jerks forward hard; Tero's pressed down on the accelerator harder than needed. "Tell me. We can help you if you're in trouble."

"We?" I ask, still not turning to look over. The last thing I want is for Theodore to know he's working with someone who is unstable. "Who is this *we*?"

"Mr. Astor—"

My head jerks toward his, my eyes narrowing. "You will not speak of this to him."

Those pastel-blue eyes narrow, his head tilting in the same manner he did outside of the building where he found me. "What is the *this* I will not speak of?"

"Just a disagreement between friends."

"Just a disagreement?" he parrots, his expression unbelieving. "You seemed scared, not angry, Gabriella."

"She was angry and said something hurtful." I shrug my shoulders, going for nonchalance, especially since I want to go home. Today has been eventful enough for me. "I'm probably overreacting to it and we'll be fine by tonight."

"If you say so." His tone says he doesn't believe me.

"I do." Turning toward him again, I plaster a small grin on my face. "Now that you have an understanding of the inner workings to the female bonding insanity, how about you take me home? I'm itching to start the planning phase of my exhibit."

"On your birthday?"

"What better day than the one I get to make the choice in how I spend it?"

"Touché." Tero laughs; the sound is loud and boisterous and a bit strange. It comes off as a wheeze and I join him, not stopping until tears spring to my eyes and I snort. Then he's laughing at me, which creates a weird cacophony inside the enclosed space, and I can't breathe by the time he's slowing down. "You are something else, Miss Moore. Never change."

"I promise *if*—"

"I take you home," he finishes for me, pulling over to the end of the street and putting the car in park. The phone, which he'd put in one of the cupholders, is now in his hands and his thumb is flying across the screen as he types a message, hits send, and then sends another. For two minutes we sit in silence until the device pings and he shows me the response.

> As you wish. Please enjoy your day and the chocolates. ~Astor

A second one comes through before he can close his phone.

> No work is allowed either. ~Astor

The latter I give an inner eye roll to and instead smile. "Thank you."

"None needed, birthday girl." Pulling off from the curb, he takes a familiar route toward my home after I give him the address, and I close my eyes. There are things that don't make sense, but I'll decipher them even if it kills me. Elise's actions, the dress, and my dreams all have to mean something, and I plan to put an end to this mystery. I can't go on like this. I can't continue being scared or doubting everything because of a recurring nightmare. "Now let's get you home."

"Once again, thank you for everything."

"I'll take a nice painting as payment in the future."

At that, I bark out a laugh. "Done. My choice on the subject, though."

"Seems like a fair trade." Another turn and my body sways with the movement, pulling me closer to the window, and I open my eyes. We're close to my home and after pulling into the driveway, Tero lets the car idle while rushing to get my boxes and then my door. I'm not given the chance to open my own, and he nods toward my door when I stay seated just watching him run around. "Or did you change your mind?"

"No." Shaking my head, I chuckle. "I'm just not used to seeing people move like that."

"Move like what?" He follows me up the three steps to my door, curiosity in his tone.

"Precise and controlled."

"Should I be looser and clown-like?"

"Not one bit." Turning the key, I let us inside and motion toward the smaller sitting room to the right of the entryway. It's the formal of the two with my TV room being at the far back near the kitchen. His eyes take in the space, nodding to himself a bit, and I can almost see a question sitting on the tip of his tongue. "Go ahead. Ask."

"Not a question, per se..."

"Then?"

"Just thought it'd be more contemporary and less flowery, is all."

"And you'd never know by my appearance that I'm fascinated by true crime documentaries. I live for that craziness and binge watch every single one I come across."

"Really?"

"Netflix ones are the best. The bloodier the better."

"I'll take your word for it." Tero places my boxes down atop the wooden coffee table. "I'm more partial to animal documentaries, snakes to be precise."

"Oh! What kind?" Because I'm a sucker for those too. That, and Shark Week.

"Pythons. Constrictors in general, really."

"They are fascinating creatures."

His smile widens and those clear eyes light up. "Finally, someone else who gets it."

"Love those shows, but I'd probably freak out if I ever saw one up close. I'm a total chicken, then." Grabbing the top box, I pull out a chocolate ganache macaron and take a bite. "God, these are so good. That bakery is about to make a killing off me if the rest is anywhere near this masterpiece."

"How deep is your sweet tooth?"

"Never ending," I manage to say before stuffing the rest in my mouth. "No shame either."

He raises a brow just as his phone pings with a text. "Yet, you chose savory instead at breakfast?"

"Breakfast, lunch, and dinner are never to be sweet. Those morsels are saved for the after."

"Noted." His cell chimes again, and he takes it out of his pocket without looking at it. This one is a smaller device than the one in the car. *How many phones does he have?* "Three, but this one is for when I don't answer the one you saw earlier, and no, you didn't say that out loud. Your facial expressions are very telling."

"Makes sense." Not really. "And the third?"

"The third is for family only." Before I can respond, he looks at the small screen and nods. "Well, this is where I leave you. The boss is calling."

"Okay." *Why am I so comfortable with him?* "I'll see you tomorrow."

"Yes, ma'am." Tero heads toward the door, reaching out for the knob but pauses when his hand touches the metal. "Would you like a lift to the gallery tomorrow? I don't mind if—"

"Yes." No hesitation from me.

"Good." He doesn't say anything else, stepping out into the early afternoon sun while I stay rooted in place. I ignore my home phone ringing from the kitchen and then the answering machine beeping with a message.

Eventually, though, curiosity wins and I head toward the device that came with the house and I've been reluctant to throw away. I kept my uncle's number too and just continued to pay the bill.

Can you please answer me already, Gabby? I'm sorry for being a jerk today, and the dress looked really beautiful on you. Please don't be mad and call me back, your best friend, who sucks at apologies.

"What are you playing at, Elise?" She made a big deal out of my dress and my behavior and my "ruining" her moment, but everything was set up by her without my input. Without my permission and relates to my business, not hers.

Why be overdramatic?

Why purposely start a fight and hurt me?

Why did I automatically think someone broke into my home when I have no proof?

Those questions keep running through my head, further cementing my need to hole up for the day with junk food and some reality TV. Something light and funny and so far removed from any kind of drama that I can relax—forget.

Mr. Pickles collar tinkles then, his chubby body trotting into the room, eyes searching every corner. He's not being himself, trembling a bit, and I don't hesitate to scoop him up in my arms while checking both his water and food dishes.

His breakfast is gone and water a bit low, so I refill both while he snuggles deeper into my neck. That cold little nose makes me giggle, and I give him a few extra scratches on his back for the innocent love he gives without asking for anything in return.

Because that's what dogs do. They give and are loyal and bring happiness even in moments when you doubt yourself. When you need it the most.

"Thank you, buddy." Another kiss to his head, and then I say the two words that make him a giddy stinker. "Walk time."

Gabriella

There's someone sitting on the porch steps, leaning against the railing and looking at her phone when we get back from our walk. She hasn't seen us yet, and I'm half tempted to turn around and come back later, but Mr. Pickles takes that decision away from me when he growls. The sound is a low rumbling that catches Elise's attention, and her eyes snap to mine.

She looks at me with a sad expression as she stands, dusting off the back of her ripped-at-the-knee jeans. "Can we talk, please? Things got really out of hand and—"

"We can."

A breath of relief leaves her. "Thank you. I know you're—"

I halt her rambling by holding my unoccupied hand up. "Coffee first, and then we'll talk."

"Deal." Not that I'm giving her a choice. I pick up my grumpy pupper and walk past her, opening my front door. Elise hasn't made an attempt to follow me, and I look back over my shoulder and offer a small smile. "You can come in, chick. No one's going to bite you."

At my words, she snorts, yet I do catch the dubious look she gives my dog—a dog that, while not overly friendly with her, has never bared his little teeth or barked. At the most, he avoids, and when left without a choice, lets her pet him with an annoyed look I find adorable.

Mr. Pickles is a bit crotchety, but he's my crotchety little guy.

We don't talk while making our way into the kitchen, nor after I let Mr. Pickles go to find something to do. Instead, she watches as I store everything we took away, the last being my cell phone, which I place atop the counter. The silence in the room is heavy, but she came to me and I wasn't in the mood to make it easy on her.

So I play the ignore game until she's ready. I busy myself by washing my hands and then pulling down our preferred mugs from my cupboards. Hers is a princess thing in bubble-gum pink that I find atrocious, while mine is black and says *The Blood Of My Enemies* in bold red.

And while the coffee percolates, I stand with my back against the counter and watch her. Right now, it feels as though I'm seeing her for the first time. I see a side that I do not like, and the grimace on her face tells me she's aware.

"Why?" I'm the first to break the silence, tired of this roundabout silence that gets us nowhere. My eyes are on hers, daring her to lie. To please help me understand this feeling of betrayal that consumes me.

"Honest truth?" My response is the arch of my brow, which pulls a deep sigh from her. Almost as if she's being forced to admit her fault, but the thing is, I'm not doing anything here. Elise came to me. "Fine. I was jealous of the attention you were getting, okay?"

I can't help but snort. "That's it? That's the best you can do?"

"It's the truth."

"Try again."

"Gabby, I'm serious." Her face pinches at this, almost as if she's smelling something foul. "I'm not trying to be mean, but look at you, and look at me."

"Not everyone likes blondes, Elise. Ever think of that?" There are other things I can point out: her attitude, unprofessionalism, and the way she practically threw herself at Theodore. *He doesn't like women like that. Like her.* My subconscious sneers the words, but I keep my expression neutral, no matter how much all this bothers me —how much my body nearly recoils at the idea of them together. "And even if that's the excuse you're choosing to go with, how you treated me—embarrassed me—is unacceptable and quite frankly, a bit sad of you."

At my words, her eyes narrow. "Not in this case. I've done my research and—"

"Are you stalking him?"

"No." She answers much too quickly, her body shifting a bit from her place across from me. Elise is on a counter stool, hands palms down on the butcher block top. "That's stupid of you to even think that. I'm just better than..."

"Me?" I end her trailed-off sentence, my own hackles rising. "Is that what you really think? That you're better than me?"

"Don't take it personally, Gabby."

"Too late." Pushing off the counter, I head to the fridge and pull out my creamer and walk back. The pot is done and I pour each of us a cup, preparing mine how I take it, while hers remains black. "You know where everything is."

"Don't be like that. Let's put this morning behind us and head out." I'm not going to bother myself with answering her and stir my coffee, adding a bit more sugar at the end because I need something sweet to combat the bitterness her words are brewing within. "Come on. Girlfriends don't argue over guys. We respect the rules and since I saw him first, you need to back off. Do so, and everything will go back to normal."

Bringing the cup to my lips, I take two sips. "That sounds like a threat."

"I don't want to fight with you."

"And yet you warn me to back off?" Once again, heavy silence fills the room and I'm more than uncomfortable with her here. God knows I'm trying to work through this—trying to understand her—but my patience is at an end. Her words have more than hit a nerve, but then a thought hits me and I start to see another angle. *What are you playing at?* "I have a question."

"Shoot."

"When was the first time you saw Theodore Astor? Did he show interest in you?" Those last words taste bitter. *I'm going to be sick if he's touched her.* It's a thought I shouldn't have but can't deny being true.

Something happened between us at the cafe. The chemistry still lingers on my skin where he innocently touched me before leaving.

"In person?"

"In general." At my question, Elise looks away and then chooses that moment to prep her own drink. She adds some sugar and milk, then takes a few sips to test it out. But what's obvious is her sudden avoidance and the twitch in her hands. "Answer me."

"How is that any of your business?"

"Answer me."

"Today was the first time physically, yet I've followed him for years. His face is kept out of the media for the most part and it's hard to track him down, but I did." That sounds stalker-ish. Elise flips her hair over her shoulder, twirling the end of one curl. "As you can imagine, he's a busy man, and your work was the opening I needed so I jumped at the chance. And he's just as handsome as the few photos I've downloaded."

"You're here telling me to back off someone you just saw with your own eyes for the first time today? Where you embarrassed me, yourself, and him?"

"That wasn't my fault! You ruined everything wearing that trashy dress—"

"Speaking of the dress..."

"What of it?"

"Did you come into my home and leave it here as a gift, or not?"

Something crosses her face, a fearful expression, but it's gone before I can fully decipher. *What are you hiding?* "So what if I did?"

"Then why have a problem with me wearing it?" Nothing. Not a peep. "A birthday gift worn on my birthday. What a crazy notion."

"It was unprofessional to wear and you—"

"To a meeting I didn't ask for nor set up, and which I only found out about an hour before I needed to be there? That meeting?" My sarcasm is heavy, my glare just as icy as hers. I'm done being pushed around. "The same meeting where Theodore Astor ignored you, asked you to be quiet, and exchanged numbers with me?"

"He saw you as easy."

"Never confuse me with yourself, Elise."

"Tell me, Gabriella. What were you thinking when you offered yourself to him?" And there's the woman I met today in the café: my friend's true colors. Her face flushes and her chest heaves, the cup slamming down atop the counter with enough force that it breaks, and all that's left behind is the handle in her hand. "Are you that desperate to lose your virginity? Isn't it *pathetic* of *you* to throw yourself at the first man who indulges your quirks and is nice?"

And yet, I'm not moved or intimidated. Instead, a part of me is angry.

So angry.

Insulted.

Hurt.

"What was I thinking?" It's rhetorical, but when she opens her mouth, I level her with a look. This surprises her; the hostility in me is new, but that little girl who grew up alone and with forced thick skin each time life knocked her down isn't having it. This feeling is one I've fought to always push back, but today I'm embracing it. It's bubbling within my veins and my heart races, I'm feeling flushed, and a deep vibration settles through every limb. "You're asking me what I was thinking?" My laugh is sardonic, so dry. "I was thinking my friend went out of her way to make a dream come true for me out of the goodness of her heart—because she loves me, and not because there was a personal agenda attached. I was thinking that it was a business meeting, not a pimp's personal catwalk where I'm used to attract a big spender and then told to bend over and take it as you please."

Elise scoffs, tossing the mug's handle onto the floor. Not the counter, but the floor as if she has a maid that majestically walks behind her to clean up each mess. *How are we even friends?* "You're being melodramatic, Gabriella. Those weren't my words."

"But it's implied. No?" Placing my coffee down, I rub a tired hand down my face. I take a moment to choose my next words carefully because even though her actions today cut, I still care. You don't stop overnight, even though this makes it hard to. "Why are you really here, Elise? What do you want, because you can fuck right off if insulting me into submission is your game? I'm not the desperate one here."

"Has anyone ever told you that you're exhausting? So much work to be your friend."

"Funny, but I understand that sentiment like no other today."

"Gabriella, I need you to listen to me." Elise points a manicured nail at me, her face looking as if she tasted something sour. The same one she had during brunch. "I need you to back off with Astor, and things will go smoothly for you. He's mine. Don't force my hand, Gabby. Please heed my warning and follow my lead on this deal. You've already made things hard enough for me as is."

"Made what hard? My paintings. My work. My deal, not yours." It's difficult, but I manage to keep my tone calm. Unaffected. "I'm thankful for your input and unsolicited help in the past, but you've more than overstepped once again. Your place in my life was that of a friend, not a manager. You don't own me, and I'm neither a puppet nor a stepping stone to whatever top you wish to reach."

"I won't repeat myself. Back off."

"And you need to leave. Now."

"As you wish." Walking past her, I head toward the front door and open it wide. She doesn't leave me standing there for long, the slap of her flip-flops loud on my floor. I'm not looking at her as she pauses beside me, I don't react when she takes my hand and gives it a squeeze before stepping through. "I'm going to give you a few days to calm down and see things my way. I need him, Gabby. Please don't ruin our friendship by forcing me to do things that can't be undone. Trust me on this."

"I did once, and this is where it's led me. Disappointed and hurt."

"Life isn't easy," she says, while my hand grabs the doorknob, grip tight. "You'll survive just fine, sweetheart. Trust me, there's plenty of other dicks in the sea."

"That's the only thing I'll agree with you on, Elise. There are plenty and life will carry on, but what won't change is that Theodore didn't give you the time of day then, and won't tomorrow no matter what you do." My words shock her and she takes a step back, just enough for me to slam the door, and that's what I do. I'm not interested in her reply or seeing her at the moment. Her words have cut deep and behind the stoic facade, I'm wounded. Her words did their damage, and no amount of apologies at the moment or threats or whatever the hell else she has up her sleeve will make a difference.

Screw her. Screw everything.

The first tear falls and then another as her hand lands on the door, a *slap, slap, slap* that's loud inside my home. I'm sobbing by the time Elise tries to open the door with her key, and my chest feels as though it's caving when I slide the side bolt in place.

Another thing to add to my already packed schedule.

New lock. New paintings...

"I can't sign with the Astor Gallery now." Another hurt-filled cry leaves me at the thought. I've put so much of myself into each finished piece, forgoing a life outside of my studio, and this is the repayment. Elise made the contact for me and if I accept, I'm using her. I'd be as pathetic as she claimed. Grabbing my cell phone from the countertop, I send out a quick message and turn it off. "This is going to hurt my career."

THEODORE

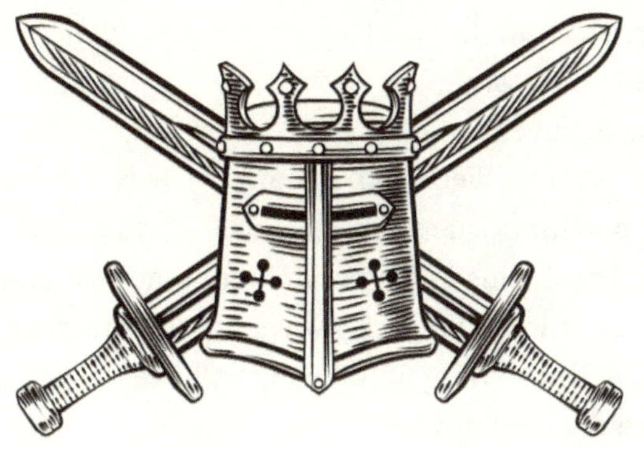

Her polite refusal incenses me, but more so because the words come across as lifeless. Almost bitter, and I have an idea of the why, and the culprit. Because Gabriella thought Tero left and drove toward my location, but the truth is, he didn't.

Under my instructions, he stayed. He watched her house, and I was right in doing so.

Miss Scott just doesn't understand the meaning of the word not interested. Not by the subtle rebuff, and much less by my outright hostility during brunch.

But then again, women like her live in a false reality where everything is catered, and the word *no* isn't in their vocabulary. I've known her kind in the past. Have seen many versions over the years, but the most consistent is the one stepping on those closest to them while climbing social ladders.

"What do I do, boss?" Tero asks, tone curt. He's very old-fashioned in that sense, believes that a man chases and the woman has the right to refuse or accept, while I'm in the somewhat alluring middle. I'll never force Gabriella, but I will romance her—seduce and then cherish. "Because from the small argument outside, Miss Scott was here to warn her off and threaten the deal."

"Is that so? Interesting."

"That she believes she has sway?"

"That she showed her hand so early." There's more to her reaction. To her pursuit of me—the unwanted flirting—when I know of her behavioral problems in the past. I'm not the first gallery owner or rich man she's flirted with; however, I am the first to show no interest or fuck her. "When will the report be ready? I need to be sure before I make my next move."

"Tomorrow morning."

"Then head home. We're done for today." Sitting back in my chair, I look out the floor-to-ceiling windows of my office and catch the final rays of sunlight. With each moment that passes, the bright colors turn dark and while the world starts its nighttime routine, I let the chips fall where they may right now. "There's nothing we can do until we talk to her face to face, and I'd like to have some proof of my suspicions before then. Gabriella's too sweet and would never think bad of her friend, no matter how hurt she is, but she needs someone to watch out for her."

"And that's you?"

"Yes."

"As you wish. Good night, boss." The line disconnects and I toss my cell aside, thinking through my options, the first being how to accidentally bump into her and start the conversation in an organic manner where she's not on the defensive.

Moreover, I can only think of one option where this might be plausible...

The bakery she went to with Tero is his favorite, and I was told her sweet tooth is a weakness—something I'm banking on her imbibing in. Emotions can be a dominating thing and after the rough day she's had, my best bet is to think she'd go through the desserts and want more.

This is my in:

Bump into her at the bakery.

Or buy her an obscene amount and deliver them later that evening.

I'm not going to hound her, but the power of persuasion is a beautiful thing when used at the right time. And that's not now. Maybe tomorrow or the next day and if not a week later, but one thing is for certain—I'm not giving up on her. She's too talented and beautiful, and I admire her stubborn streak that believes by taking my offer she's indebted to her friend.

I'll let her sleep on it.

"Tomorrow is another day."

I'VE BEEN SITTING inside the bakery shop for the last two hours, nursing my drink. The place is packed, the tables full, and yet I have the perfect view of the front door.

I also have incredible luck when at fifty past nine, Gabriella steps through the door with an AirPod in each ear and a slightly grumpy expression on her face. *Not a morning person, I see.*

She's wearing a Ramones crop top that leaves just enough skin on display to tempt and a pair of cargo pants that have seen better days low on her hips. They're paint-stained and have a hole at the knee, but with the way she walks to the counter and orders—the way heads turn her way and the cashier smiles—you'd swear she was on a catwalk.

So beautiful. So unaware.

"Should I stay or leave?" Tero, outside of being my assistant, is one of my oldest friends. Much too observant too. "No problem on my end."

"Stay. She'll be more comfortable that way."

"Of course, although I'd say seeing you right now would be very welcomed." His head tilts in her direction and I look, eyes narrowing at what I find. There's a man beside her now, trying to shift closer, and the pinched look on her face screams discomfort. He's blind to this, though, too busy letting his eyes roam her face and a little lower—

I don't answer Tero. Don't acknowledge his low chuckle, and before the idiot can send another flirtatious smile in her direction, I'm next to her.

"Hello, stranger."

"Theodore," it's a shaky whisper tinged with gratitude and relief before our eyes meet. Her smile is genuine and soft, and the asshole on her other side notices. He also coughs, but her sole focus is on me. "What are you doing here?"

"Same as you." For a second, my eyes flick to the man wearing a uniform, khaki pants and red polo with some store's name I don't bother to read, and he stumbles back. Almost drops his coffee and exits, for once using his common sense. "Needed copious amounts of sugar after being up all night re-examining the proposed showing you declined."

Her cheeks turn pink while those green orbs give me an apologetic look. "I'm really sorry about all that. If you need me to pay for—"

"I'd never take your money."

"But I did make you waste your time."

"Not really." That piqued her interest, her brows furrowing while my smile broadens. "Will you give me a few minutes of your time to explain? I swear it'll be worth your while."

"I don't know..."

"Aren't you curious about who I'm replacing you with?" Gabriella's reaction to my words is instantaneous. Her eyes narrow and lips thin, hand clenching a bit around her cup. It causes the lid to pop a bit and a few drops to drip down her fingers. "I mean, she's not our first choice—"

"Sure. Let's go talk *about my replacement.*" The latest half is muttered under her breath, and fuck me, her sour expression is adorable. Makes me want to bite her. To wrap those red locks around my fist. "Where's your...never mind."

And I follow those thick hips toward the table Tero's sitting at, his light blue eyes filled with a mirth he won't display. Her scent swirls around me, pulls me in closer, and I'm only content when my hand meets the small of her back.

I let it linger there and she doesn't complain, gifting me with the small feel of warm skin on my fingertips.

"Miss Moore."

"Uh huh." Gabriella waits beside a chair, and I pull it out for her before taking a seat myself. Her fingernails drum on the wooden top, eyes searching the two contracts in plain sight. "So, that's her?"

"Yes."

"I see."

"What's that supposed to mean? Is there something I'm unaware of?" I'm not lying to her. This is my backup plan, but I won't deny playing dirty in order to change her mind. Because no one likes to be replaced and she's no different, reading down *Cecily Marie's* achievements and sales figures to her last show in the states. "Please speak up if there is. Whatever you say stays here."

"She's brilliant, no denying that."

"But?"

"Her reputation is one of diva status and problematic with both staff and clientele. That's on you if you want that headache on your hands."

A smile threatens to escape but I hold it back, nodding instead as though understanding. "I've heard a few things but have been left with little to no choice. The artist and dates will be announced this week. I don't have time to scour the country for the next up-and-coming gem."

"You could still do better."

"Cecily Marie isn't my first choice, but..."

At my trail off, her arms cross over her chest and lips purse. "Oh, you're good."

"How so?" I ask, giving her a perplexed look. Feeding her an innocent lie.

"Tero, how—"

"I'm just an observer here." The man holds both hands up, almost tipping over his coffee cup in his haste. "That, and he does sign my check."

"You both suck." Petulant behavior has never been a trait I find attractive, but with her it's endearing. But then again, there's nothing I don't like. No part of her I don't want or crave.

"That's mean."

"You've given me no choice, Gabriella. I do need to fill the spot and—"

"Don't."

"Don't what?"

"Just give me a good enough reason. Just one."

"Because you earned this, Gabriella. Simple as that." At my words, tears spring to her eyes but she blinks them back, not allowing them to fall. She's also quiet, her emotions unreadable, but the small catch in her throat is a sign I'm getting through to her. The way she lets me grab her hand, entwining our fingers together, is a step in the right direction. "Your work speaks for itself, while your *reputation* is one of professionalism and dependability. Elise didn't give you this—fuck that. The only reason I agreed to that brunch was you. Without Gabriella Moore there is no deal, and that's a truth that can't be negated or changed."

"Are you just saying that so I—"

"Gabriella, I want you. No one else."

There are many ways she can take that, and the fact is they're all accurate. She's what I want. All of her.

In any capacity. In any way.

"Okay," she says after a minute of silence. It's low, almost too low, but I hear her as if she'd shouted this from a rooftop. Gabriella takes in a deep breath before letting it out slowly. Her shoulders straighten out while her head lifts a little higher, a small smile finally stretching across those sweet lips. "Okay. I'll do it."

"Are you sure?" I ask while from the corner of my eye, Tero produces a pen for her to sign. Cecily's contract is beside hers and the sums of money are blatantly unfair, Miss Moore being the clear victor—further proof of my choice always being her.

"Give me the contract."

"You didn't answer my question."

"You're going to be demoted to number six in the first impression chart if you don't let me sign, Mr. Astor." The little tease, innocent or not, makes my cock jerk behind the confines of my pants. *Sassy little thing.* "What's it going to be?"

My answer is to rip the other contract in half after placing Gabriella's in front of her. My beautiful little artist doesn't disappoint either, grinning at my action before signing her name at the three designated areas.

It takes less than sixty seconds.

The binding agreement is set in stone.

You're mine, gorgeous.

Gabriella

I knew what he was doing the moment I sat down at their table, and I'm not ashamed to admit I'm thankful. Relieved. So grateful, because missing out on this opportunity would've hurt me.

Emotionally. Career wise.

Something that Theodore saw and rectified when he preyed on my humanity. Because jealousy is a part of life, and the feelings that overcame me—the ones that made me sign after arguing someone else's merit—aren't ones I'm proud of. Nor do I negate them, because I know I'm better even though she's a bigger name than me.

However, two questions still remain, run rampant through my head. *Why her? Why was he there?*

I'd gone to the bakery that morning because simply put, I devoured the extra surprise the shop owner had placed in a box. These flaky little chocolate croissants with a hint of spice in the hazelnut spread she'd baked within were delicious, and after not getting any sleep, I went back for more.

I also wasn't lying about his chosen painter's attitude and diva-like personality. I've seen both firsthand. Have been in the same room and dealt with her criticisms while she flirted with a gallery curator to be given the rights to show at their location.

"What's done is done, and I don't regret it," I say out loud, walking up the stairs to my studio with Mr. Pickles close behind late the next afternoon. He's been with me all day, my little shadow since I came home from my impromptu meetup with Theodore, and it's been nice. We ate an early dinner together, watched the movie *Secret Window*, and then went to bed. Not fancy, but a nice quiet day that I desperately needed. "No sign of Elise either."

Today has been much of the same thus far, too. Except for the excitement coursing through me.

I'm thinking. Planning. Already forming each piece in my mind.

And while I'm divided between two subjects, my original and private muse, they both revolve around predators.

Human. Animal. Both beasts led by different impulses.

Stepping inside my studio, I turn on the lights and then walk to the window, pulling apart the curtains. At once the room brightens, the small rays dancing across each finished painting as well as the canvas still sitting on an easel at the center.

Just like all the others in this room.

My inspiration since the nightmares began has been a faceless man and the chaos that surrounds him. His settings are always dark like the room I see in my dreams—some with blood and some black as night—the lingering emotions of fear coming across each stroke as death lies at his feet in different forms. His weapons also vary.

A knife.

A gun.

His bloodied hands.

But the one that has always worried me, made me question my own sanity, is the face in profile where drops of red come from his mouth and stain his white shirt. That one stays inside the room's closet; it's never to be seen by anyone but me.

Looking down at Mr. Pickles, I arch my head toward the unfinished one where the man I'm calling the "Gate's Keeper" stands at the top of a mountain of bodies, no faces on any of them. "You think this would scare Theodore if he saw it? Too much for a show?" His answer is a bark, a deep one that shakes his little body. "I agree. This is morbid."

Then why do I keep coming back? Why would I even consider this? Questions I have no answer for. I'm also not ready to stop.

Something beckons me. Something controls me.

Another yip and I look down, bending a bit to scratch his head.

"Sticking to the original thought it is, then." Standing back to my full height, I grab the half-done painting and place it against the farthest wall with the others before I start doing inventory. The Astor Gallery wants seven, and I have everything I need except a few paint supplies I need to stock up on. "Feel like going for a ride, or being lazy on the couch?"

As the last word leaves my mouth, my stomach rumbles. It's already a little past five by the time I finished with today's mission, and when I turn to head toward the door, my dog takes off like a bat out of hell.

His growls lead me to the kitchen where he's standing in front of the back door, scratching at it.

"What the heck is wrong with you?" I'm rushing toward him when the doorknob jiggles and my instincts kick in. "Who the hell is there?" I yell out, and the movements stop and a few seconds later Mr. Pickles relaxes, sitting with his back facing me. A protective position. "It's okay, boy. Let me just check."

There's a small window at the door with a roman shade that gives me privacy, and I pull it up, giving me sight to the vast backyard. There's no one there, but I do find a note on the ground. It's made out to me in that same stationary that Elise uses and I find a little tacky.

Why was she here?

Opening the door, I find the keys I'd given her half broken in the lock. She's been trying to come inside. Makes me wonder how many times in the past she's done this too.

I pick up the note and open it, reading the two lines that make my blood go from ice to pure fire.

Congratulations on signing yesterday, Gabriella.
Smart move on your behalf.
I'll be in touch for both my payment and your help
with Theodore.

Best Friends For Life.
XoXo

I'm on autopilot when I walk back inside while pulling out my cell phone. His number is the one I click, and it's his voice that picks up after the second ring.

"I didn't think I'd hear from you today, Gabriella." Theodore's voice comes through the line, his timbre always smooth as whiskey. "It's a nice surprise."

"I wish it was under better circumstances, but this isn't a friendly call."

"No?" There's rustling on his end, a door opening and closing. "Are you okay?"

A deep sigh escapes me, and the note crumbles in my grip. "Yes and no."

"Explain."

"Do you have a company you trust to change some locks for me? I know it's late in the day, but maybe you have a locksmith on file who takes emergency calls?"

"What happened, Gabriella? What aren't you telling me?" It sounds like car keys jiggling on his end, and the wind has picked up too.

"Elise has keys, and I want everything changed."

"Then I'll be there in forty and with the locks in hand."

"You'll be here?"

"I think you should know I'm quite handy, Miss Moore."

Only he could make me laugh right now, and I do. A giggle slips through without my approval. "Is that right? A regular old Handy Manny?"

"More like jack of all trades and master of all."

"We'll see about that." My dog whines then, his body looking between me and the outside. He's needing to go out and see for himself that it's safe. "I'll see you when you get here. Just come around to the back. I'll be back there with Mr. Pickles seeing if she left anything else behind—"

"Anything else?" This leaves him on a low growl, and my brows furrow. *Why does that upset him? He isn't aware of our fight a few days ago, just my reservations after the disastrous brunch.*

"Elise left a note." There's an uncomfortable feeling in my chest, this pressure that comes and goes as it pleases, and no amount of medical test over the years have found anything wrong with me. And yet, when I'm stressed, it makes its presence known like now.

"About?"

"A personal matter. Please leave it at that."

"As you wish, Miss Moore. I'll be there soon." The call cuts out a few seconds later, and my guilt begins to grow right after. I shouldn't feel that way, but I do, and I'm left stewing in my emotions while my dog runs around the yard.

And as the seconds on the clock tick by and my restlessness grows, one thing becomes certain while further confusing me: I don't like him being upset.

"Still have your doubts?" His smug expression makes me roll my eyes a few hours later. "Are you ready to admit you were wrong?

"Never." I'd never tell him I find the way his large, muscular hands grip the drill sexy. Nor the way he licks his lip, biting the bottom one while concentrating a weakness. Instead, I shrug while pretending to criticize his work. Like I'm secretly not impressed and my thighs didn't clench a few times. "This is mediocre at best."

"Liar." Theodore is quick to call me on it, standing to full height from his hunched position where he'd been drilling in the last two screws to my front door. He's already done the back, checked the bottom floor's window locks, and now I'm the owner of some fancy-techy locks that work with my phone and a personal code. His amber orbs traverse my short frame slowly from head to toe while pointing at me with the drill in his hand. "Tell the truth, or I'll be charging you double."

"I only pay with treats," is my cheeky reply, and for a second something flashes in his eyes. They become darker. Hooded. But then it's gone when he blinks, and I'm left wondering if my mind is playing tricks on me. *I saw hunger there. I know I did.*

"What kind of treats? You bake?" His voice, though, is a little deeper. Rougher, and I swallow hard, pretending I'm not affected, and fix my messy bun for the third time in fifteen minutes. Pretend that the damn thing isn't staying in place when what I need is a cold shower and a priest to clear my thoughts.

Because watching him work has been torture. Unmercifully so.

"Not to save my life, but my pantry is always full of candy." Tilting my head to the side, I tap my lips. A move he follows. "Do you prefer Snickers or Twix as part of our deal?"

Laughter builds in his strong chest and rumbles out, the sound loud and boisterous. And I find myself liking the sound. Liking him more than I should. "You are too precious, Gabriella."

"I'm going to take that as a compliment."

"Please do. You have no idea how endearing I find everything you do." At once my face heats up, his words making me smile, but before I can respond he's taking a step back. There's a low vibration coming from his wrist, his watch signaling an alarm while my amusement dies. *What just happened?* "Raincheck on this very intriguing topic?"

"I guess." Because I've got nothing else.

"Good." Bending a bit, he places the drill on the floor and then stands, bringing both hands to my face. The skin is a bit rough, manly, and they feel heavenly as his thumbs rub back and forth across my cheeks. "Has Pickles gone out for the night?" Verbally I can't respond, too focused on the almost reverent touch, but I do nod. *My mind can't be playing tricks on me. This is real.* "Then I want you to head inside and lock the door for me. I want to hear the mechanism engage before I leave. Can you do that for me?"

"Yes."

"Thank you." Neither of us move after, our stares unwavering. "God, you're beautiful." Anything I could've said after dies on my tongue because his next action stuns me, completely and utterly leaves me breathless while those lips I've been looking at, memorizing the way they enunciate each word, press against my forehead. Their plumpness lingers there, but it's his deep inhale that sends a shiver down my spine. Theodore Astor is taking my scent into his lungs, his mouth is kissing me, and right before I have to grip onto his shirt for support, the smug man pulls back and grins down at me. "Good night, Gabriella."

"Good night."

"Please head inside, sweetheart. I need to make sure you're safe."

"Okay." And true to his word, he doesn't leave my front porch until I'm locked in and everything works, leaving behind a different mess altogether. I'm a bit shaky as I turn off the lights and walk up the stairs toward my room.

I don't acknowledge Mr. Pickles, who chooses to sleep in my studio.

I don't bother slipping into a pair of pajamas after stripping down to just my panties.

I don't bother taking either of my sleep medications.

All I *do* know is the feel of his lips followed me the entire time until sleep claimed me.

Gabriella

Warm fingertips glide up my thighs and hips, pausing just long enough to dig their nails in deeper, earning a hiss from me. I'm sensitive—I'm desperate—while the man behind me continues his torture.

His bare chest is against my naked back. My chest is on display to the open air inside a room that today promises pleasure, not pain or fear.

The walls still drip in red.

The furniture is still black and gothic.

The air is sweet, yet death lingers at its door.

And yet, I'm home. So at peace as I throw my head back and moan my approval, my hips gyrating against a strong torso with nothing covering his manhood or my slick little holes.

I'm ready for him. Need him in a way that's borderline psychotic, but I'm made to wait as lips trail up my neck, pausing over my veins which throb in time with the pulsing of my clit.

"Always, my pretty girl." Another pass, another open-mouthed *kiss, yet this time his right hand rakes down the center of my chest, leaving a fiery trail behind that makes me shiver. My skin feels flushed and my bottom lip is caught between my teeth, and right as I decide to turn my head—to see my lover—his teeth nip me. "Don't, Gabriella. Do that again, and I stop."*

"I need it."

"Soon, but not yet." The room is cold and my nipples tighten further, the little peaks craving the attention they don't get. This is the third pass of his fingers just over my hips, almost featherlike—

"Oh God," I cry out, my entire body coiling as his large hand cups my core, thick fingers parting my lips. They slide from my entrance to my sensitive nub, creating the most delicious friction. "Please."

"Please what?" It's a deep rumble up his chest, the vibration traveling through me. "Tell me."

"I need you." My confession is met with a hum before a fingertip slips inside, my entrance clenching—trying to pull it in deeper, but I'm being denied time and time again, and frustration sets in. "Or maybe I don't. Maybe all I need is...oh fuck!"

Another finger enters me, and his pace isn't gentle like a second ago. Now, he slams in and out in a punishing pace, the palm of his hand smacking my clit with each stroke.

My thighs tremble, walls pulsing as he hits a spot inside I've heard about but never experienced.

Something unintelligible leaves me—a moan or grunt, I don't know—because every cell in my body is coiling tight. Tighter, almost violently, and then nothing, not a damn thing as he pulls them out just when my orgasm was prickling near.

"You were saying?" the man snarls while placing those wet fingers, my scent, around my throat. I try to turn my head, to see him, but they tighten a bit and I feel it everywhere. My skin tingles, goose bumps dancing along my sweat-slick flesh as I'm denied once again.

"I—"

"Belong to you."

"Please." I'm begging. Needing the release more than my next breath.

"Say it, Gabriella. Say you belong to me." His cock slips between my wet thighs, rubbing the length of my slick labia as another rush of wetness leaves me. Christ, he feels good. Too good, and my eyes roll back when the blunt head caresses my entrance. "Tell me you're mine."

"I'm yours."

"Always, pretty girl." And then he slams into me, and I'm left on the precipice of pleasure and pain. On this thin ledge where everything around me stills and my screams echo through the vast space.

I'm floating. My body feels sensitive and wet, and there's a burning sensation on my chest that contrasts against the bliss between my thighs. The two merge and overwhelm my senses while this man I've yet to see face to face takes me like a savage beast.

Each stroke is punishing, his cock pistoning in and out while I can barely stand. There's no lead-up. No way to describe the sudden wave of euphoria I experience when his sweaty chest vibrates with his groan, the sound of his pleasure breaking me into a million pieces.

He fucks me harder. He's merciless and I come, pushing my hips back and meeting him thrust for thrust.

"Good girl. Let me feel you."

"You have me." The response leaves me before I can understand what I'm promising. To whom. Because all I know in that singular instance is that I don't want this to end. To lose him.

"Not yet."

My brows furrow as my walls contract around him, pulling him in deeper. "Not yet?"

"Not until you see what I see." His hold on my neck tightens and his mouth presses against my ear, his exhale rough. His cock stretches me a little more, and I raise onto the tips of my toes. "I'll have you, Gabriella. But first, I need you to focus...look down, pretty girl. Feel me come, coat you with my seed, as reality hits."

I follow his instructions and scream.

Red. All I see is red. All of it coming from me.

From a gash deep across my chest that bathes the room in my life's essence.

I'm bleeding out. My skin is flayed open, and a burning coldness fills me—I'm suddenly freezing and can barely breathe. Each hollowed breath hurts, and yet I'm aware of his come dripping down my labia and thighs.

Aware of the tender way, he places a kiss just below my ear.

It's all I can cling to as my knees go weak.

As my vision starts to fade and just before darkness claims me, I hear him one last time. "They did this to us."

My eyes snap open, and a scream rips from my throat. I'm shaking, clutching my chest with my left hand while the right is trapped between my clenching thighs.

I still feel him. It was so real.

Small aftershocks course through my body without my permission while my mind can't escape the image of me bleeding out. The gash—the burning sensation accompanied with a steadying pain—while his cock flexed against my walls.

This is too much. Not normal.

Am I suffering from night terrors?

Because what kind of person has a wet dream where they're killed? Because if that were to happen in real life, I'd be dead. *I'm scaring myself.*

"I need help." Slowly, I pull my hand out of my panties, ignoring how slick each fingertip is. The realization hurts, but I can't continue ignoring that maybe the dreams and stress are affecting me more than I thought. "There has to be a scientific reason this is happening. Someone who can help me."

They did this to us.

They did this to us.

They did this to us.

I can hear him in my head. It's on repeat and my skin heats, my heart skipping a beat while beads of sweat fall down my temple. They mix with my tears, this uncontrollable sob that escapes my chest, and I curl into myself.

It takes me a while to calm down, to breathe normally, and when I do, I don't hesitate to grab my phone and ring my therapist's office.

They have an opening for two today.

I take it.

Something has to give.

"THE DOCTOR WILL SEE you now, Miss Moore," the mid-thirties nurse standing at the door leading to his office calls out to the practically empty waiting room later that afternoon. It's just me and a man. Older. Jittery. And who I've avoided making eye contact with each time he looks my way.

I've been here a few times over the last twelve months to treat my insomnia at the suggestion of my primary physician. There have been small windows of times I've refused to go to sleep in order to avoid entering that dream and felt ill. That is, until my doctor told me how damaging it is to the body—promised that the prescribed anti-anxiety medication to help me sleep/relax would limit my recollection of each episode.

How there was a chance, minimal but there, that a deep-enough relaxed state of sleep would leave me without dreams.

Bullshit. All of it.

I do dream. Vividly.

And yet, here I am, nodding while walking toward her. She's smiling, so happy and carefree, and at the moment I'm hating her for it. "Thank you."

"Of course. Right this way, Miss Moore." We don't talk after, and once near to the open door where my doctor waits, she pauses and waves me forward. "Go right ahead. I'll see you on the way out."

"Right." Another fake smile and hers widens, nodding at me as if

I'd sent her blessings of health and more money than she could spend in ten lifetimes. The interaction lasts less than ten seconds at most and then she's gone, speed walking back toward the front while I'm hating every moment of being here. "Come on, Gabriella. Get it together."

Not the best pep talk, but I turn and walk into Dr. Silva's office, while the man himself is behind his desk. He's leaning back with his dark brown eyes on the door, and the light dusting of silver hair that adorned his temples has spread in the last year. With each visit, it has become a little more prominent until encompassing his entire head.

"Nice to see you, Miss Moore. Please take a seat."

"Glad to be here?"

My psychiatrist laughs at my question and nods, already writing something down in his ever-present notepad. "And how have you been since your last appointment..." his eyes shift to his laptop screen where he squints "...four months ago? It also says here you owe me lab work and a progress report on those dreams and their frequency, if any have occurred."

"I've been busy and just signed the contract for my next show."

"Congratulations." The painting to his right is mine, a commissioned piece of his favorite place in the world: a lighthouse in North Carolina. "That's great news, and we'll get back to that; I'd love to attend."

"Once I have the dates, I'll let you know."

"Perfect." Then silence. A long and awkward one, until I cough and he raises a bushy brow. "Answer the question, Gabriella. Are you still having that one recurring dream?"

"I am."

"How often?"

"Enough that I am here questioning my sanity."

"How so? Please explain." Dr. Silva pushes his glasses up a bit, his face so neutral. Not so much as a twitch or smile, fake or not. "Have you been taking your meds as prescribed?"

"I have." A lie, and he nods as if he knows I'm lying. "One tablet every night an hour before bedtime, and yet, the dreams are getting worse. I've gone from wandering through a strange room and empty halls to being sliced open and bleeding out. This isn't normal, doctor. I really think I'm suffering from night terrors."

"Let's go back a bit, Gabriella," he says, hand gliding across the page of his notebook, the ink filling up line after line. "When you started seeing me, these dreams had a twice-a-week frequency with sometimes bouts of self-induced insomnia in between. No?"

"Yes."

"Six months ago, they had become a three to four per week occurrence. No?"

"Yes."

"And now?"

"Almost every night."

"Almost?" His brow raises, and I know what's coming next. "Have you been staying awake for days? The truth, please."

"The last three weeks, I've been having trouble falling asleep."

"Elaborate, please."

Running a tired hand down my face, I let out a harsh breath. "Sometimes, the meds don't work. Sometimes the Melatonin doesn't so much as make me yawn." He goes to open his mouth, but I hold up a hand. "And then there are those nights when I try them together and fall asleep only to wake up with my heart beating out of my chest two hours after crashing."

"Why didn't you call the office? We need to know these things." His lips purse, and he begins to type something on his laptop, his lips moving but I can't make out what he's mouthing. "I'm going to send in a new script for a different medication to your pharmacy on file, and you'll be discontinuing the other. This one's just for sleeping and should keep you there throughout the night. You'll also be leaving here with one for bloodwork."

I grumble. "Hate needles."

"And I hate the smell of lavender, but my wife insists we use it in every room of our home." At that, I laugh and he chuckles a bit, yet his amusement dies just as fast as it came. "And your stress levels? How are you managing? Are you working out or walking—"

"What are the possible side effects?" Cutting him off is rude, but I'd rather he answer my question instead. This one matters. "Because the last one always made me sick the next day."

"That's something that varies from medication to medication. We won't know until you try it, but please call my office right away if you experience any sudden headaches or bleeding from your nose and mouth."

"Jesus," I mutter under my breath but he heard, his sad nod telling me as much. "What about the possibility of these being night terrors? Don't you have some form of testing that can be done to rule it out?"

"I'd rather you start the new medication and see how it goes. If no change, we will move on to the next step."

"Next step?"

"Another medication, and if that doesn't work, we'll do an MRI scan to rule out a physical cause. If neither is found to lead us anywhere, then we will begin a series of tests—polysomnography— to determine if you are indeed suffering from night terrors."

"How long before we can reach that stage?"

"I'd like to see you in a month again. That is, unless you're having a problem with this new prescription."

"Thirty days?" My laugh is sardonic, my chest tightening, and I rub the area. I'm sure he can sense the ire beginning to mount within. "Are you kidding me?"

"I'm sorry if that's not the answer you were looking for, but there's a procedure to each treatment that must be followed." Dr. Silva takes his glasses off and places them on his desk along with his pen. Both are atop that stupid notebook I want to smack him with and then burn. "Please trust us, Gabriella. Trust me that I will do what's best for you and your mental and physical health."

"Sure." Because what else can I say? He won't listen.

My primary didn't either.

They think it's stress related. That it's manifesting in vivid dreams.

"Great." He stands and so do I, following him to the door that he holds open for me. "I'll see you in a month, and I think you'll have good news for me. And please remember, keep the stress levels down and always take your meds."

Gabriella

"Black. I'm going to need a lot of black," I whisper to myself, standing in the middle of the acrylic paint section of a specialty art store while debating brands four days later. After my walk around the block with Mr. Pickles today, I've felt energized yet restless. I'm also running on nothing but coffee, determination, and the hour-and-a-half power nap I allow myself once a day.

No sleeping at night. No meds; the new or old ones.

Not a damn thing. This is the euphoric stage right before I crash, but I'm willing to take the risk. After getting home that day, I looked up the side effects to my new "night time" supplement and it's much the same as the last, but with the added possibility of oral bleeding and headaches from hell. It's in rare cases, I understand that, but I'm just not in the mood to add to my already heavy plate of bullshit.

So instead, I'm evading while sticking to the primary objective for my pieces. Because there's this uncontrollable beckoning that's leaning toward a dark and depraved setting where few have truly ventured into: the jungle. Be it the Amazon or Sri Lanka or any other large rainforest, there are legends of tribes and animals who live on these sacred grounds where money means nothing and you hunt to survive. It's a delicate balance, perfected since the beginning of existence, and I'm giving in to this temptation.

More so after recalling my conversation with Tero about snakes.

Because they are majestic. Animals that solely survive on instinct and have no need for greed. They kill to sustain themselves, not for gluttony or power.

That is something they wield naturally without anything more than existing.

"Hunter versus prey. Life and death." In my mind, I see trees and vines in different shades of green and contrast with a single predator highlighted in each piece. Both human and animal. "Now, which shade fits best for the base?"

There are two that I love and use, but a new one on the market has just a hint of metallic that my eyes are drawn to. It'd be perfect for the night sky, and will stand out, become reflective with the lighting being used.

"A lot of customers are choosing that tone this week," comes from a male voice just behind me and I shriek, dropping the bottles in my hand. They don't break, but instead roll beneath the gondola likely never to be found again unless someone gets on their knees, and with the man wearing a store uniform standing close, that person won't be me. "My apologies."

"You scared three years off my life." At my grumble, he holds his hands up but makes no move to step back. He's too close, and I don't like it. He also doesn't say anything after, and I'm confused by his just standing there. *Just like the coffee house a few days ago.* How uncomfortable he made me feel then too. "Can I help you?"

"You can..."

Stepping back, I bump into the shelf and then wave my hand in a *hurry up* action. "How?"

"You're very pretty." Not what I'm expecting, and it also heightens my unease. I'm not dressed to impress right now in an old paint-stained sweatshirt and denim cutoff shorts with a messy bun to top it off. Nor do I feel up to making polite conversation, but that choice is taken from me as he leans against another shelf.

The man is easily in his mid-twenties and taller than me with dark brown hair, blue eyes, and a slim build with the slightest pouch in his midsection. Ordinary. Nothing that would draw me in physically, and while I can overlook that and let him down in a gentle manner, the lecherous way he's watching me spikes my anxiety.

"Thank you," I say to be polite and move the cart beside me closer to create separation. We're alone in this row, no one near from the sound of it, which is strange. When I walked in, there were plenty of clients strolling the aisles. "And I'm fine. No help needed as I know what I'm here to buy."

"Are you sure? Spending my shift with you wouldn't be a chore at all." His name tag reads *Tim,* and the title of shift manager is printed beneath it. "You know, I've seen you here before, always in the paint section. Always unaware of the stares you receive just like around town."

"Okay." *That's not creepy at all.*

"I could keep others away if you'd like?" Tim looks at the items in my cart with interest. "A struggling artist?"

"No." My one-word response doesn't register at all. Nor my frown or the way I grip the metal kitty multi tool meant to protect if need be that I carry on my keychain; the ears are pointy and sharp enough to penetrate flesh.

"How about I cut you a deal, sweetheart. I'll let you use..." Tim lifts a hand toward my face and I cringe back "...my employee discount and you cook—"

"You have two seconds to walk away," a voice booms to my left, and I let out a breath I didn't know I was holding. Without turning my head, I know it's Theodore and I've never been more grateful to see another human being. My unrest evaporates, and when his hand touches the crook of my elbow, pulling me in closer, I nearly melt into him. I'm not questioning how he affects me when the creepy employee across from me has ruined what was supposed to be a fun trip.

"I'm just doing my job, sir—"

"Last warning." This time it leaves his chest on a growl, his muscles coiling beside me. His anger is palpable. His strength is visible in the cords of muscle that flex. "Walk away before you're unable to." The threat is there. It lingers heavily between the three of us, and Tim is smart enough to heed the warning, tucking tail and rushing away as if someone called him for help. This is the second time; it would've been an amusing sight had he not ruined my shopping. "Are you okay?"

Turning my head and meeting Mr. Astor's stare, I find his expression as soft as the tone he used with me. No traces of his ire left. "I don't know what you're doing here or how you found me, but thank you. That was beyond uncomfortable for me."

Are you following me? And more importantly, why don't I care if you are?

If anything, I feel a little safer thinking I have my own knight in shining armor.

"I'm glad I heard your voice when I did. I'd been heading toward the specialty vinyl area."

A snort escapes me. I'm also not buying it. "You own a Cricut machine?"

"No." He grins at me, those amber eyes crinkling a bit at the corner, and it only serves to make him more handsome. It's then that I take in his change of clothing, and my body gives a small shiver he mistakes for unease over what's happened. Jesus, this man is dangerous, and I let my eyes subtly give him a once over. And if I thought Theodore Astor in an all-black suit was handsome, this simple pair of lightly faded black jeans and plain grey T-shirt just might kill me. He's bulging muscles and raw masculinity with a scent that invades my pores and dominates each and every one of my senses. "...but Tero's wife does, and it's her birthday tomorrow."

"That's very sweet of you," I mumble, still appreciating his perfect male form. However, the moment his answer clicks, I'm left blushing in embarrassment. For assuming.

"I can be, depending on the person or moment." The last word hasn't passed through his lips when his brows furrow and lips thin into a line. *Even that is sexy.* "Did he touch you?"

"What?" I'm flustered, and this seems to aggravate him for some reason.

"Did Tim touch you?" he asks again, and this time, it's on a low hiss.

"No." Taking in a deep breath, I let it out slowly. My face pinches tight, though, and for a second the memory of his hand coming toward my face flashes through my mind. "You stopped him before he could."

Theodore nods, but he doesn't say anything else and turns his attention to my cart. "Did you find everything you needed? Or are you still—"

"Black." Christ, I blurted that out like an idiot, which he only raises a brow to. "I mean, I need black paint and was in the middle of picking a shade, when he interrupted."

"Shade?"

"Yes, shade." Giving him my back, I turn toward the shelf I'd been picking apart my options on. "They each have a slight variation and would work to serve a different purpose depending on the subject of each painting and main colors used. Like this one. It has a slight hint of purple to it."

"I see." Nothing more, but I hear the hint of amusement there. There's also his body heat that penetrates my clothing and sears my flesh, a caress that makes me flush from the tip of my hair to my hard little nipples pressing against the cotton of my sweatshirt.

"See this one?" There's a low *yes* from him, his hand now on my lower back as he looks from over my shoulder. God, he affects me like no one else ever has. I've seen this man a handful of times in my life, and yet, this attraction seems to grow. It also makes me question how relaxed I am around him, what just happened with Tim no longer a concern. *Why?* "This is the one I'd been debating on prior to being interrupted. I like the metallic hint, but need to find the right place to use it."

"And have you found it?" Theodore moves slightly closer now, but with him I welcome the move—I'm smiling. His hand on my back traces my spine and then fingers the edge of my hood, giving it one small tug. "Have you found what you've been searching for all this time?"

"Yes." I don't move, but I do allow him to take the bottles from my hand and place them inside the semi-full cart. I already have the canvases back in my studio, my brushes come from a specialty online store, but the acrylic paint and gold leaf packets I was dangerously low on—this shop is a godsend, excluding today's obnoxious employee. "I'm ready to check out."

He exhales roughly, breath fanning across the crown of my head. "Good."

"Good?" It leaves me on a shaky whisper right before his warmth disappears.

"Look at me," Theodore commands, and my body complies before I'm given the opportunity to deny him. Instead, I turn and fully face the handsome man and meet those eyes that always seem to draw me in and hold me captive. "Why do you look so exhausted? Are you sleeping okay, Gabriella?"

"Just had a few rough nights. No biggie."

Theodore brings his hand to my face and runs the pad of his thumbs under each eye. "You need a few days off. No work, and please try to get some sleep."

"Believe it or not, this is relaxing for me."

"So is lounging on your couch while munching on chocolates and binge-watching Netflix documentaries."

I take a step back and mock glare, crossing my arms over my

chest while meeting his hard stare. "Someone's been snitching, or have you been asking?"

"I will neither confirm nor deny this, but I will counter the question with one of my own."

"That's not how any of this works."

"Yet it will happen nonetheless." He takes my silence as a win and tilts his head toward the end of the aisle where the center of the store is located en route to the registers. We make it to the line to pay when he looks over again, chuckling at my annoyance for being left in wait. "Have you had dinner yet?"

"No, but here's one of my own..."

"Go on."

"Are you going to buy what you came for?"

"I'll order it online." Then, his amber eyes scrutinize me. "Have you eaten at all?"

"Again, no."

"What are you in the mood for? I'll—"

"I've already placed an order for pickup at seven and I'll swing by the place after I pay for this."

"Where?"

"Why?" I ask, studying his profile and memorizing each detail. The more I'm around him, the bigger the compulsion to draw him becomes. To recreate each line—his angular jaw and pouty lips—and add him to my line for the Astor Gallery. *Would he get mad?* "What's it to you?"

He snorts, and the sound seems so out of character. Makes him cute to me. "You're not paying for anything on your birthday."

"Buddy, that day came and went like a hurricane. It's been a little over a week now."

"Well, I'm making up for it." The girl at the register smiles at him, never once saying anything in greeting or asking the customary *did you find everything okay* because she's too busy doing what I am. Listening. Watching. Having an inner swoon moment that while making me want to glare at her, I understand. "Now, tell me where, and I'll have Tero pick it up."

"That's abuse of power. Shouldn't he be off by now?"

"He isn't."

"But—"

"Tell me, Gabriella." A full-body shiver runs through me at the way he says my name. There's this tinge of reverence that makes no sense to me and his eyes look at me with hunger. It's all there for a split second, but on my next blink, it's as if I've imagined it all. His handsome face is blank and his facial expression expectant. "What did you order, and from where?"

My tongue seems tied for some reason, but I do hand over my phone before he asks again, leaving open my Uber Eats pick-up screen with my pending order. "This Indian place isn't far at all. It'll be at your door before you reach it."

"Why?"

Theodore hands over his card blindly to the cashier while I wait. He grabs my bags and then has me lead the way to my car without answering my question. It isn't until everything's inside the trunk of my car and I'm behind the wheel that I'm graced with another charming smile.

It's alarming how easily that action disarms me.

"Everything I do, Miss Moore, is because I want to. Simple as that." He raps the top of my car twice and pulls back. "Drive safely, and I'd like to see you at the gallery tomorrow around ten."

"Why?"

"It's a surprise."

"Will I like this surprise? That's the important question here."

He shakes his head, a smirk curling at his lips. "You'll have to show up and see."

"That's no fun."

"It is for me, sweet Gabriella." And then he walks away without letting me respond. Not that I could, because once again I'm left watching him. Too occupied with his muscled back just like the rest of him, the cords of muscles beneath the thin grey shirt are a distraction I can't escape from.

This also leaves me with two very important observations...

How easily distracted I am in his presence.

How easily I forget all my problems the moment he's near.

KING

I 've been watching my pretty girl from the shadows for a little over a week. I've been listening to the world around us appreciate and take note—discover what I've known all along—that Gabriella Moore is a gem walking amongst filth.

The Astor Galleries know this.

Her best friend has always been jealous of it.

Men around her covet what belongs to me, and my patience is beginning to run thin. I've been accepting of her teasing and allowing key players to participate. Love the thrill of being taunted by those around her to come a little closer and expose myself, even though I won't. Not yet.

Instead, I play the game she innocently isn't aware of participating in and anticipate her every turn.

She moves. I move.

Gabriella is unaware of the demon whose strike outweighs her gentle moral compass. A lesson she'll learn soon enough as I'll always devour my prey whole. No empathy. No soul.

But then again, it's been this way since the first time our paths crossed.

Her shallow breaths are coquettish.

Her walk is sensuous without trying.

My pretty girl is the definition of effortless and I'm only but so strong to resist such a gift. Even with eyes full of unshed tears and a pale complexion a few days ago—the result of shock from her nightmare and the stress brought on by those around her—the little artist is exquisite and much too trusting. She's innocent in her search for acceptance, and I'll teach her just how useless that way of thinking is.

My girl is above all others, never an equal.

She's a queen. My queen.

Soft music plays from her dimly lit bedroom window tonight, and I smile. *Are you giving into sleep, little one?* I know her habits—routine—and this one always leads to her passing out. This is how she decompresses after a stressful day and right now, she's up on her bed drawing in a private sketchbook comparable to a diary while our guest on the ground whimpers at my feet.

He's scared. A shaking, pathetic excuse for a male, and my lip curls in disgust.

How did he ever think he'd be good enough? How can a man who pisses himself at the sight of me end up any other way but as he is now:

Tied up and gagged. Scared and shaking.

"This is the only chance you get to explain, Mr. Roy." There's an indiscernible noise that escapes him, his throat bobbing harshly. "What's that, Tim? I can't hear you."

"Please." It's the only word I can make out, and it serves to make the blood within my veins throb in anger. The ire that's been slowly building since he accosted Gabriella rises and my eyes narrow, lip curling over my teeth as a growl rumbles up my chest. "I learned my—"

He's cut off by the rubber sole of my boot driving into his mouth, breaking a few teeth. At once, his head snaps back and his body arches—nearly toppling over—but the bound position he's in keeps him on his haunches. Tim's eyes are wide, tears falling down his dirty cheeks while he chokes, and I pat his head as one would an ornery child.

And I wait patiently as a father does for his breathing to calm. I give him a dignified moment to collect himself before squatting down to his eye level. "We are going to try this again. Understood?" At his nod, I give a small tug and the cloth covering his bleeding mouth falls, exposing the damage. The four teeth in the front are broken and a large, deep slit is on his bottom lip, causing his chin and neck to be bathed in red. "Talk."

His lips tremble, face becoming paler the closer I get. "I didn't know she had a boyfriend."

"Continue." A pretty little voice comes from Gabriella's room, and I catch a small peek of her walking in front of the window toward her closet. It's why I chose this position near the tree line in her backyard. It gives me just enough of a vantage point to see a glimpse of her here and there if she crosses from one side to the other. And right now, she's heading toward the same closet where I left a second gift for her to find in due time, but for now, I hold a single finger over my lips while standing to my full height.

Those disgusting cries of his die down as both our heads turn and watch the shadows dance across the wall, and then we get a glorious peek of her padding back toward the bed. It's brief, but that singular second is an act of mercy from me to Mr. Roy. A gift, because his end is near.

The lights go out but the music stays on, the volume rising just a little more. She's listening to a classical composition, the melody slightly haunting as the piano becomes the focal point as it reaches its crescendo.

"She wouldn't approve of this," Tim whimpers so low I almost miss it, but don't.

"Is that so?" He doesn't take heed of my hiss or the way my teeth clench as he nods. He doesn't take in the special pair of gloves I've slipped on with metal tips at the end of my pointer and middle fingers sharp enough to filet flesh. "Please do share how well you know her. How intimate you are with her day to day."

"I'm—"

He's cut off by my hand shooting out, grabbing a fistful of hair and tearing a chunk clear off. I'm forcing his head back, the angle painful, and I don't speak until our eyes meet. "Don't lie."

"I'm not." Another low cry, the sound of a wounded animal meeting its end.

"Final chance." My nails dig in, cutting into his scalp. Blood rushes to the surface, matting his hair and dripping down his neck, and my nostrils flare at the sight. *So easily overpowered.* "How well do you know Gabriella Moore?"

"I've been a fan for a while." His voice is no higher than a whisper, the truth finally passed through his injured mouth. "Follow all her social media."

"Keep going." I let him go and Tim falls forward, spitting on the ground, and the remnants of his teeth land on the grass with quite a bit of bloody spittle. He's coughing between disappointing sobs, trying to clear his airways, and my nose wrinkles in disgust when all he manages to do is vomit from the action. "Can I have some water?"

Pitiful. Simply pitiful.

"Ninety seconds."

That stops his hacking, his entire body freezing. "It was an honest mistake. I thought she was single and—"

"Stalking her became a hobby," I finish for him; the demon within takes his rightful place. I'm here as a judge and executioner as I don't believe in the jury system. There's only one set of laws in the world, and it's mine. His cardinal sins go against each commandment —his lust for her flesh and bank account are liberties he took while disrespecting me. "How long before it became more?"

"She always comes in alone and ignores anyone that tries to start a conversation." His eyes avoid mine, his body shaking from his position on the grass. Kneeling. "Today was the first time, I swear. It'll never happen again."

"I know." Before he can blink, I've landed another kick, this time to his midsection forcing him to tip back in an uncomfortable position. His arms are tied behind him while his legs are in a forced squat, leaving him flat on his back with knees bent. Then I land a stomp, and the first rib cracks under the pressure. I can hear it snap clearly, feel the bone give beneath my shoe, and I rub the sole against the injured area. "Now, finish your story. Enlighten me."

"I'll leave." His voice cracks, a broken whisper as trails of tears adorn his face.

"You will." Pressing a little harder, a second rib cracks and he's smart enough not to yell. Little whimpers escape his lips and I smile, chest rumbling into a low chuckle. "But you'll have a chance to say goodbye. This is my promise to you."

"I'd rather just disappear. You'll never see me alive again."

"No one will." Before his next intake of painful breath, I mount his chest and extend all five fingers. The metal shines in the darkness, the light of the moon glinting off the bloodied tips. "Apologize."

"Don't kill me."

"Apologize."

Tim swallows hard, eyes shifting from my hand to my face. "I'm sorry."

"May you never find peace." He doesn't get to utter a single syllable, his gurgling scream lasting only but a second as I slice clear across his flesh. It's a straight line that spurts his life's essence onto my face and neck, staining my clothes. The feel of it on my face is warm and the cooling night breeze quickly forms the substance into a sticky calling that I lick off.

Those vacant eyes stare back at me with pure horror stretched across his expression as I do, a haunting sight of understanding I revel in before standing up, undoing his bindings, and dragging his frail corpse toward her back door.

He'll greet her in the morning. I promised a final goodbye.

Eerie silence follows as two beady eyes slither into the backyard, passing me as I head toward the exit. There's a secret door behind a large overgrowth of tall cedar trees that makes the back end look more like a tree farm and not a residential area. And yet, they're well taken care of, covering the metal exit at the center of the brick fence with iron trim that leads to a back alley and side street.

"Not a trace." At my command, the backyard's newest guest gives a nod, its white skin glistening in the moonlight while I'm cloaked in darkness. And while I'll forgo my goodnight kiss tonight, I'll take her soon enough and savor her sweetness.

My pretty girl is worth the wait.

Gabriella

I *miss you, pretty girl.*

My eyes snap open at those words coming from a voice that tonight doesn't elicit fear, but familiarity. I'm not shaking or sweating, and the room around me isn't the one from my dreams where blood touches every single corner as if caressing a fond memory.

Instead, I'm left panting inside *my* home and on *my* bed as I recall the heavy feel of eyes on me—watching me—while I dared to finger the edge of a bed which felt familiar, yet I know I'd never seen it much less touched it before. There was also the warmth of secrets shared between *those* walls and the dream version of myself, because tonight I wasn't a visitor looking around in fright, but instead a willing participant reminiscing with an old friend.

Maybe I fell and hit my head months back, and this is the insane dreaming of someone trapped in a coma? I muse right before a familiar grunt pulls me away from my thoughts and I look over at my companion of choice. Mr. Pickles is looking up at me from my right, and it's an expression I'm all too familiar with on his chubby little scrunched-up face: hunger and the need to potty.

"You want to go out?" His response doesn't come from a verbal cue, but a boop to my arm with his cold nose. "I'll take that as a yes. Come on, chubby."

Another noise of complaint before I can throw my legs over the edge of the bed, he jumps off and sits in front of the door. Mr. Pickles eyes me while I stand and stretch, little grumbles of annoyance passing through his lips while I shimmy my sleep shorts off and toss them aside before grabbing a comfy pair of sweats. I leave the plain grey tank top on with the built-in bra and rush to the bathroom after grabbing my cell, brushing my teeth in a haste while the impatient pup grumbles outside the door.

He eyes me from the threshold the entire time until we're heading downstairs. Now, he wiggles from beside me with an extra pep in his trot until we reach the bottom step and I lose him as he runs out before me.

The back of my home sits on a decent-sized lot with no neighbor to my left and two large open yards at the side and back of the property. It's overrun by trees planted by my uncle, and I haven't had the heart to clear them out because they also protect me from the occasional nosy neighbor or passerby strolling down the sidewalk.

However, the closer to the door we get, my dog starts to shiver. There's also a bit of warning in his bark. The low growl comes out, and he ignores the leash I picked up from the hook on the wall for our possible walk down the block. He's not looking at me, but staring at the wooden door as if waiting for something to appear.

"Quit being silly and sit." Mr. Pickles looks back but doesn't listen. "Sit, buddy." Again, he barks and this time bares his teeth, an action that is very uncommon for him, which puts me on edge. I don't hear anything or see past the small shade on the windowpane so I pull it up, and everything seems as it does every day: green and more green with a hint of brown from the wooden deck. With him not listening, it's hard to open the door so I pick him up, squirming and fighting in my hold, and walk us into the laundry room where I keep the travel dog crate. "Sorry, little guy. Let me check everything out, and I'll be back to release you."

In reply, his lips curl over his teeth and his eyes shift around. *What the hell?*

Closing the door to his crate, I step back into the kitchen and head straight for the back door without pause. My hand is on the knob and I turn it, pulling it open, and then let out a loud shriek.

Something falls back with a heavy thud. Its hair grazes my shin and when I look down, every cell in my body vibrates and a scream lodges itself in my throat, yet this time no sound comes out. Fear and shock overtake my senses and my anxiety spikes as wide, dead eyes look up at me from the floor.

His eyes are vacant. His face is a swollen, bloodied mess. The sole identifier on him is a small plastic name tag on his uniform shirt.

I take a step back and then another.

My legs shake. My chest rises and falls fast, not enough air entering its passageways as recognition strikes me.

Tim is dead. The same salesperson who just yesterday accosted me inside the art supply store and Theodore saved me from.

How? Why the hell is he here?

His throat is sliced clear across and the skin around it has what looks like small teeth marks embedded across the marred flesh. Several bites. Not human. He's pale and tied up—a horror-struck expression on his face as the pain registered before his last breath.

"Call the cops," I say, ordering myself with a steady voice that is devoid of the true panic building within. Every inhale is becoming harder. Every blink is failing to clear the sudden fuzziness in my vision, but it's the slithering of something large and white making its presence known that breaks me.

My steps back are clumsy. Like a newborn colt without control of its extremities, and I trip, a helpless cry leaving my throat as I crash to the floor butt first. The sudden impact hurts, the pain shooting up my coccyx shocking me into a frozen state as I take in its appearance.

The animal's eyes are on mine with its forked tongue flicking in and out, sensing the air around us. Its posture is unthreatening, yet it moves closer as it crawls over the dead body half lying within my home and half on the back porch.

I've never seen a snake like this, but I can automatically tell it's an albino constrictor, though if it's a python or boa eludes me. Moreover, no matter how hard my heart beats inside my chest, I press my lips hard together and remain still. Its movements are majestic, a predator knowing it has no threat here, and I've seen enough animal shows to know snakes sense movement and prey through their tongues.

And the last thing I want is for it to strike.

I want to appear bigger and unafraid. I want to get up and run. God knows I do, but I'm unable to so much as flinch while trapped in its gaze. The large body slides off the cadaver a few inches from me, coiling into itself while the head and a few feet of its body stand upright. Eyes a milky blue, the snake lifts its head and tilts it to the side, then waits. And waits.

No movement. No striking.

The only signs of its menacing power are the dead man and the albino skin wearing splatters of blood along the body and drying across its mouth. *How did Tim get here? How did this snake end up here, killing him?*

My rational mind isn't looking at the gash across the man's neck, but instead focusing on the bite marks and ripped skin straight across. Was it the pressure of a constrictor's hold that forced the skin to split open, which he then further ripped apart with its jagged teeth?

A possibility? Yes. I've seen enough wild animal documentaries to know that they're powerful and once the teeth sink in, tearing the flesh apart is the sole way to extract them.

Even as my mind conjures scenarios, the snake continues its

perusal of me—judging my reactions while flicking its tongue lazily in and out. We stay like this for a while, without so much as a muscle twitching. A few beads of sweat dot my upper lip and brow, and yet, the animal isn't showing any signs of aggression. His body is unmoving—watching.

I wait for the right time, psyching myself up to run toward the laundry room, when my cell phone rings. The sound is loud and the animal's reaction is swift, turning away from me and slithering down the back porch area and then disappearing into the trees. This catches me off guard; one second it's staring at me and the next, it's gone, completely lost within the greenery and limbs of trees—the leaves on the ground.

I'm unable to move. I have no idea how long I stay with my eyes set on the area the constrictor disappeared to.

Again my phone rings and I ignore it until a loud banging at my front door accompanies it. Then, there's the Ring alert telling me someone is at my door, and only then do I stand, noticing how much warmer the morning feels. My movements are on autopilot while my reaction is cold, eyes sweeping across the dead body before walking in the direction of the noise.

I don't know how to act. I can't even comprehend that this is real. *Is it, though? Could I still be asleep?*

"This nightmare sure took a twist tonight," I mutter under my breath, glaring at my front door as it comes into view. Someone is pressing incessantly on the doorbell, fist pounding, and I'm tempted to punch the person for making an even weirder dream more annoying. Without pause, I open the door and glare. "What now?"

At my outburst, Tero stops all movements, eyes wide. "Are you okay?"

"No." A bubble of laughter escapes me; the sound is shrill and a bit manic. "There's a dead body in the back, a snake tried to charm me, and I've completely accepted that insanity has overtaken me. This is all probably a hallucination, and you aren't even here."

"Can I come in?" He's talking to me as if I were a scared animal. Unpredictable.

"Sure. Be my guest." I wave my hand in a gesture to proceed, and then frown when I catch Theodore standing by the all-black SUV outside my door. "Why are you here?"

"You didn't show up and didn't answer your texts. Mr. Astor has been trying to get ahold of you for the past hour; it's midday now." He's walking deeper into my home, almost following the growls of my dog, and I'm right behind him. His footsteps don't make a single sound, something I find odd and reaffirms my belief it's all a dream, but the presence now behind me refutes the thought.

Theodore doesn't have to utter a single word, but I feel him. His touch seeps into my bones, making my heart race. His scent makes my mouth water, the temptation almost too great, and I catch myself before turning around and embarrassing myself.

There's something about his presence that overtakes my senses—pulls me closer—and when his warm, large hand grips my arm and tugs me back a step, reality smacks into me with the force of a freight train.

This is all real. This. Is. Not. A. Dream.

I'm awake.

There's a dead body...

"Oh, God." A sob slips past my trembling lips as my legs threaten to give out. I'm shaking, teeth chattering as I try to explain —say anything to Theodore who's holding me close to his chest— but can't. The sounds leaving me are full of fear and sorrow, and I'm fighting against my fight or flight that demands I do something.

Anything.

To save myself.

"Breathe in, Gabriella." The deep baritone of his voice breaks through my mental fog, but doesn't break the invisible binds tightening around my neck as I recall the time I spent this morning watching a snake while a corpse lay at my feet. "Come on, beautiful. I need you to breathe and—"

"Snake." Somehow I manage to utter the one word past my harsh breaths and the loud curse that comes from Tero. Not that Theodore moves us any further or asks his assistant what happened. Instead, he places his large palm across the center of my chest while pulling me closer.

"Breathe." One word, and I feel the way his broad chest expands against my back, holding the air trapped inside his lungs until I follow, and only then he releases. He keeps me like this, pushing me to follow the cadence of his warm breaths, and I do without hesitation as if commanded to do so. "Good girl. Just like that..." his lips are at the crown of my head and I shiver when he leaves a tiny kiss there "...you're doing so well."

In the distance, I hear the sirens. They're coming closer and closer until doors slam closed and heavy footfalls follow. There's shouting. I can make out the click of guns and instructions are being followed, and yet, I don't move from his embrace and continue to match my breathing to his.

I'm trapped by fear, and he's my lifeline.

I need him to anchor me because I'm close to crumbling.

"Police!" a male voice calls into my home, his hard raps against the door making me whimper.

"Come in." Theodore doesn't stop his calming ministrations. Instead, I feel him turn his head in the officer's direction. "My assistant is in the back and will fill you in. No one here is armed."

"Is she okay? Does she require medical attention?" Theodore answers him with a shake of his head, but the man seems to need more and from me. I sense him come closer. I feel his hand hover on my shoulder, and my panic rises once again. "Miss, are you harmed? Can you tell us what happened this morning?"

"Dead." Another sob. The small amount of relief in my chest once again tightens and I cough, scratching at my neck. "He's dead. He's dead and a snake—" Something in me snaps at that moment, the tethered string of consciousness withering into nothing, and when I meet the man's eyes for the first time, everything goes black.

Gabriella

Music plays in the background, the cacophony of instruments creating a melodic cadence that most inside the room sway to. In pairs, they twirl in a circular fashion while spectators talk quietly amongst themselves dressed in their best garments—sizing up their counterparts.

Some with greed.

Some with lust.

Some with a calculative stare while I watch from my seat at the center of it all.

The choreography follows the light tone playing from a small band of musicians entertaining the crowd, keeping those within the circle twirling and counting steps, switching partners between well-practiced hand maneuvers before tapering to a more sophisticated waltz.

Each couple falls in line and their forms, the sophisticated posture in the stance, become poised and full of finesse. Each step is refined, their pivots regal while onlookers give a small applause that *lasts no longer than three heartbeats before silence ensues and all eyes remain on the crowd of dancers.*

They do their best to ignore my presence atop a small, elevated platform where two intricate black chairs occupy most of its space. One throne is empty. One has me perched atop while dressed in an extravagant gown a deep shade of red reminiscent of the color of blood with a golden lace overlay. It's strapless, the bodice tight from my chest to my knees where it then flares out a bit. The silk feels soft against my skin while the lace is light and eye catching, provocative, and nothing like the dresses the women in attendance are wearing.

I'm modern to their Victorian modesty.

As my eyes traverse the room, my head is held high and shoulders are pulled slightly back. I make out many faces, all strangers, and yet, I don't feel out of place. If anything, this amuses me, and I find myself making a game out of catching the eye of someone daring enough to look my way.

"Not very nice of you, pretty girl," a husky voice says from behind my chair, his finger caressing the skin from my right shoulder across to the left. Goose bumps rise and a small illicit shiver rushes through my every limb. "You want me to paint the walls red?"

"Well, you're no fun tonight." There's a pout on my lips, which causes the man I've yet to see to chuckle. I'm being coquettish. I'm so comfortable with him, more than I've ever been with anyone in my life, and it's so outside my normal behavior. "I thought indulging me was the highlight of your life?"

"It is." Sharp fingernails leave a small trail of goose bumps, dipping ever so slightly beneath the thin material of my dress over the ridges of my spine. "But you must go back now."

"Back where? You're not—"

Screams rend the air and four male bodies fall on their knees, each one simultaneously cupping their necks. Blood pours from a thin line, their clothes quickly drenched in the crimson shade while those around them laugh.

So much laughter. So much morbid glee at the sight, and what's worse, I'm not affected. Not like I should be.

"Are you ready?" he asks, his breath fanning my cheek.

"Ready for what?"

"To wake up, pretty girl."

I'm pulled to consciousness with a harsh start. The noise inside the room is loud and matches my rapidly rising chest; a *beep, beep, beep* that fully awakens me, bringing into focus the white walls and lone window with partially opened curtains. The view showcases that I'm on a high floor and no longer in a ballroom where high society beauty—opulence—fill every corner. Instead, there are machines all around me, the blanket atop my bare legs is a bit scratchy, and I gasp when my eyes land on the lone figure sitting in an uncomfortable-looking chair to my left.

Theodore's leaning awkwardly with his head lulling to the side. His breathing is deep and hair an absolute mess, but in a way that's attractive while dressed in casual clothes like yesterday when—

Tim's body. The bloody snake. *Oh God.*

"Shit," I whisper rubbing my chest area, my voice almost indiscernible, and yet, Mr. Astor's eyes snap open at once. They meet mine; amber on green, and in them I find concern and understanding, two things that bring tears to my eyes. Not that I let them fall. I've embarrassed myself enough by passing out and who knows what happened after that. "It's nothing, really. This is all just one of those bizarre things that happen and become some anecdote I share as an old lady."

"Shouldn't I ask the question before you lie?"

Instead of denying his claim, I turn my face and pretend to take in the one-bed hospital room. "How did I get here?"

"You had a panic attack and passed out," he says, voice low, yet there's a hidden scolding there for looking away. "The officers at the scene called in the paramedics who brought you here. That was five hours ago."

I cringe, my cheeks turning pink. "Five?"

"You're safe, Gabriella."

"Am I?" The question slips from me before I can stop it, showing a man I barely know—a stranger—how vulnerable I feel.

"No one will ever touch you. Please trust me." I don't miss the emphasis on the word *you*.

"No one is fully safe, Mr. Astor, and tomorrow is never guaranteed."

"Look at me."

The sun has begun to set, the blue sky turning a gorgeous shade of orange with hints of pinks and purples. It reminds me of the subject matter for my showing, how danger always lurks and comes out to play in the dark.

The dark. Why didn't I think about the motion sensor cameras!

"Where's my phone?" I'm still not meeting his gaze. Instead, I catalog the changes in hues. "How long will I need to be here, or can I—"

"Look at me." It's a command this time and I follow, my face snapping toward his without conscious thought. And damn him, I'm once again hit with tenderness and concern. With understanding, without him uttering a single encouraging word. For a few minutes we stay this way, slowly leaning toward each other, and I let out a low gasp when his large hand cups my cheek. "You've done nothing wrong. You are safe."

"But—"

"I'll take care of it. I promise."

Those words put me at ease for no reason at all, but maybe it's someone caring that helps my mind cease its dreary movie reel. I grew up with no one defending me, much less giving me comfort, because in a group home where nine other kids are in your same position, the youngest are always shown off to potential adopters while the rest are left to figure it out.

For years, all I did was manage. Worked small jobs and fed myself, and even with the money and home my uncle left behind,

I've been frugal and low maintenance because the future can be volatile and unpredictable.

Elise herself has never been involved in my life outside of my work or social settings where I'm invited. And I've been accepting of this. Have allowed her to go in my place multiple times because it was the easier alternative.

Because her whine is something I'd rather not deal with.

Never again, though. Her actions as of late show a side I'm not fond of nor need around me.

Hell, I don't think she'd sit here with me while I slept after a panic attack.

Taking in a deep breath, I let it out slowly and nod. I'm choosing to believe him. I'm choosing to breathe in deeply and gather my thoughts and think rationally, and not like the frazzled girl I've become as of late. "Thank you, Mr. Astor—"

"Theodore to you. Always Theodore." His thumbs caress my cheeks twice before he sits back in his seat, the action abrupt while creating a bit of space between us. My lips part, the question sitting on the tip of my tongue. "After. Ask me after."

I nod, even though he makes no sense.

"Miss Moore," a male voice calls out before tapping twice on my room door, and my gaze turns to him. He steps inside without prompting, without explaining why he's here, and when he notices my fingers about to press over the red button for the nurse, the stranger whips out a badge. "I'm here to talk about what happened—"

I cut him off by holding a hand up. "First, I'd like your name, that of your precinct, and under what guise you are here. If you are here to get my account, you are more than welcome to stay, but if I'm being suspected of any wrongdoing, then it can wait until I am discharged and in better form to withstand your line of questioning."

Where my sudden bout of confidence comes from, I don't know or question it. And while I'm guiding myself based on crime shows watched with a bit of common sense mixed in after having had a panic attack years ago—the doctor then demanding I avoid stressful situations—I wait for his reply. I doubt he's taking kindly to my demands, his pinched face telling me as much, but I won't back down. Something has to give after the hellish crap I just lived through.

"That isn't up to you." The tone isn't one of warm regard while his posture is a bit threatening. "You are the last person to see Mr. Roy alive and—"

"That is a lie and we both know it." Theodore places a hand on the bed right beside my own, not touching me but leaning forward. His expression is hard, eyes narrowed on the detective who's yet to introduce himself. "Now, answer her questions and state your business. This will be her call on how you proceed, and if you want to test that theory, be my guest. The doctor can have you escorted out, citing unneeded duress being placed upon his patient and you'll have to abide by the penal code which ties your hands on all accounts."

"Who are you to interfere with a—"

"Theodore Astor."

The man swallows hard, his face losing a bit of color while taking a step back. "I didn't come here to create a problem for her. I'm just doing my job, nothing more."

"Then answer her questions."

My fingers drum against his hand to gain his attention. "Thank you."

The anger of a few seconds ago vanishes the moment our eyes meet. His face softens, and a small smile curls his lips. "Never thank me for taking care of you."

"I can, and I will."

"Is that so?"

"Yes." In that moment, everything disappears and all noises stop. I'm trapped in his stare, in the small flutter of butterflies in my stomach and how the tips of my fingers tingle from where I tapped his hand. *Why does he affect me so?* I've never been a prude, but no man has ever made me want the things Theodore does.

I've never wanted a man to claim my virginity. To touch me.

A throat clears then, and I feel my cheeks warm as I watch Theodore's grin widen. He's aware of the effect he has on me. "Miss Moore, I'm detective Ricardo Consuelos and I've been assigned this case. Mr. Tim Roy was found on your property this morning by you —is that correct?

"That's correct."

"Okay." He takes two steps closer and pauses, pulling out a small notebook. The action reminds me of my therapist, and I frown a bit, something Theodore catches but before he can ask, I'm shaking my head. "Miss Moore, I want you to know that while I don't suspect foul play, I do need to investigate and eliminate any possible doubt. Do you understand and agree to this?"

"Yes."

"Do I have your permission to question you now?"

"You do, but I have something that should make this simple." Both men look at me, one with surprise and the other with knowledge in those warm honey eyes.

"How so? Better yet, let's start with why you didn't call 911 immediately after finding the body." That comes from the detective. His curiosity is mixed with reproach while I look over at Theodore.

"Do you know where my phone is? Or can I borrow yours?"

"You can use mine." From his pocket, Theodore takes out a small device that reminds me of Tero's second cell, which he claimed was for family, and hands it over. Nothing fancy. It's basic. "Code is 1982."

Nodding, I punch in the code and open the internet app once the interface comes to the screen. The search is quick and even quicker is logging in and looking for the video in question. And while I do this, neither man speaks but they watch me, and only once I turn the phone toward Detective Consuelos does he understand my rush.

The timecard started recording around two a.m. and continues in intervals as the motion sensor cameras pick up movement. There's only a lull between videos that lasts ten minutes, but I'll leave that up to them to investigate.

I don't want to see him die.

I don't want to see that image ever again.

"You had cameras running?"

"That should've been picked up by the officers on the scene, Detective." Theodore takes the phone from me and hands it over to the unprepared man. "This should clear everything up for you—go ahead and look through the recordings. I'm sure Miss Moore will be more than willing to give you her login information when you're done."

"Of course. Thank you." Consuelos does just that, and for a few minutes I watch from my hospital bed as he goes through video after video from different camera angles, not bothering to mute the sound or his reactions to the horror-filled scream captured on each. *How did I not hear this? Is going deaf for hours a side-effect of my medication?*

To be honest, I don't even remember taking anything last night.

However, this happened, and I can only imagine what the detective is seeing, telling myself that it's a movie and not real life, but the haunting sound fills every square inch of this room and I shudder. My throat constricts a bit, and I can't stop myself from bringing a hand up to the area, which Theodore catches.

"Take the device outside," he hisses out from between clenched teeth, causing the detective to nearly drop the phone. "Can't you see what that's doing to her?"

Detective Consuelos looks at me then with a horror-stricken face, and I'm sure mine mimics his. "My apologies, Miss. This was both unprofessional and careless of me. I didn't mean to cause you any stress. We have more than enough evidence to clear you of any wrongdoing, not that you were directly being investigated, and we'll commence a different type of search. Do we have permission to bring in someone from animal control to catch the snake? Traps will be set up for your protection and to remove and relocate the animal who was probably released by an exotic pet owner."

"Yes," I manage to croak out, taking the glass of water from Theodore and then taking a few sips. "Please do."

"You have my word that we will catch it, Miss Moore. You'll be safe again." With that, he leaves and it's just myself and the handsome man watching me carefully. And while I have so many questions that need answers, exhaustion hits me hard and I close my eyes. The need to rest is nearly overwhelming, and the last thing I hear is so low I'm afraid it's all in my imagination.

You'll be staying in my home tonight.

THEODORE

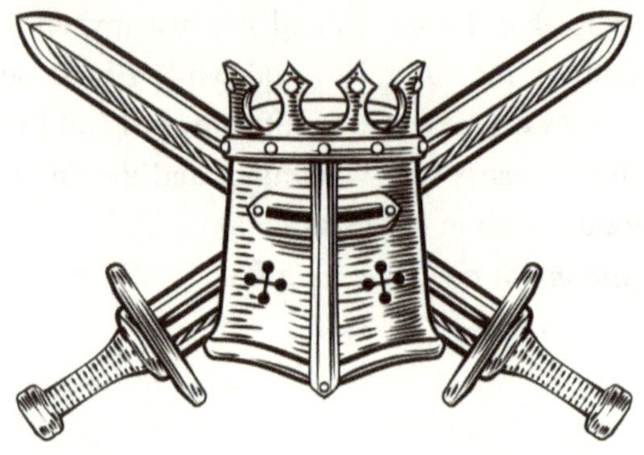

She looks so defenseless and small on that bed, but more so as the detective overlooking the murder case interrogated her a little after waking up. I wanted to safeguard her from this, to break his jaw when he insinuated wrongdoing for not calling it in right away, but Gabriella handled herself perfectly. So prettily.

She knew her limits and rights and made it known, especially when handing over the security password where two motion sensor cameras captured the event. I'll also be looking at the footage later while she rests in my home, because that's where she'll sleep tonight.

Under my roof. My care.

I'm not letting her out of my sight. Not today. Not tomorrow.

I'm a firm believer in fate, and it's led me to her. This is a predestined path we all must follow, and my admiration for her work has led to an infatuation with the little beauty that's been building for years. Her paintings are an extension of that inherent mouthiness that makes her all the more attractive.

I like her blushing tendencies.

I like her sassy responses.

She's naturally stunning and without pretentiousness; what you see is what you get. It's there in her expressive eyes and body language. There's no need to guess with her, and that's more than refreshing. It's so fucking sexy.

"Am I crazy?" she whispers while asleep and I chuckle, taking in the slow rise and fall of her chest. How her eyelids flutter and goose bumps spread down her arms. *So, little Gabriella naturally talks in her sleep? Adorable.* "Feels like it. Everything is out of my control."

"You're not," I answer even though the question wasn't for me—who knows what's going on in her dreamlike state, but if she can hear me, my hope is that I bring her comfort. Taking a hold of her hand, I slowly bring it to my lips and place a kiss over each knuckle. "I promise."

"But these dreams and the voice—"

"Dreams are just dreams, sweetheart. Nothing is wrong with you." My lips are against her skin, loving the softness of her hand. How delicate and small it is in my own. "You're perfect as is. Always have been."

Soft footfalls make a squeaking sound the closer to the room they get, and I turn to look at the door a second before the on-call attending peeks his head in. He's on the younger side and with wandering eyes that sweep across her face a little longer than what's appropriate and he knows it.

The asshole smirks to himself and walks in, but stops when he notices me. Blue eyes widen and a tan complexion becomes a bit pale; he backs down faster than he blinks.

"I'm sorry. I didn't know anyone was—"

"When will she be discharged?" I interrupt his meaningless apology. I'm not a man of useless words or platitudes; I say only what I mean, and nothing less. Anything else is a waste of time. He stares at me but doesn't speak for a few minutes and my patience is running thin, too thin to play this game. "Answer me."

The man swallows hard, nodding fast. "As soon as she wakes up.

Her vitals are stable, and other than exhaustion, Miss Moore is fine." Dr. Frausu, as his name tag reads, hasn't bothered to look at the machines monitoring her or the notes left behind by the nurse an hour ago. My jaw ticks and the hand not holding hers clenches, nails digging into my palm. "I'll have the paperwork ready for whenever she wakes up. Does that work?"

"You do that." There's a slight jerk to her hand and her breathing has changed. My eyes flick to her, and I notice the faster rise and fall of her chest. She's alert. *And yet Gabriella's playing asleep to listen in. Bad girl.*

"Of course, sir. I just need to check—"

"Get out." The words come out on a low growl, and I notice him flinch from the corner of my eye. He's also looking at the floor. "Send the nurse to check her as your incompetence isn't welcomed in this room. Understood?"

"I'm her doc—"

My head snaps in his direction, eyes narrowed. "I don't like to repeat myself. Understood?"

"Yes." He nods before I finish and then scurries off before I can acknowledge his response. Pathetic.

"That was mean." A low chuckle greets my ears, and I tilt my head in her direction while watching the door close. "And here I thought you were harmless."

"So is pretending to be asleep in order to spy on the conversation, Miss Moore."

"Which sin is worse?" she asks while I turn to face her, my body leaning closer.

"The one where you doubt my abilities to protect you at all costs." My words cause her to blush, and yet I also notice I ruffled some feathers. She's glaring while biting that damn bottom lip I yearn to lick. "Something on your mind, Gabriella?"

She scoffs, a challenging brow raised. "How is it rude when the conversation is about me?"

I don't miss her avoidance and mimic the action. "Easy."

"I'm waiting."

"I know." Keeping my eyes on hers, I get just close enough to make her gasp. For goose bumps to rise across her soft skin while I bite back a grin. "It's rude because it's beneath you. It's rude because I'll never hide anything from you, Gabriella. Ask me, and I'll always answer."

"Trust isn't freely given by me. Nor does this make sense." A red curl has gotten loose from her messy updo, and I push it back behind her ear with a single finger. She shivers. Shakes a little. "We don't know each other, and this makes no sense."

I nod at her low response. "We don't, and it does."

"How so?"

"Because sometimes life places a gift in your path that you'd be an idiot to ignore. Because there's something between us, more than this sudden attraction, that I won't ignore."

"And I'm that gift?"

"You are more than that."

"THIS IS MY HOME," I say after entering my penthouse apartment in the Belltown area a few hours later. She's been discharged into my care, per the nurse's request to be monitored and a bit of negotiating on my behalf. She doesn't know me well enough yet, and I was more than accommodating in sending a message to the detective working the case via her phone and mine explaining where Gabriella is and the why.

Elise also knows, but not by our doing. She'd found us leaving the hospital—were almost inside my car—when her false best-friend-instincts arose, and she tried to take Gabriella with her. Not that the blonde idiot cared or wanted to help, something the beauty beside me knows, but more to prevent this.

Miss Moore in my home. Close to me.

"Come on, Gabby," Elise says with the fakest smile on her face,

her hand reaching out toward the stiff woman beside me. "Let me get you home and settled in so Theodore can return to his busy day. I'm sure he doesn't have time to babysit you."

"How did you know we were here, Miss Scott?"

Her eyes flicker to mine, batting her lashes before attempting to seem concerned. Lies. A motherfucking lie. "Didn't Gabriella tell you she called me? She said she needed a ride home and I came down right away."

"Is that so?"

"Ask her yourself, Theodore. Right, Gabby?" Both sets of eyes turn toward the quiet woman beside me who promptly rolls her eyes at Elise while holding her hand out silently for my car keys. We are but a few steps from it, almost within reach if you lean over enough, and I hand them over without a second thought. "Gabriella! We spoke about this and have an agreement."

There's a hidden meaning behind those words, a tinge of a threat, but my girl's response is to unlock the door and get in, closing it with a bit more force than necessary, but the answer is in her actions. She wasn't going anywhere with her. Not that I would've allowed it either.

Gabriella could've left, could've let Elise manipulate her, but I was proud of her for not saying a single word. Moreover, I'm expecting her so-called friend's call. Because after our brunch fiasco, I've done my own bit of research and know more than she wants—what is beneficial to her.

"And you live here alone?" Gabriella asks out of nowhere and I bite back a smile. What she doesn't ask outright is if I'm dating anyone.

"I do. There hasn't been anyone in my life for a long time."

"And now?"

"And now you'll get a tour." This is the largest unit in this area and those surrounding, with over fifty-seven hundred square feet of living space, a wrap-around terrace, and an ostentatious master bath that I can see her enjoying. It's where I relax when in the city, and the interior reflects that with clean lines, minimal gold accents, and black-on-black everything.

All shades. All styles.

Modern. Mid-century. There's even a touch of farmhouse in the soft chenille blankets Tero's wife insisted I keep in a leather basket of the same color when she decorated the place.

"Trust me, Theodore," she'd said with a knowing grin. *"You will thank me later."*

I've always favored this color, and she sees that as I walk us in deeper with a hand on the small of her back. We pause at the entrance of the living room where the Space Needle greets her and the waters of Lake Union can also be seen depending on which way you look.

"Wow," is all she says, taking in everything. The Seattle skyline is the backdrop and its lights the sole hint of color dancing across my walls. "And you made it seem as though you didn't understand the difference in shades."

It's hard to keep a straight face at her jest; I know exactly what she's talking about, and I'm also proud of her for joking after everything that's happened. She saw Tim both alive and dead mere hours apart but is keeping her composure and trying to move past it. But that might also have to do with the medications given to her before we left, which should last the night; tomorrow is another day, and I'll help her through it.

Nothing that happened was her fault.

"When did I do that?" She tugs on my arm to face her and when I do, that small hand goes to her hip. Gabriella cocks it, watching me through a mock glare, and this time my lips twitch. The woman is refreshing. So adorable. "Is there a question hidden within that pose?"

"At the supply store..."

"What of it?" I know what she's insinuating, but it's much more fun to annoy her a bit. And it's because of the rough night that I push a little more, to keep her from going back to the awful memory. "All

I did was hear you go on and on while not interrupting. Temperamental artists hate that."

"You jerk!" But then her brows furrow, lips thinning into a line. "I can't believe she said that during a meeting, and that sadly, I still considered her a friend up until recently. I'm beyond embarrassed by Elise's behavior."

"That reflected on her, not you." Walking us deeper into my home, I take her into the kitchen while keeping my opinions on the woman to myself. Not now. She'll see for herself soon enough. Know everything. "Are you hungry? Thirsty?"

"Thank you for saying that, and no. I'm just tired and should probably..." Gabriella trails off, her eyes wide while slapping her forehead. The sound is loud, and I bite back my disapproval. "I can't believe I just—"

Taking the few steps between us, I cage her face in my hands and lift it up. She shivers a bit but also pulls in closer, which I more than approve of. "What's wrong? Is this about your dog?"

"Please take me home." The unshed tears in her eyes hit me in the gut. I don't like to see her like this, even if at times unpreventable. "I'll be fine, and I need to take care of him."

"No," I say the word low, softly. "You need to rest, and he is safe." Gabriella tries to interrupt me, but stops at the shake of my head. "Tero has him and will bring him in the morning."

"He has him?"

"Yes."

"And you didn't tell me this earlier because?" And fuck me if her huff and annoyance aren't cute to me. "Also, why are you so hellbent on me staying here? I'm okay, I swear, and—"

"I want you here because I'm worried for you. I want you here because I care and can't get you out of my head, Gabriella." Those luscious lips part, and a small gasp escapes them. "And I want you here because this unexplainable pull won't allow it to be any other way."

"Okay."

"Okay?" I chuckle, earning a roll of her eyes. "That easy?"

"I'm too tired to argue over who is right and who's gone insane." At her response, I rub my thumb across her cheeks. I love how soft she is and the way she reacts with another small shiver. "Besides, I'm just as curious about you as you are me and this weird attraction that I won't deny. That, and the detective and Elise..." the annoyance in her tone as she mentions the ex-friend nearly makes me laugh "...know where I am. You try something funny, and it will be you they look for."

"Is that a threat?"

A small shrug. "More like an honest observation."

"A very smart one," I agree and then drop my hands from her face. "Which is why I insist you eat and then get some rest. It's late, and you've had a long day."

"Not really hungry," she says through a sudden small yawn.

"But can I tempt you with anything?" At once, her skin flushes and it takes every ounce of self-control in my body not to nip her bottom lip. To taste her. "Tell me, and I'll make it happen."

"I'm fine."

"Fine is the code word for 'I'm not really okay' so speak up."

Her eyes flicker away from mine and toward the clock on my left, and the only reason I don't complain is how quickly they shift back. *I'm always so unlike myself around her.* "What I'd like is nearly impossible to get at this time. No use in arguing, but can I FaceTime my dog instead?"

"Tell me."

"No."

"Try me."

"Has anyone told you before just how pushy you are?" My response is a non-caring shrug. "Ughh, fine. Pie."

"Pie?"

"Yes, pie." My mouth waters at the response, my mind going straight for the sweet little slice of heaven between her thighs that I've yet to devour. Because I will. Not today, but I will, and it's hard to pull myself from those dangerous thoughts when I'm hard and hungry. Her saving grace is the rough day she's had and the hospital visit. "I want a piece of the PB&J masterpiece from the Pie Bar."

There's this wistfulness in her eyes as she tells me, almost as if tasting the treat, and I jerk hard behind the confines of my zipper. *Such an unknowing tease. So sweet.*

"Anything else?" It comes out a bit gruff, but Gabriella doesn't pay any mind, too lost in her thoughts of dessert. "Can I get you to eat something heartier first?"

"No. Just pie."

"Done."

THEODORE

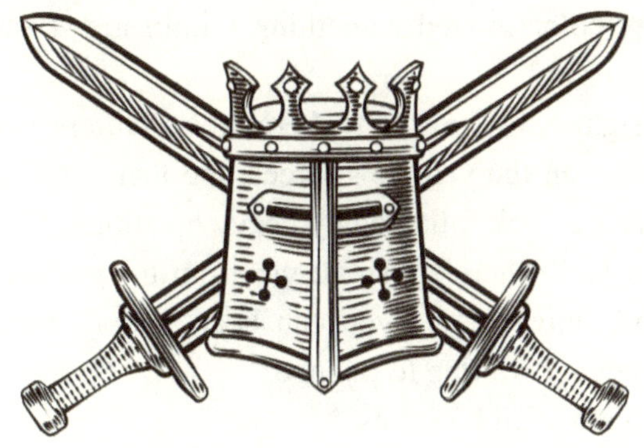

Gabriella's taking a shower when I step out of the penthouse and head down to the garage, the low moan as the water meets her skin becoming almost too much to bear. She was unaware of my presence inside the guest room while I dropped off a pair of sweatpants and a soft cotton shirt for her to wear.

I also left a note atop the bed telling her I'd be right back. That my house is hers to use as she pleases while ignoring how close she was.

Naked.

Wet.

Motherfucking mine.

I'd wanted to give her something that would make her comfortable, and instead, I received the gift of her sighing in contentment. That blissful sound made my already-hard cock throb, pulsing in pain for the release I denied it once again.

Soon, I whisper into the empty cab of my car while driving toward the Pie Bar like the easily manipulated man she's made me; something the beautiful woman is unaware of. Ignorant of the many ways I admire her and have for longer than she knows—I've wanted her since seeing the first stroke of her brush on a blank canvas.

Each new color moved something within me. I saw the world through her eyes.

Turning right onto the street where the restaurant is located, I hit the number two on the vehicle's screen and then wait. It rings once, and then there's a click followed by heavy breathing. "Tero."

"Evening, sir." There's a small yip from his end, and the owner doesn't sound amused. "As you can hear, I don't have a fan as a guest but an enemy waiting to pounce."

"He can pounce all he wants."

"I'm already aware of being his personal chew toy."

A bark of laughter escapes me as I pull into a parking space, putting the car in park. "She'll want to video call him in a bit to make sure he's okay. I'll need you to stay awake as long as it's necessary, my friend."

Even though I can't see him, I can almost imagine Tero nodding his head. "Will I be taking him into the office with me or—"

"No. Bring him to the penthouse at ten."

"Understood." There's a heavy silence afterward and then the sound of a door closing. For a few beats, I wait for him to gather his thoughts, but nothing. Instead, my patience grows thin and right before asking him to say whatever's on his mind, he lets out a frustrated sigh. "Elise called the office as you predicted a few minutes before it closed, demanding to know where you live and why Miss Moore is at your home. She was downright hostile toward Meera."

I close my eyes and tilt my head back, scratching my jaw. "I'm to assume she didn't ask how Gabriella's doing?"

"That was the least of her worries," he hisses out, tone heavy with disgust. "That woman is a rat in the grass without honor. Most pests hunt for survival while she leeches off friends to gain social status."

"Is that a personal observation?" I ask, already knowing the answer. His judgement is one I trust. "Or did you do your own analysis?"

"Both."

"Speak up as my friend, not an employee."

"They didn't meet by chance or accident, Theodore. Something else is at play here, and I'm worried for her safety."

"I know." There's a beep coming from the dash alerting me to the car turning off in thirty seconds if I don't press the okay button, but I ignore it. It's not important. "Someone wanted Elise to befriend her for a reason I've yet to uncover, but I will. No one will touch a hair on Gabriella's head."

"And I'll do what must be done, Theodore."

"You have my blessing."

MY EYES FOLLOW the smooth glide of her fork past those berry lips and then the slow tick of her jaw as she chews the bite of pie, emitting a low kittenish sound of approval at the taste. And fuck me, I find myself a little jealous of the inanimate object.

I'm hard in my seat. Fucking throbbing.

And yet, I don't make a sound or move while imagining those plump lips wrapped around my shaft, head bobbing up and down while that soft tongue traces the underside.

"God, this is hitting the spot after today's shit show." Another groan, her tired body wiggling a bit in the chair I placed her in. Each noise is a temptation. Each smile a caress across the head of my cock, the bulbous tip leaking for her. "Is there more?"

I pour myself a second glass of red wine. "An entire pie, if you behave."

"What does behaving entail?" The sass in her tone is alluring, but I hold myself back and instead focus on the red-rimmed eyes that look so tired. On the small sigh she tries to hide and the tense way she holds the fork.

"It entails your promise to sleep right after or at the very least, relax while watching a movie in the guest bedroom downstairs."

"That's it?"

"That's it." Her sharp brow lifts, but it's the grateful expression I'm captivated by. *What have they done to you, sweet girl?* "This is all I'll ask of you."

"Thank you." The tension in her body drains, and a bashful smile takes place. "You got yourself a deal, and I want another piece, please."

"I'm a man of my word." Standing from the table, I walk into the kitchen and pick up the pie she chose and take it back with me, placing it before her to take another slice. And she does so without prompting, opting for the larger cut while I'm left swallowing hard and reminding myself that I need to go slow for her.

I'm an obsessed man with this beautiful girl.

I'm going to enamor her until I'm the only thing she can focus on and allow as a distraction.

"Seriously, this place is a gem. Makes everything temporarily better."

"How can I make that feeling everlasting?" Picking up my wine glass, I take a sip of the sweet red liquid. "We can do this at your pace, Gabriella, but please know I'm here for you. I will listen and help you get through this as best as I can."

She swallows her bite, nodding her head. "I know."

"Do you?"

"Yes."

"And are you ready to talk?"

"No." Even though the one word shuts down the subject, her tone is apologetic and the last thing I want is for her to feel remorse of any kind. Extending a hand toward her, I wiggle my fingers until she smiles and places her warm hand in mine. "Now what?"

"Now, you breathe and eat and then lay down. In that order." Her fingers squeeze mine at that. "I will not push you to talk tonight, but tomorrow is another day. At some point you'll need to, and I hope you trust me enough to accept my help."

"Thank you."

"None needed, but if you don't hurry up with that, I'll be stealing —" I'm cut off by her pretending to stab my hand with the fork.

"Touch it and die."

"Dare me."

"You wouldn't dare harm my sensitive mind tonight, would you? Someone under traumatic stress?" I'm surprised by her humor but don't let on and instead, grab her plate with the pie and pull it toward me. Gabriella doesn't approve and growls at me, the sound so damn cute, and I smirk. "Put it back."

"Apologize."

"Sorry," she mumbles under her breath, face pinched. "Now give it."

"Only because you're just as sweet."

"You suck." A bark of laughter rumbles through my chest while she giggles. It goes on like this for a while; the harder I chuckle, she does too. Tears spring to her eyes and Gabriella wipes away the few that fall, shaking her head as her amusement lingers. "I needed that, you know."

"Needed what?"

"To laugh, because all I've done today is pretend." Gabriella takes her hand from mine and runs it down her face, the action showing me a glimpse of her true emotions. There's frustration but also fear. "I keep telling myself that it's not real. That this is a dream, but it's not, and the fact remains that a man was killed in my back-yard and I stared down a large snake while discovering the body. There's no getting rid of that mental picture. There are no words to calm down the panic I feel at just the thought of going home, but tomorrow I will because facing my problems head on is what I've always done. This is just another disturbing blip in my road."

"You don't have to do it alone this time."

"That's where you're wrong, Theodore. Sadly, I do."

Gabriella

There's something so comforting about finding someone with the same affinity as you. To stumble across the same similarities while opening yourself up to the possibility of more even in the midst of chaos. It gives you an anchor. A reason to ignore reality, even if it's for a few minutes.

What that more is, I don't know. Maybe I'll never quite figure it out, but today he's brought me peace within a whirlwind of fear that's made me thankful—susceptible to his every charm.

It's in the simplicity of a look or a conversation about the preference he has for the color black, one that matches my own. Because colors and shades are things I understand, and within his home and our conversation I found a bit of normalcy, a tranquil middle ground for my mind that's fighting back panic while high on whatever concoction the ER department gave me.

And while I appreciate the reprieve these medications have given me, they're not long lasting nor do they erase the damage done.

My eyes shift, and I look from right to left and right again. I take in the elegant wallpaper on one wall with what looks to be a black lattice design and then toward the gold sconces, giving the living room a warm feel. There's opulence here and from my quick glance, I can tell that these items are made out of real gold and not painted metal. At least, to a degree, as the karat and thickness and other materials used all come into play.

Every square inch of his home is decorated in different shades of the lustrous color—contrasting beautifully against each other while bringing its uniqueness to the forefront. The items give his home a gothic Victorian aura, a sense of what's dark and edgy, yet to me, it also feels homey. It puts me at ease.

Is it smart of me to even be here? No.

Do I find myself caring? No. At the moment, I don't.

Instead, I follow him down a dark hallway toward a large door where he stops and then turns to face me. His expression is soft and eyes hold so much understanding. Not pity. Theodore doesn't think of me as weak and shows me this by giving me the time to work out my thoughts before I can express them.

"This room is yours for as long as you need."

"Thank you."

"Don't thank me for taking care of you." He brushes past me on his way back toward the main living area, but before he can take more than three steps, my hand on his arm makes him pause. For a minute neither of us says anything, but the ball is in my court now and I walk around his tall frame and stop where I can meet his warm eyes.

"I do have to thank you, Theodore." There's an automatic twitch to his lips, the need to deny his act of chivalry, however, the truth remains the same. He owes me nothing, yet stayed by my side. He brought me to his home without knowing me without asking for anything in return. "For the first time, I had someone beside me in my time of need, and that's something I could never repay you for. And while it might sound silly to you, you being here makes it better. I wasn't alone."

Theodore stands there surprised by my words, and I take advantage, standing on the tips of my toes to reach his chin. The man is tall, so tall, and I'm barely able to press a light kiss to his skin while taking his scent into my lungs. It happens so fast and I'm inside of the room before he can utter a single word, back pressed against the door while my chest rises and falls fast.

There's no denying the shock of electricity that flows through me from the simple touch. The way my lips tingle and nipples stand at hard little peaks as I push off the structure and take in the room in detail this time, not the semi-high pass through I did before and after showering. *Distract yourself. Don't think about him.*

Easier said than done. Especially when it seems as though his scent—that man and earth with a hint of woodsy spice, infiltrates my senses and weakens my knees.

"He's a god in human form," I whisper to the room before forcing myself to concentrate, to not seek him out and ask for a goodnight hug. Instead, I look around the room I'll be sleeping in. At the center of the large space is a four-poster bed in wood that seems to have been burned to get that Shou Sugi Ban treatment, taking it to the point of being a step before charring so the grains would become more pronounced. Then, you have the matching nightstands and the feather-down black bedding, the thick fabric looking inviting—cozy —while the gothic pendants and chandelier give a romantic vibe. "This is beautiful."

Further into the room is the bathroom and closet, both stunning and following the same scheme of the home with more wood and dark stone and expensive lighting. *Definitely making use of that tub before I leave. It's perfect for added decompression.* My eyes continue their nosy sweep and land on a painting on the wall to the left of the bed, admiring the simplicity, yet the emotion behind the piece is there.

It's the sole source of color within this room that is not the customary black throughout the home. The backdrop is a blood red while the silhouette of a naked woman with long hair, her back to the artist, is highlighted in white.

And I find myself drawn to it.

It speaks to the artist in me and signals eroticism within purity. Freedom and love.

I wonder who the artist is? There's no signature that I can see, and while the curiosity kills me, I stay where I am and don't investigate further. The last thing I need is to have it slip through my fingers and land on the floor if I go searching for a name on the back. "Bed it is, then..." nodding to myself, I walk back over "...before I get myself in trouble." The comforter has already been turned down, and I don't hesitate to slip between the cool sheets, grabbing the remote to my left that's within reach and pressing the power button.

At once, a smile spreads across my lips when the screen clears and a Nat Geo special on the Amazon plays. It's then that I relax. Give in to my exhaustion. *Christ, this bed is heaven.* Comfortable, I find myself sinking into the plushness as some wild bird *caw caws* from what seems like a great distance.

It becomes lower with each inhale and exhale.

So low I almost don't hear it.

And when the jumbled words of the narrator start again, I hum before everything goes black.

THE NEXT TIME I come into awareness, there's a low hissing sound near me, then that of crunching leaves, and a squeak in the distance that causes my eyes to snap open. Immediately, I fear the worst, almost shielding my face with both hands as yesterday morning's encounter comes to mind and my body betrays me.

And yet, my reality is different. It's nothing more than another animal documentary playing on the television, and this time, on venomous snakes.

On cobras, to be precise.

The narrator is busy explaining their ophiophagy tendencies while my heart races and palms sweat. His voice drones on in the background, giving off some fact or another that doesn't compute in my head as I watch this predator eat its own kind after fighting to the death.

Her reason evades those responsible for the nature show as just moments ago she was bedded by the male counterpart. But then again, maybe this is nothing more than a show of survival instincts— a strike first without questioning his motives.

This moment on camera is cannibalism at its finest, and yet, her poise is unapologetic and majestic. There's beauty in her strength, a command to her presence that I understand on a level that's confusing, and more so is the sudden appearance of these beasts at every turn.

"Maybe I should be watching cooking shows instead? Baking seems innocent enough," I say aloud a second before there's a knock on the door. It's gentle, three quick raps that are followed by a low call of my name. "Coming!"

"I'll wait," he says, then mutters something else that I don't quite catch while I'm too busy scrambling off the bed and rushing over without caring what I look like. I also move too quickly and bump into the solid wood corner, my toe paying the price—the shooting pain nearly taking my breath away.

"Shit!" I cry out, hopping back and almost falling off the edge of the mattress when the door slams open and a worried Theodore finds my eyes. He's beside me in four long strides and picking me up, cradling me against his bare chest while walking out without a single word.

His body's so warm against mine. Feels so good, and it's easier to pretend my whimper is one of pain and not this uncontrollable attraction.

Being in his arms overrides my senses, and I quickly forget why he's carrying me in the first place. I forget about the hurt toe and that I'm only in his shirt, having kicked off the pants in the middle of the night when it got too warm.

All I can focus on is the feeling of his muscles surrounding my flesh and the feverish sensations that travel through each of my limbs.

We enter his living room and bypass the couch as he heads into the kitchen, placing me atop the granite countertop. There's a slight chill that makes me gasp, but I'm quickly warmed up by the hand massaging my thigh, squeezing in a way meant to be comforting when all it does is raise the temperature in the room.

I'm in tune with his movements. With the way his eyes traverse my short frame, from the crown of my head to the tips of my toes and back again.

And what I find more disconcerting is the absence of my shyness.

Where did it go? Why is it that I feel so at home with a man that for all intents and purposes is a stranger to me, in nothing but the oversized shirt he gave me? No panties. No bottoms. Nothing but the threat of the slickness on my thighs leaving a spot for him to find after I get down.

He's dangerous. So dangerous for me.

"Let me see your foot." Not a question, but a command. Amber eyes on mine, he glides the tips of two fingers down my injured leg until reaching my foot. Goose bumps rise across my body; his touch spreads through every limb and then settles in my core.

Christ, I clench. Hard. It nearly hurts and I bite my bottom lip, something he takes for pain and not the unknowing pleasure I feel. "It's just a bruise. It'll be good in a day or two."

He ignores the breathiness in my tone, choosing instead to drop to his haunches and inspect the area. Theodore is so close. A subtle shift of my hips and I'd be nothing more than a virgin offering, but I squeeze my thighs instead and hold my breath.

"It's so pink and already swollen." Tone gravelly, his nose flares a bit when he swipes a finger across the tender spot, pulling a hiss from me. I also move a bit without thinking, not that he'll see anything. At least I hope I'm not flashing him. "Would me kissing it make you feel better?"

Around him, my mind lives in the naughtiest of spaces and I almost beg him to. Almost. But I'm sure what I'm thinking and what he said have two very different connotations.

"That's okay."

"Are you sure?" He's looking up at me through thick black lashes and God help me, I bite my cheek to keep in the embarrassing sound that almost slips through. I even find the way his throat bobs harshly so sexy. "A kiss and ice would fix you right up."

I'd definitely need the ice to cool off. You're killing me. "Yes."

"As you wish." But then he does something that's so much worse. It's a total destruction of my senses. One small and tender flick of his tongue makes me forget the world around me and my bare pussy; I can't stop the way my back arches and hips jut forward a bit, just enough to flash him a second before he stands and hovers over me.

Right against me. Trapping me.

Theodore's clenched hands are on the stone countertop and his face a few centimeters from mine. His exhales become my inhale, and the hooded look in his eyes makes me shake. I tingle from head to toe—clit throbbing—and the man has barely touched me.

I need to stop this. But won't. Can't.

"Better?" he asks, coming a little closer, his stare flicking between my green eyes and my lips. Something unintelligible leaves me as a response, and he nods as if it were the most eloquent thing he's ever heard. There's also a bit of a smirk, the knowing look of a man who knows he's a walking temptation. "Then you should get dressed and meet me back in the living room in ten. Tero should be on his way up with your pup soon."

"Okay."

"I've also ordered breakfast for you."

"Okay."

"After he leaves, I'll drive you home myself..." his cheek rubs against mine, lips at my ear "...and make sure everything's okay for you to go back. Do you trust me to do so, Gabriella? To take care of you any way I see fit?"

"Okay," I say again, too distracted by his nearness.

"Good girl."

THEODORE

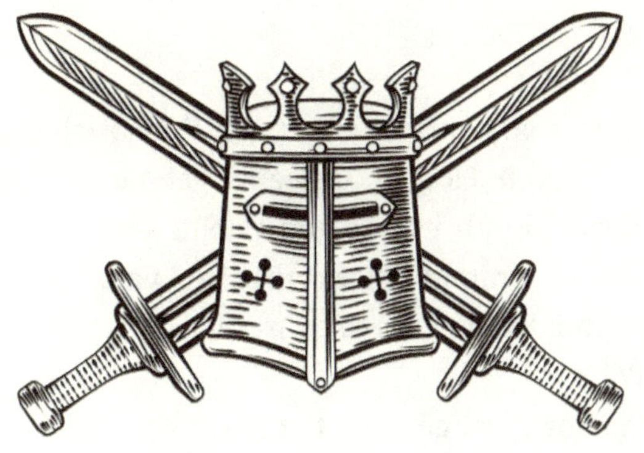

She's sitting beside me with her ever-loyal companion on her lap; he eyes me while she stares outside the window, lost in thought. Every once in a while her lips move but no sound comes out, her nose scrunches up but I don't know why and it's driving me insane.

Because with her—when it comes to her—there's always this innate need to know it all. Every last thought. Every reason behind her actions. To be the one that is there while helping her when the time comes.

"Are you okay?" I ask, my voice low inside the car so as to not startle her.

"What?" Her head turns in my direction and her expression is calm. She looks at peace. *So fucking gorgeous, and at the same time unaware.* Still wearing my clothes that are clearly several sizes too large, Gabriella is the epitome of stunning in her natural splendor. No makeup or perfume or revealing clothing is needed to showcase her ethereal beauty. "Did you ask something?"

"I did." Taking the next left, I turn down the street of her home. It's located at the end and on the corner with the driveway to the left of her front door where a garage remains closed. Pulling in, I put the car in park and then turn to look at her. "What's going on? You seem lost in your head."

"Thinking."

"About?" I hedge.

"That I need some coffee desperately." Gabriella is lying, but I don't call her out on it. Not yet. Instead, I get out of the car and come around to her side. I pull it open and extend a hand. "Come on. You make that coffee while I check the backyard and property for anything left behind that needs to be trashed."

"Trashed?"

"Police tape or garbage from the day." Her expression is one of confusion, and after helping her and the dog in her arms down from the car, I walk us up the front steps with her bag from the hospital in my hand. From the corner of her eyes, she squints at me in waiting. "Yes?"

"Be more specific, please."

"I will after you answer my question first," I say, which she furrows her brows at, but then the realization hits soon enough and I'm slapped in the arm. "Violence doesn't solve anything, Miss Moore."

"Quit being too good at turning things around on me."

"Then be a little more open and don't make me use the power of the Jedi mind trick on you."

"Seriously?" Laughter bubbles out of Gabriella, her head thrown back and shoulders shaking. "Jedi mind trick?"

"Are you mocking me, woman?"

"I can't breathe!" Another slap to my arm and then she's putting the dog on the ground as she bends forward, hands on her knees. She's cracking up, completely overtaken by something that isn't that funny, but if it's what she needs, I'll gladly supply the amusement.

Seeing her like this warms my chest. So carefree. So at ease.

"Are you done?"

"Almost. I swear." Another bout of giggles. She's wiping her eyes while straightening up, her expression a bit sheepish. "I have no idea why I find that so funny coming from you."

"Why?"

"Just can't see you as a Star Wars fan...that's all." Gabriella unlocks her door and Mr. Pickles is the first to enter, not sparing us a second look while hightailing it somewhere up the stairs. "Huh. Usually, he's whining for a treat right about now."

"A treat?" We walk straight through the main living areas and into the kitchen where I place her bag with the few belongings she had at the hospital. "What kind of snacks do dogs eat?"

I'm playing along with her, taking the opening as it presents itself. And this is one of those instances because while I might not own a dog, I do understand the reward system for a trusted companion. Human or animal, it's all the same, and you give to those that are truthful and deserving of your time and affection.

"Not a pet person?"

"I am, but not the conventional kind." My answer piques her interest, and I can almost see the questions forming in her mind, but shake my head. "I'm still waiting for an answer, Miss Moore. Tit for tat is the only way I play."

"You sly devil." It's a bit of a sneer, but I smirk at her veiled insult. So cute. "Fine. But I swear you asked for this, and I need some coffee first. Do you want a cup?"

"No, thank you."

Green eyes give me a questioning look. "I didn't see you eat or drink anything today."

"That's because I rose at seven and you slept in until late. My schedule can be quite rigid, and that includes eating."

"Oh." That's all she says, but I can tell there's more she wants to ask.

"Go ahead, sweetheart." My words cause a small tinge of pink to blossom on her cheeks, and the color is lovely on her skin. I'd like to see it in other places—her perky ass being one of them. "I'll answer any questions you may have."

"Are you on some kind of special diet?"

"You can say that, but it's more of a lifestyle change. The more organized I am in all aspects of my life, the more I accomplish."

"A lifestyle?"

"Rise early, meals only during certain hours, and eight hours of sleep every night, no excuse."

"Oh! You mean like fasting?"

"Yes."

"Cool beans. Does it work?" Gabriella walks to the coffee machine and sets it up, grabbing a large cup from the cupboard with some design on the front. "The fasting, I mean. It was trending all over social media a few months back and I was pretty curious, but when it comes to food, I'm too weak to abstain if a chocolate cupcake was to appear before me."

I shake my head, a chuckle slipping past my lips. "It's like everything else in life. You struggle at first, and then it becomes second nature."

"That's true, but..."

She trails off as I walk toward her, stopping only when we're face to face. Almost chest to chest. "Gabriella, answer my questions. What were you thinking about in the car that had you so lost inside your head?" I cup her face with my right hand, thumb caressing her jaw. "Are you in trouble? Do you need help?"

"It's nothing like that..." she swallows hard, eyes becoming a slightly darker shade of green "...it's silly, I swear."

"Tell me."

"Can't a girl have secrets?"

"She can when I know it doesn't involve her safety, Gabriella. That's something I'll never gamble on."

"I have nightmares, Theodore."

"Nightmares?"

"Yeah." Again, she blushes while attempting to duck her head but I don't allow her to. There's nothing to be embarrassed about with me. Never with me.

"Go on, beautiful. I'm here to listen and will never judge you."

Gabriella takes in a deep breath and nods, letting it out slowly after. Her eyes are on mine. "I've been having the craziest dreams for a year now and it's always the same, or lately, a variation of it." When I don't say anything, she takes that as a sign to continue. "Same room. Same house. The same voice asking me questions or talking to me as if we know each other intimately, and yet, last night, nothing. Without taking my sleeping medication, I literally passed out and just slept, and Theodore, for the first time in a long time, I feel rested. Truly rested."

"That's a good thing."

"That's an amazing thing, and what I was thinking about on the drive." Before I can reply, there's a sudden crash upstairs and the sound of something heavy falling over. Those innocent eyes widen, and I take off before she can attempt to do the same. Mr. Pickles is barking, his little growls not intimidating in the least, but I'll give the guy credit for bravado.

Footsteps follow me up the stairs and onto the landing, but before she can attempt to move past me, I place a hand on her stomach. "Wait here."

"Are you crazy, that's my dog and—"

"Gabriella, I'm not asking. We don't know what's in there, so wait here." My voice comes out harsher than I intend, but the situation hits home for her. We don't know what or who is here, and I'd rather she stay out here where it's safe. "I'll be back."

"Don't let anything happen to my dog."

"He'll always be safe with me." When she gives me her nod, I follow the sound of her dog's bark inside the last room on this floor. His body's half in the room and half out, his yips a little funny, but I understand once I'm at the door. "Oh, buddy. You're in trouble now."

The culprit is none other than her dog and a paint can, the latter splattered all over the floor of what looks to be her home studio. The shade is bright blue and has stained him, leaving little paw prints on the wood and when she steps beside me, I feel bad for him.

"Mr. Pickles!" she yells out, causing him to stop and look up with the most pathetic eyes I've ever seen on an animal. "What did I tell you about touching my experiment jar? This is the third time, dude, and now it's bath time before a timeout."

And bath time sets him off, the little shit running off and disappearing down the hall and into another room.

Gabriella isn't happy, huffing while walking past me. "I swear, if it's not one thing, it's another. My life was never so exciting before, and I miss the quiet."

"The joy of pets."

"Is this why you don't have any?" She grabs a bottle of some cleaning solution and sprays the area, nearly drenching it before grabbing an old towel from the same place. Gabriella wipes it down, and the frown on her face while mumbling about her dog is quite cute.

"My pets can't be housed like domesticated ones can be."

Her hand pauses its cleaning action, and her head turns toward me. "What's that supposed to mean?"

"I'm the private owner of a conservation outside of the country that houses the largest collection of exotic animals in the world. These are animals that were once pets and when the owners couldn't afford the maintenance or the city demanded they get rid of them, I took them in."

"You're kidding," she asks, her mess on the floor now forgotten.

"Not at all."

"For real, or are you yanking my—"

"I'm serious."

"Wow." Her expressions flicker from shock to curious to awe in the span of five seconds. Gabriella rises onto the tips of her toes, jumping in place, and I can't help but look at her breasts. The way they bounce. How perky they are with tiny little points that press against the fabric of my shirt she's still wearing. "...visit it?

"I'm sorry, what?" There's no shame in my expression, and she doesn't catch me looking either. The woman is too excited, rambling a bit, and I hold up both hands to pause her. "Slower, sweetheart. What were you saying?"

"I said, *Mr. Astor*...is it open to the public?"

"Yes and no."

Her perfectly sculpted brows furrow. "Yes and no?"

"It's not open to the public but would be for you. We can go after you—" This time, I'm interrupted and it's Tero's ringtone. He's not one to interrupt me unless it's important, and I don't hesitate to pull a different phone from the one I let the detective use at the hospital. Only he and his wife have this number. "What?"

"My apologies for the interruption. I know you're still with Miss Moore, but something has come up that you need to see." He sounds a little out of breath. Agitated. "Can I meet you at the office or penthouse in an hour?"

"Office, and clear the building," I say, my eyes watching Gabriella. She's curious, a little worried, but tries to pretend she isn't listening while bending to pick up the ruined towel. That one is tossed in the wastebasket before she grabs another, spraying more solution on the floor and repeating the process until it's clean. "Can you swing by the penthouse and pick up the file atop my desk? There's something in there we need to go over as well."

"Done." The sound of a car door closing comes through the line before the start of an engine. "I'll see you soon, and again, my apologies for the interruption."

"None needed. See you soon."

"If you need to go, it's okay." Picking up her cleaning supplies, she puts everything back where it goes and then turns to face me again, her hands twisting in front of her. "We've been here a while now and everything seems fine."

"Unfortunately, something work related does need my attention, but I'm not leaving yet."

"No?"

"No." Holding a hand up, I let my eyes wander around the room and take in a few pieces. She's truly gifted. Has a certain emotional touch to each painting that comes through the canvas and settles in your bones. "First, I promised you I'd look around and make sure that the cleanup crew I hired removed the mess left behind."

"What mess? Everything looks fine, and please don't run late because of me."

"The forensics team was here, and your home was searched from top to bottom, especially the downstairs doors and backyard, for clues. They dusted for fingerprints while others combed the yard for any clue as to how he got here in the first place. All procedural, but I don't want you to have to see or handle that."

"You're too kind, Theodore." There's a hint of relief mixed with so much gratitude in her tone. She makes me feel like the saint I'm not. If anything, I'm selfish in my need to care for her, to shield her as best I can from what cannot be stopped. "Has anyone ever told you that?"

"Only with you, Gabriella." Taking the steps between us, I lean down and place my lips on her forehead. I breathe her in. Her natural sweetness with a hint of vanilla and cherries still lingers after showering at my home. "Only with you."

KING

My pretty girl. My poor, trusting pretty girl.

Because souls like hers aren't meant for this world. No. They should only exist in a reality where they're protected—cherished—and yet, most are destroyed before they've had the chance to shine.

To grow and love. To relish in their freedom.

To discover what makes them different from everyone in the crowd, but then again, there's a beautiful lesson to be learned about true emotions. Because honest and pure don't exist, but loyalty and death are two things that will never fail you.

Someone who is loyal will never leave your side in sickness and in health. For richer or in your time of destitution.

And it's because I love her with a sickness that I do what I do. What I must.

My loyalty will break Gabriella and then put her back together again.

She will never leave me. Not again. Not by choice or circumstance.

Moreover, no amount of time walking this earth will ever erase how I feel about the whimpering woman before me, thrashing in her bed as she dreams of me. Of the darkness I control, and she will join, but only after I've broken her down to nothing. When I've stripped her of every ounce of innocence and unleash the demoness that's crawling beneath her soft, fragrant skin.

"I'm here, Gabriella." At my words, a whimper passes through her plump lips, her chest arching slightly off the bed before settling back down. Her legs, though, kick off the bedsheet and I catch a glimpse of the nearly bare pussy between her thighs. The shine of slickness that merges with her cherry vanilla scent, creating the perfect ambrosia. "Fuck, pretty girl. How you tempt me."

My mouth waters at the sight, and my teeth dig into my bottom lip, I want her. Yearn to hold her in my arms again and the time is drawing near, but not yet, and this is all I can take at the moment. To hover above her bed while watching. To lightly run the pad of two fingers up her thighs to her hip bone and then pause long enough to draw in another deep breath.

She's in the air all around me, her essence pulling me in closer.

"Where are you? Why can't I see you?" she murmurs in her sleep, head moving from side to side, and I smile. Soon she'll never have to wonder where I am or what I want as my need will be tattooed on her flesh for every motherfucker to see. "Show yourself, dammit."

Her impatience is a turn-on.

"Soon." A promise. A threat. My patience runs thin every single second I don't have her in my arms. "The world will weep blood before I lay it at your feet. They will all pay for what they've done."

But first, I have a game we are going to play. A scavenger hunt.

I'll leave my clues, and she will follow.

And for every item found, I'll gift her the revenge she unknowingly seeks.

Slowly. Methodically. Painfully.

Her enemies, known or not, are mine, and I take care of what belongs to me.

Because my love for her will never be soft or innocent, but it is honest. It's passionate and cruel to anyone who rises against my pretty girl. So for now, Theodore Astor is useful and brings her comfort, which I'll allow, but that will only last but so long. I'll let him watch out for her until it's time. I'll let him check the corners of her home—comb through her yard for anything being out of place—while I leave behind traces of my presence that can only be found by her.

Like the one she's yet to uncover in her closet.

Like the small charm I just added to her bracelet.

Like the black rose I placed atop her mail pile with a note attached while she bathed her dog earlier. The perfect distraction to slip inside and watch for a few minutes, to bring the shirt she left atop an oversized chair to my face and inhale deeply, nearly drowning in her maddening scent. His mischief granted me that moment of reprieve, and I'll thank him kindly for it in the future.

Moreover, the police never saw me in her yard through the cameras easily bypassed by its own technology when I hacked the system. They have no recollection of the man that's always near and watching, of the way I hunt with methodical movements while revealing each piece of the puzzle my pretty girl will soon understand.

"Long live the queen."

Gabriella

My phone pings from beside me and I look over at the screen, pausing mid-shadowing. It vibrates and then stops, only to alert me once again that I haven't read it within a minute. Theodore's name flashes and my heart skips a literal beat.

There's something about him that I can't stop thinking about. An attraction I don't want to fight off.

For the first time in my life, I want to be selfish and claim something as mine, no matter the cost.

Sliding my finger across the screen, I enter my PIN and click on the new message, smiling when I read it.

> Be ready by nine. Dress comfortable and to walk.
> ~Theodore

So bossy.

"I'm not going to give in so easily, Mr. Astor."

> Sorry. Have plans. ~Gabriella

His replies are instant, and my grin widens.

> Consider whatever you had planned now canceled. ~Theodore

> You're mine today. ~Theodore.

Grabbing my now lukewarm coffee, I take a sip and look at my sketch. The outline for my jaguar is done, I'm mimicking a pose from an animal documentary that showed the animal literally fighting off a gator and then dragging him up onto the shore. There's something about the design that's bothering me, though, and I think it might be the eyes. *I think they need to be enlarged.*

Another three dots and then a message.

> Don't ignore me, beautiful. We're going on a hunt today. ~Theodore

Putting my sketchpad down, I stand and stretch. "God, that's good," I groan as my muscles pop loose after being in one position for so long. It's a little after eight and there's time to shower and feel human, but what to wear?

"Closet first." Taking my coffee with me, I walk to my room and head straight for the closet. My style is comfy meets artist and paint splatters aren't outside the norm for me. I really don't own a lot of clothes without some kind of accident on it, and I release a drawn-out sigh. "I really need to start wearing overalls in there, instead."

Skirt? No.

Dress. No.

I own a lot of jeans and cargo pants, but neither is catching my attention and after going back and forth between capris and cutoffs, I go with the latter. They're a blacked denim style with the pockets falling out of the leg and I pair it with a black and white tie-dye shirt that I'll knot at the waist.

"My black Converse will work just fine." Tossing the items on the bed, I flick my eyes to my bedside table and let out a low *fuck me*. It's now 8:35 a.m. and I'm not even showered. *I also didn't respond to his last message!* "Next time, he needs to let me know of said plans to kidnap me a day in advance."

> In the shower now. Don't be late. ~Gabriella

I almost trip in my haste, catching myself at the last minute. The phone pings as I push my hair back from my face, already exhausted and we haven't even left. *Being a girl is hard.*

Another text alert and I open them once I'm inside the bathroom and have the water in my shower running. Steam begins to billow around me while my grin widens. Such a man.

> I'm already downstairs and waiting. ~Theodore

> Although I'm suddenly tempted to stay in and have a drink. I'm parched. ~Theodore

My response back is a picture of my hand under the water and then I toss the device aside, taking the fastest shower known to mankind. Literally in, lather, rinse, and out without enjoying the pure bliss that is standing beneath the near-boiling water while you contemplate life.

I'm inside less than ten minutes and have another two messages when I step out.

> Would you forgive me if I break and enter? ~Theodore

> I'll buy your forgiveness in the form of art supplies and my services as a personal assistant for forty-eight hours. ~Theodore

"Very tempting offer," I muse, towel wrapped around my body as

I walk out of the bathroom and into my bedroom. Usually, I'd lie in bed and air dry for a bit, loving the cool breeze over my skin after a hot shower, but today I have no time and run the towel down my body.

It takes me another fifteen minutes to get dressed, perfumed, and then add the tiny bit of makeup I use. Just some winged liner and a bit of cherry tinted lip-gloss to make my full lips a little plumper. My hair though is the one thing I have no idea what to do with, but decide last minute on two French braids with the ends laying on either side of my neck and down to the top of my breasts.

"That's as good as it's going to get." *I hope he likes it.*

"YOU BROUGHT ME TO THE ZOO?" I ask, a little awe in my tone when he comes around my side and opens the door. We're at the Woodland Park Zoo and I'm as giddy as a kid at Disney. "Really?"

"Is that okay?" He knows the answer, though. The smirk on his face says it all. He's pleased with himself. "Or would you rather go—"

"You can go if you want, but I'm staying."

"Good girl." Theodore offers a hand which I take, letting him pull me out of the reserved spot near the entrance. We don't get in line to purchase tickets, but instead walk right through the main gate while employees nod at him. It's a bit odd, but I don't ask and choose to believe this is all part of being rich.

He probably donated money to an exhibit, and they let him in for free. "Which area are we heading to first?" I ask, grabbing a map from one of the tourist stations. "Are we going to begin in Africa and work our way through or...hey!"

"We don't need this, sweetheart." At my perplexed expression, he taps my nose with the tip of his index finger. "I know the place well, Gabriella. I've also set us up to have the Rainforest area to ourselves. You'll have all the time you need to study predators, draw if you like, while I get to watch you in your element."

"Really," I squeak a bit, beyond excited. "That's amazing..." but then my excitement dies just as quick "...wish I'd known. I would've brought my sketchpad with me; I was actually working on a jaguar this morning when you sent the first text."

"Come with me." Theodore intertwines our fingers, tugging me along behind him as we walk toward some area of the park. I've been here a few times in the past, a long time ago on school field trips, and still have no clue where he's going. The people around us turn our way, a few murmuring to themselves, but he pays them no mind and doesn't stop until we reach the entrance to the Rainforest attraction. "Do you trust me?"

"I do." Not a lie. Something inside me begs me to, without hesitation.

"Then you should know I'm a man who's always prepared, and that includes our date." My heart flutters at that word. That he describes our little outing with an intimate connotation. "I have everything you'll need inside."

"Still letting it slip you were a Boy Scout, I see." I'm smiling so big—probably look insane—but I'm so touched that he went to all this trouble for me. "Or is this part of being a CEO?"

"More like I want you to be happy." *Christ*, that answer makes every muscle below my belly button clench. There's something so attractive about an attentive man. It's sexier than his looks. "Ready to head in?"

"Lead the way." If he notices that my voice came out a bit breathy, he doesn't mention it. Instead, Theodore walks us into the *closed for a private tour* exhibit and goose bumps rise as the first grunt of an animal is heard. It's a playback of some sort coming through the speakers, but it has the same effect.

The first thing I see after crossing the threshold is a small table and two chairs set up with art supplies atop it. He wasn't kidding that

I'd have everything: charcoal, colored pencils, regular pencils, paints, a few brushes, and even three large canvases sit atop.

My lips part and I shift my eyes to his. "Wow."

"Told you."

His smug expression makes me want to pinch him, but I don't. Instead, I roll my eyes while waving the hand not in his, in front of me while fighting back a giggle. "I definitely see."

"But are you ready?" He picks up a leather-bound notebook and a set of mechanical pencils, the same ones I have at home. All the while my hand remains in his, he refuses to let go or doesn't notice. I'll also be damned if I tell him. "The yellow anaconda should be feeding soon."

"Are you serious?" I ask, even though by now I shouldn't be surprised. "We get to see that?"

He nods, his amusement clear to see. "Two words."

"Private tour?"

"More like date 101."

"The 101 of that answer isn't a word."

Even his careless shrug is attractive. "Well, I'm treating it as one."

"Then lead the way, Mr. 101. Seems you're in charge today." My sass earns me a wink and then we're walking, his body always close to mine as we make our way to the serpent area. It's large and my eyes keep skimming between the different species, taking in their colors and lengths—the patterns that set the venomous apart from their possible harmless counterpart.

Some glass enclosures are larger than others, but when we reach the anacondas, I'm in awe.

Completely enthralled and I don't realize I'm stepping forward, almost standing against the thick glass, until the animal's head snaps up and our eyes meet. It's curious. Its large body is half lying, lazily, on the shallow water surrounding a rock formation meant to mimic a wild setting.

No coiling. No sticking its tongue out.

Instead, the animal lowers its head while Theo wraps an arm around my shoulder. "They'll be here in a few minutes. You want me to grab you a chair?"

"No." I can't look away from this animal. So much power. So much strength. And yet, right now it seems docile while keeping those dark eyes set on us. *Why am I not afraid?* "Do you know what they feed it?"

"From my understanding it's rodents and rabbits. All pre-killed before being put in the enclosure." And right on cue, a small door opens, and a metal claw-like stick appears holding a limp rabbit from its grip. The animal is plump, probably fattened up for the snake, and yet the anaconda stays in place.

They drop the rabbit near the water's edge, causing a small splash. And that does catch its attention, the large snake striking before the pole used to feed exits. Its mouth opens, a lightning-fast move before locking in place and the coiling begins. Tighter. Tighter. It's morbid to watch, but my fascination outweighs the disturbing sight and I find myself sketching before he begins to swallow.

My drawing is of a proud animal, head up high and eyes straight ahead. It's unafraid. Hungry.

"That's amazing, Gabriella," Theodore's voice comes from beside me, his lips near my temple. "Very detailed."

Turning to look at him, I lift my head and almost gasp at how close we are. Our lips are almost touching, and heat spreads across my cheeks. "Thank you."

"Will that be one of the paintings?"

"I think so." My eyes flick to the animal. I'm a little nervous having him so close, but look away just as quick. The animal is mid bite now, and it's a grotesque sight. "How about another exhibit?"

His chuckle fills the space. "More reptiles? Or how about we head toward the ape area." I love gorillas, but there is another animal I'd rather see more.

"How about a big cat instead?"

"A jaguar?"

"Please."

"I'm here to please you, sweetheart." Heat flashes in his eyes, and they darken for a moment—the length of time it takes a person to blink, before it's gone—and I'm left wondering if I ever saw it. "All you ever have to do is ask."

"No matter the request?" I ask, and the room goes from freezing cold to hot. My body reacts, nipples tightening at the possible meaning, even though his expression doesn't give anything away. "That might be a dangerous offer, Mr. Astor."

"It is, but I'm more than prepared to pay." Then I'm being pulled out of the snake encounter and we're walking toward an open-air area that houses the jungle cat in question. He doesn't say anything and neither do I, but the words still hang in the air.

They make me smile. They make butterflies appear in my stomach.

"Ready to have your mind blown again?" he says, taking me out of my thoughts and right back into a present where I'm in front of a beautiful animal with this gorgeous man beside me. How did I miss us stopping in front of the glass? But more than that, the jaguar in question is standing near the glass lying down and licking his paw without a care in the world. "Meet the real king of the jungle, Miss Moore. He's been waiting to greet you."

Gabriella

"Avoiding me now, Gabriella. How mature of you." Elise says just as I lock my front door a few days later. I've been holed up inside my studio for seventy-two hours since getting back from the dictionary equivalent of a perfect date. That amazing day where Theodore blew my mind throughout, always so attentive—making sure I had everything at my disposal to brainstorm my next line of paintings for his gallery.

Moreover, I've also been busy getting the base coat done for each. They'll fall within the same scheme: dark with a gradient effect that will end with the darkest shade at the bottom and that new tone I'd found at the craft store, creating a halo effect.

So far, they're perfect after the initial trials—a few pieces that looked horrendously lifeless no matter which way I attempted to add some vibrancy through shades of dark blues and purples. My mind wasn't in the right place that first night back, still dealing with the insanity my life has become, and it took a binge-watching session of old-school cartoons to clear my head.

Now, the hint of luminescence coming through within the darkened room and strategic lighting I've mock-placed for that purpose jump out of the canvas, depicting a jungle-inspired night with stars on the horizon in the shape of my favorite astrology signs. They've kept me occupied, consumed, and I've ignored the outside world for my work

Not a first for me, not by a longshot, but Elise seems very angry by this. *Where was she when everything happened and my panic attack right after? But more importantly, how did she know where to find us when I was discharged?*

My so-called best friend was nowhere to be found after our last conversation, and it's been almost two weeks since then. That time when she accused me of being cheap, a bit pathetic, and demeaned me for still being a virgin. Funny, how is someone with their hymen intact a whore?

"That coming from someone who didn't have the decency to call and ask how their friend is coping? Not so much as a text either after once again embarrassing me in front of Theodore." Pocketing the keys, I adjust my messenger bag and turn to face someone I thought of as a friend for so long. As my family. "Or how about the lack of apology after insulting and belittling me? Or trying to enter my home without permission?"

"What happened at Theodore's?" she asks instead again—same as last time—ignoring my claims while inspecting her broken acrylic nail. *She doesn't know about our date.* I'm also not going to share. "What did you do there?"

"Why are you here?" I counter with just as much iciness, taking in how messy she looks. This isn't the woman I know. The same one that dresses to the nines at all times of the day and throws shade at anyone who doesn't follow her fashion-forward protocols. "And don't lie, or add in fake concern for me. That ship has sailed."

Her hand clenches, and the smile on her face is sardonic. "Going against me is a grave error, Gabby."

"No. That was not seeing you for what you truly are." Her face pales at that, eyes widening a bit as they meet my own for the first time. Such a weird reaction to a statement about hypocrisy. "You lied to me, Elise, over and over again, and I'm done." *Prove to me that I'm wrong and you aren't the kind of person you're behaving like.*

"I made you who you are." At this, I scoff, bored with this conversation. It's taken me some self-reflection, but I've come to terms with her true feelings—understand those little quirks that for so long I made excuses for. Moreover, those words shred the last little bit of hope I held that she was concerned and nothing else. "The Astor Galleries would've never so much as looked at your garbage portfolio without my assistance. You needed me, and I did what needed to be done in order to rise to the top."

Those words show me her true colors.

Greed. Selfishness. Envy.

It hurts. The betrayal stings, but the fact I've been too stupid to see past the *I have a friend* syndrome embarrasses me. Makes me question who I am to allow this.

"You faked being my friend all this time. Used me." Swallowing back my emotions, I level her with an indifferent stare. I can see this bothers her. And I also smirk at how easily ruffled she is. *How did I not see this before?* "What do you get out of all this crap?"

"That's not your concern, Gabby." It's a hiss through clenched teeth, her eyes narrowing. Elise's posture is meant to intimidate, and yet, I find myself matching her movements. I'm not budging or backing down, much less asking her to forgive me. I'm not going to cower, and when she brings a finger up to my face, I don't hesitate to grip her wrist in my hand and squeeze tightly. "Let go."

"What do you gain?"

"Just know that in this game, I'll always win. I've done so many times already." The woman sounds like a crazy person.

"What does that even mean?"

"Let go." She steps into my personal space, yet fails to remove her arm from my grip. Instead, the closer she gets, the more I tighten my hold, and I don't miss the look of surprise that flashes across her face. "You're pushing your luck today. Last warning."

"Answer me."

"It means you're out of your league, little girl."

"That's where you are wrong, Miss Scott," a male voice says and both our faces turn, finding Tero standing not far from us with both hands in his pockets. He's dressed for a day at the office, yet no blazer, and the tie is long gone, it seems. "Now, why don't you share with her the illegal move you tried to accomplish three days ago after seeing that pathetic man who worked as a copyright lawyer."

"This doesn't concern you."

"Oh, but it does, mulher. Você está fodido."

Once again, Elise tries to snatch her arm back, and I relent after her second failed attempt, stepping off to the side. Tero also takes his place beside me, leaving her ample room to walk back the way she came, and after another glare, she does. There's no explanation from her over his accusation, and dread fills my stomach.

"Why would she go see a lawyer? What is—"

"We need to talk, Gabriella. Let's take a walk."

"Only after you tell me what you told her in another language?" I'm already heading down the pathway with him close behind, almost like a guard dog protecting my steps. "And where is Theodore? I haven't heard from—"

"One at a time, Miss Moore."

"Cut the formalities, Tero." Rolling my eyes, I head toward the park nearby. This deviation is going to put me behind schedule, my much-needed trip to the supply store will be a tight one, but he has to be here for a reason. "Spill."

"All I said is that she's fucked in Portuguese."

"And I learned something new." Laughter, loud and high-pitched, bursts forth and I'm unapologetic in it. Thank God he doesn't get offended, and instead chuckles beside me, shoulders shaking. We stand like that for a few minutes on the sidewalk, both finding hilarity in the stupidest thing, but then another thought pops into my head. "Is that your native tongue?"

"You could say that since I was born in Brazil." He's smiling, the look on his face one of reminiscing while pointing toward the park's entrance. I'm following his lead, and we walk until reaching an open area with benches along the path. No one is there and before I can ask, he bumps his shoulder into mine. "Besides, you'll probably have worse to say when—"

"One, are you stalling? And two, most definitely."

"You could say so, but—"

"I'll take it from here, Tero."

His voice never fails to send shivers down my spine and harden my nipples. It's soothing, yet feels like molten lava flowing across my senses, a dominating presence that's undeniably man. Sensual. Commanding.

"Theodore."

"Hello, beautiful." He steps beside me and bends down just enough to lay a kiss on my cheek as the other man leaves; his lips hover there a second longer than what's considered the norm. My skin also tingles there. My body wants to feel them again. "How have you been these last few days?"

"Relentlessly working."

"On my pieces?"

"Yeah." Theodore attempts to ask me something else but I shake my head, holding a hand up. "But I have a feeling that what you need to share is far more important than my delving into the wonderful world of bases and setups."

"True." He doesn't chuckle as I expect, and my stomach twists. "Please have a seat."

"How bad?"

"Take a look, and I'll tell you what I think." It's then I notice a folder already placed on the bench, and I sit on the edge before picking it up with a bit of hesitation. My eyes go from it to Theodore's, and he nods, encouraging me to open up and read down the first page. He chooses to remain standing while I flip to the next page and the next, not truly wanting to believe what I'm reading while I'm once again smacked in the face by betrayal. *Why, Elise?*

"Jesus." Because what else can I say as the papers in front of me depict how Elise tried to copyright my artwork as her own. The filing is here. It's her name on the dotted line. "How the hell could she do this? Does this mean she owns my currently available work? What about the pieces already sold or commissioned?"

Is this part of her threat? What she's using to warn me off with?

Tears gather at my eyes, and my heart clenches so painfully tight that I gasp, the papers falling from my grasp. All my hard work. All the sacrifices and hours spent in my studio.

"No." His one-word response causes me to look up at him through blurry eyes. "She will not get away with this, Gabriella. That's my promise to you."

"But what can I do? If she's approved and—"

"My lawyers have already submitted the paperwork necessary to prove that she's lied on the application along with a signed affidavit from her crooked attorney stating this."

"How?" I ask, because what person would willingly admit to filing an unlawful form with the intent to harm knowing this could cause him to be possibly sued or fined. "Why would he do that?"

"I'm persuasive, and we'll leave it at that."

"What did you do?"

"Scared a good twenty years off his life," he says, his eyes alight with amusement, and I can't help but smile even though a part of me just died. Even though I surely look like a mess, eyes watery and cheeks blotchy, I'm relieved by his words. I also have no way to pay him back for his kindness. "And whatever you're thinking, stop it. I'm sure karma will deal with them both and fairly."

"I'm still so thankful."

"And I promised to take care of you. Did I not?" At my nod, he takes my hand not clutching the folder and stands me up. Just one tug and I'm against his chest. His arms snake around my waist, and his unoccupied hand lifts my chin. Those lips are so close to my own, his touch so comforting when I should be a crying mess. "It's also why I had Tero follow her since yesterday and came over when he called to tell me where she was heading. I'm willing to fight all your battles, Gabriella. To be what you need in whatever shape you need me to be—be it a friend or the devil himself, but please know that everything I do is with your best interest at heart."

THEODORE

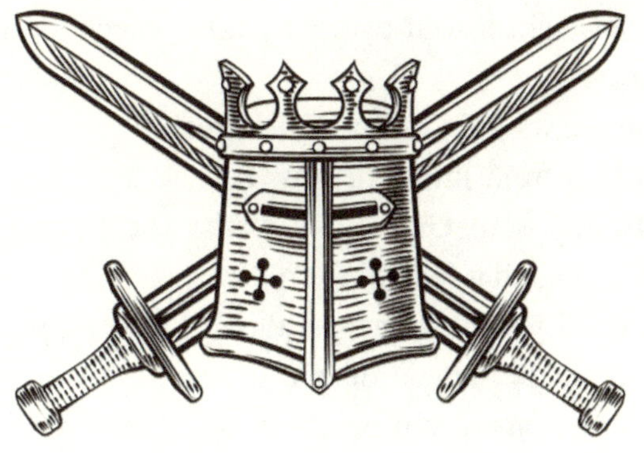

Tero's waiting for me inside my office when I walk in. The gallery is empty except for the two of us and his wife who sits in the lobby while reading through some paperwork. Meera's inquisitive gaze follows me, I know she has questions but waits until prudent, to ask them.

"What did you find?" I take a seat behind my desk, my chair creaking when I lean back.

"Not me, but Meera." At the raise of my brow, Tero pushes a black folder across my desk. "You might want to take a look at that."

The first page is one with quotes from five different law offices, and each one deals with copyright law. The numbers are high for all, but the last one is the only one willing to take on the case without proof of ownership. "Who is he?"

"Turn to the next page."

And when I do, my blood boils as a standard contract sits before me between Elise Scott and one David Hall from Hall and Hall Associates in Portland. Something that in and of itself throws a few red flags up as he's been in trouble before for fraud, a case that made the national news sites. And two, why not someone local and with a better reputation?

"How many laws does this contract break?"

"At least five from initial review, but the largest is illegal intent to acquire the rights to Gabriella's work. The government doesn't take kindly to lying on a federal form."

"And how did you come across this?" I ask, flipping to the next page and reading the details of every item listed in the over forty copyright submissions. From paintings to a handful of sculptures to the right to my commissioned pieces. "The conniving bitch."

"Elise is worse than that, but she's not acting alone." At my nod, he lets out a small chuckle. "And to answer your previous question, my wife was looking into one filed for the gallery and randomly made a search under Gabriella Moore. This is what came back as Miss Scott was cocky enough to attempt and take ownership of Gabriella's name as if it were her pseudonym."

"I imagine Meera's upset."

"You know where her—our—loyalties lie, Mr. Astor."

"That I do." Skimming a bit lower on the document, I find something that's a bit odd. "And where's the lawyer now?"

"Being interrogated as we speak by a friend of mine in a Portland precinct."

Nodding, I take out my phone and check the time. "My guess is he's spending the night?"

"Correct."

"What about the identity of the third party involved?"

"It's a pair, and we've had a sighting. They're close, but not showing their faces yet."

"Thank you." Tero looks like he has something else to say but heeds the warning in my tone and walks out of my office. My desk has three files in total: two sinners and one saint, but the latter seems to always pay the price since birth. Sitting back, I scratch my jaw while eyeing each name—the male and female that seem to need something from my girl. "Why do they want you, Gabriella? What hand haven't they shown yet?"

———————

PRESENT...

She's in shock.

The look on her face is one of deep loss, and I'm angry for her, at her, for letting someone so unworthy so close. A disgusting woman who believes in self-service and destroying anything in her path. But then again, Gabriella's too sweet and trusting, two qualities that don't exist in the world we live in anymore.

"Talk to me." My voice is low, yet it still carries a bit of ire. It's a tumultuous feeling as my desire is ever-present, but right now all I can think about is sweeping her into my arms and shielding her from the pain. However, the anguish she's in is necessary no matter how much I wish it wasn't. It's her path. Part of her growth.

Her eyes have been shut for so long. Her intuition is lost by choosing to trust others.

"To be honest, Theodore, I don't know what to think. Her betrayal is setting in now—punching me in the face—and my mind can't stop questioning her motives and my stupidity."

"You two are worlds apart, sweetheart."

"How so?" Those sad green eyes look at me from beneath long lashes, her posture so defeated. "Please, help me understand. Help me not fall apart."

"I'd catch you as you fall, Gabriella. Each and every time." A lone tear falls from her eye and my chest aches, something that I'd feel for no other. No woman or man has ever affected me as she does with a single look, and it's been this way since I first set my eyes on her. "But this is part of life, sweetheart. You live and learn and become a bit harder after each lesson. No one is inherently good. No one deserves your blind trust until they've proven themselves."

"And how does someone prove themselves? How can I—"

"By paying attention." Her lips purse, and had this been any other time, I would've kissed her. Would've taken the very breath from her lungs and fed my soul with her taste, but I don't. Instead, I tuck her head under my chin and give her the comfort she needs. And when I feel the tension leave her body, I kiss the crown of her head, speaking into it. "Your heart has always been beautiful, even toward those who have never deserved your empathy. But the time has come, Gabriella, to not give until you receive. To open those gorgeous green eyes and see the world for what it is, and while you learn, I'll hold your hand. When you stumble, I'll teach you to hold your ground. But what I won't do, not today or in the future, is let you carry a cross that isn't your burden."

"But doesn't that defeat the purpose of not trusting easily if I give in to you?"

"It does." Won't deny it. "And trust me, I'm the worst of all."

Her head shifts, and our eyes meet once again. "What does that even mean?"

"It means I'm the worst beast of all because it's your heart that I'm after. Because I want all of you, not leaving a single molecule of your DNA untouched. But know this: just like I'll devour you, I'll never leave your side. You'll own me as irrecoverably as I'll own you."

"Anything you want to watch?" Gabriella asks an hour later after changing into a pair of sleep shorts and a tank top. We're in her family room and on the couch, sitting side by side while sharing a blanket. Her choice. She hasn't talked much after my confession; not in an uncomfortable way, but more contemplative —dissecting what she learned and my admission, because I want her.

All of her. Every soft inch.

Every sigh. Every moan. Every tear.

"I doubt you'll enjoy what I decompress to."

"Try me." The streaming app is open and her avatar is quite cute in a purple-ish shade and superhero costume. "You'll be surprised at what I enjoy."

I'm more surprised with her need to have me close. The sweet way she asked me to stay.

Walking her to the door, I step to the side and wait for her to unlock it. "Will you be okay?"

Gabriella doesn't answer at first, turning and pushing the doorknob instead before pivoting to face me from the other side of the threshold. "Are you leaving?"

"I'm not going to assume you want me here, beautiful. You've had a rough day, and I'll give you space."

Her brows furrow. "But I don't want you to leave."

"Are you sure? I'm only a phone call away."

"This is my way of asking you."

"I need to hear you say the words, Gabriella. I'm not going to assume."

"Theodore, come inside and lock the door behind you..." she's walking away, calling from over her shoulder while her hips sway from side to side "...I'm not in the mood for more surprise visits."

"Just pick something. I'll be right back." Gabriella stands from her place beside me and heads toward her kitchen, the opening of her fridge following soon after. "Do you want anything? It's all sugary and bad for you."

"No, thank you," I call back and then scroll through her *Watch Again* selection, quite impressed with her choices. She is a little morbid, and that makes me smile as it's nothing but dangerous animals and serial killers with the occasional cultural documentary.

No romance or comedy or even a cooking show. "Fuck, she's perfect."

Something plastic is being opened and then another door opens; my guess is the microwave, and my suspicion is confirmed a few seconds later when the smell of popcorn permeates the air. "Did you pick yet? If not, it's my choice when I get back."

"I have."

"What?" Her head sticks out of the entrance, nose scrunched up in the cutest way.

"This." A few clicks and the opening to a docu-series I've watched a few times comes onto the screen.

"Wait! I'm not ready yet."

"You have sixty seconds before I hit start."

"You're in my home. You wait for the hostess."

"Fifty," I chuckle.

"Not funny."

"Forty-three."

"You suck," she huffs, rushing back with a large bowl of popcorn and a Dr. Pepper in her hands. The innuendo sits on the tip of my tongue. I want her to know I'd gladly lick, bite, and suck every inch of her body, but instead hit play. The intro starts, and she raises her brow. "What's this about?"

"It's the story of a man who rises to power by using religion as his shield for the crimes committed," I say as the beautiful woman next to me scoots a little closer, her arm brushing mine. My hands clench, nails digging into my palms while she tests me. My self-control. The need to possess her every kiss is maddening, but she's had a rough day and I'd be just as disgusting as those around her who take without care. So instead, I look at her and smile. "He lies and steals and eventually fucks every adult member of his *church* before slaughtering the poor souls that followed him out onto that island."

"I've heard of this one, but never watched it. A false prophet?"

"You can call him that."

"How gruesome is it?" Gabriella munches on a few kernels before taking a sip from her drink. Her legs are tucked beneath her, body leaning another inch closer. *Innocent tease.* "Scale of one to ten?"

"Solid four. To me it's more informative than scary."

"Boring, then?"

"More like getting to know the mind of a killer."

"Ahh, a good one, then." Then she turns her attention to the screen while I watch her. Take notice of the way her eyes widen and each shake of her head as the start of his rise to power plays on the screen. There are a few snorts here and there, the *are you fucking kidding me* look that all women possess and have perfected after decades of testing, and finally she moves and rests her head on my shoulder.

The bowl is half gone and the soda placed on the table. Volume on low, we sit in silence and when her face nuzzles my arm, I turn a bit and pull her against my chest. She's half lying on me—so warm and soft—her small body tucking perfectly against me.

It feels right.

Everything does.

And when her breathing evens out and I move us to a more laying down position, I'm rewarded by gorgeous green eyes opening just long enough to lay the smallest kiss on my lips. It's brief, a tease, but I can't help the low chuckle that leaves me as a few seconds later, when I seek them out for more, a low snore meets my ears.

Gabriella

Warm lips trail down my neck, leaving small stinging bites along my skin. I'm flushed, so sensitive, and I arch into the stranger's touch. Silently I ask for more, nearly crying when the warmth of his mouth lifts and a tsking sound leaves the back of his throat.

The sound is admonishing with just the hint of teasing, and I whine pathetically like the needy girl he makes me. I still can't see his face, his body above mine as I lay face down on an oversized, ornate bed with plush bedding in red this time. A change. A tease. It's soft beneath me and the more I sink in, give in to its comforting feel, the more he taunts with flicks of his tongue and soft bites.

We're in a dark room, unlike the others I've visited in my dreams before, yet the dangerous edge lingers. Surrounds me. The sole source of light is coming from a fireplace, the roaring fire contrasting—casting a hedonistic glow that dances across the dark walls in an array of orange and red, the tones alight with teasing.

It's warm in here. A comforting difference to other times when *fear consumed my every limb. Instead, I'm being held against my will by his lips. By the reverence in which they skim my skin. Taste me.*

"Please?" A plea—a truth that exposes my desperate need, and I cry out when a large hand grips my asscheek, squeezing to the point of pain. The feeling reverberates through my senses like a tsunami, and I beg for more. For anything he can do. "I need you."

My hips undulate, seeking that which is being denied, and I sigh when a lone finger parts my labia, stroking through my wetness until slipping into my clenching little hole. "It hurts when you don't touch me."

"I'll always be here, Gabriella." Fingertips dance across my neck, a light touch, and my eyes snap open at the sudden change. Theodore is gazing at me from our position on the couch—we're lying pressed against the other with my core clenching each time he roughly exhales. I can't stop it. I can't ignore this need burning me from the inside while his stare is heated—hungry. I'm still feeling the last dredges of my dream flow through, but now they merge with the desire pooling for this man. It's confusing. Overwhelming. "Are you okay?"

"Yes." Heat floods my cheeks, my mouth dry while I can't help but look from his rich amber orbs to his lips and back again. "Sorry."

"Don't." His gravelly tone settles across my sensitive skin and instinctively, I arch against his hold, those strong arms tightening. We're fully lying down now in the darkened room, the TV app's *are you still there* question the only lighting source, and yet it's as if the room was bathed in pure white light. There's a heavy current traveling between us, maybe a carry-over from my dream as I look at him, my stare unable to hide my want.

I'm also unable to avoid the raw desire in his.

Theodore's eyes are hooded, his pink tongue swiping across his bottom lip while he does the same thing I do. Watch. Wait. However, it's the flex of his length against my core that breaks me.

He's big. Thick. And the feel of him right there makes me whimper, my mouth immediately searching out his.

"Gabriella." It's a heavy grunt, a warning. "Sweetheart, are you sure?"

"Please."

"Please what?" Fingertips dig into my hips, holding me in place while I peck his lips between unnecessary words. "Tell me what you need."

"Touch me."

"Fuck." It's a rough exhale, his own truth and need coming clear across the one-word response. With the hand not on my hip, Theodore lifts my chin a little more. I'm breathing in his every exhale. "Say it again. I need to hear it."

"I need you to touch me." The last word hasn't passed through my lips when his mouth crashes down on mine. His kiss is almost punishing, and I feel the same. Reckless. Wild. *Home.* I'm clinging to him, tongue intertwining as my nails rake down his scalp, fisting the soft strands at the nape. "Please, Theo. Give me what I need."

"My beautiful girl." And then I'm under him, my body pinned beneath his muscled form. I'm the softness to his harsher planes, a complete opposite, and yet my curves mold to him. I'm pliant and needy and spread my thighs to accommodate his hips.

They flex against mine, his cock rubbing along the sensitive flesh trembling for him.

Lust is a powerful emotion and I'm drowning, overcome with a need so overwhelming that he shivers. His hands tremble as he cups my cheek with one hand and the other tugs my shorts off. They're tossed somewhere behind me with my tank following a few seconds after, the sound of a picture frame falling only serving to heighten my excitement.

Theodore looks down my body in adoration. "Motherfucking perfect," he hisses out, sitting back on his knees so he can palm himself through his jeans. The way he squeezes is rough, almost brutal, while I lay panting in nothing but a nude mesh bra and panty set. Nipples hard. Pussy wet. "I've wanted you like this for so long. At my mercy."

"How long?"

"Since the first moment I laid eyes on you." No elaboration, and I don't know if he means my picture or the cafe, but at this moment it doesn't change the palpable heat between us. "You're all I think about, Gabriella." Leaning forward, he holds himself up by one arm, careful not to crush me even though all I want is to feel him. All of him. "You're all I want in this life."

"Isn't it soon?" The question slips without conscious thought and I bite my lip, hoping I didn't ruin the moment.

"Never." Those amber orbs traverse my body, lingering on my breasts and pebbled little tips before straying to the juncture of my thighs. There, he exhales roughly—nose flaring while taking my hips in his grasp, holding tight. Blunt fingernails dig in, a slight tinge of pain running through me, but I find myself attracted to the feeling.

To the way it settles in my core, causing me to clench with need.

And he sees this. All of me.

Neither of us talks. Words aren't needed, but I do give him a nod. My permission to take and own. It's my surrender, and with a growled *fuck* Theodore tugs at the two small strings holding my panties in place, tearing the flimsy fabric clean off.

They dig in, marking my skin in the most delicious way, and I can't help the whimper that escapes nor the rise of my hips in offering. An offering he caresses with the tips of two fingers, spreading my wetness around while lowering his face to my chest.

He's not removing my bra, rather flicking his tongue over the sheer material that hides nothing from him, earning a hiss from me. "Something wrong, Miss Moore?"

"No," I whimper, voice shaky. "Just feeling very needy."

"You have no idea what true need is, sweetheart." Theodore blows warm air across the sensitive skin and goose bumps rise across my flesh, my breasts heaving. The tip of his tongue traces my right breast, nipping my nipple before giving the same treatment to the left. "How long I've denied myself. How long I've been patient and waiting."

"Tell me."

"Not yet," he hisses out before tearing the near nonexistent material covering my chest, the small triangle dangling from his teeth. Theodore takes the fabric in his hand and puts the piece in a back pocket before biting the underside of both breasts, dragging his tongue across each before following the path down the center to my mound.

There he pauses with eyes closed and lip caught between his teeth.

He breathes in deeply and holds it.

His cheek rubs across the wet, bare skin above my clit and shivers.

This beautiful, strong, and at times demanding man trembles above me as if holding on to a control that's slipping. As if he's teetering on the edge, his face contorted in a reverent pain, and damn me if that doesn't cause another rush of wetness to coat my lips.

"Theo, I—"

"Say it again. Call me that again."

"Theo."

"Fuck," he snarls against my flesh, his mouth moving to where he hovers, and those eyes hold my stare. I can't close my eyes or look away. I can't move or plead. All I'm able to do is watch as his pink tongue touches my clit, a feather-light caress, and cry out as pleasure seizes my every nerve ending.

He holds it there. Pressing a little more firmly with each tick of the clock until his lips part and he's sucking my tender flesh between his teeth. The sharp suction makes my eyes roll back, an action he doesn't like, and lands a smack to my thigh. It's loud, the sting landing right where his tongue is worshipping, licking me from my trembling bundle of nerves to my clenching entrance and back again, before sucking my lips and drawing them out.

Theodore is hungry, a deep rumbling groan escaping as he dips the tip of his tongue inside me. Lapping. Biting. Sucking until my lower body rises off the couch and moves against his mouth.

"Don't move." The hold on my hips tightens, pinning me down, but I only fight harder. Angry at being kept in place when all I want to do is ride his mouth. To do what my body is begging me to do naturally—seek my own release using him—but his denial is a double-edged sword. "You taste like Heaven and sent from Hell. Which one are you, sweet girl? My prize or my incarceration?"

How words and actions turn me on while simultaneously pissing me off.

But then he's circling my clit with a building pressure, light at first and then harshly, dragging the flat of his tongue until my stomach clenches and I fist the cushions. All thoughts leave my mind. Nothing but his scent and touch exist. There's a heat rising through me. This electric feeling as he releases one hip and brings a single finger to my entrance.

He circles the opening, toying with me while his mouth never ceases his attack on my clit. Flicking, nipping, sucking it between his lips while moving his head from side to side. And I'm thrashing, my whimpers turning into screams while my thighs squeeze around his head. It's an action he doesn't approve of, and when he pulls back and shakes his head at me while four fingers smack my pussy, I nearly pass out.

Then he does it again.

A total of four times, and I'm a sweaty panting mess. Wet. So wet it drips from my entrance to rosebud and onto the couch.

"Theo, I'm so close. Just a little...*fuck*!"

"That's my girl," he coos as my orgasm slams into me and I scream, my eyes rolling back while I lose control of my body. I'm crying, tears gathering at the corners of my eyes while he continues his assault, never pausing to let me breathe. He eats me through each shiver, through each hard clench of my walls, and right when the waves begin to ebb and small aftershocks remain, he slips his finger back in and fucks me with hard, punishing strokes while pinning my body with his own. "Give me one more."

"But what about you?" He hasn't come and is still in his clothes. Doesn't he want to—

"My pleasure lies in pleasing you," he grits out, chest vibrating from the guttural sound. "And right now is all about you, Gabriella. What I need from you."

"Oh, God...I...*Theo!*"

"Again, Gabriella." He curls the finger inside me, and I seize mid aftershock, my muscles coiling tight while a strange pressure mounts. It's building rapidly and my eyes widen because it feels like I need to pee, but when I try to push his hands away, Theo pins both of mine in one of his over my head. "Don't. Just give me one more."

"I-I think I need to—"

"Let go, beautiful. Show me how that pretty pussy squirts."

"I don't know how!"

"You have no choice," he growls out and presses harder, the palm of his hand connecting with my sensitive clit. The sensation is new and scary but damn him, it feels amazing in the most perverse way and when he adds a second finger, I'm gone.

I'm overwhelmed by this electrifying rush of pleasure that overtakes every cell in my body and then the release. It's an explosion, a hard shock to my system that ends with me sobbing—shaking—while his pants and shirt are soaked in me.

My lips are moving, and I know I can hear myself, but rationality has gone and I'm tired. I'm already half asleep when he gathers me in his arms and takes me up the stairs to my room. Theodore lays me on the bed and leans down to kiss my cheek as though he's leaving, but before he can pull away, I tug him down to me. He lets me, too, without protest, simply acknowledging my need without me having to ask. Theo simply removes his pants and shirt, leaving him in his boxer briefs.

A sight I'll admire in the morning, but right now, all I want is to cuddle. To feel secure in his arms and I do just that, with my head on his strong chest and his arm around my back, drawing lazy circles up my spine, I close my eyes and give in to my exhaustion.

Gabriella

"Will you be okay?" Theodore asks standing in my doorway the next day around one in the afternoon, having slept in late with me. It's a cloudy day, the overcast giving me a slight headache, but I keep the smile on my face. I hate that he's leaving. I hate that he'll be in Los Angeles for a few days, and more so after what happened last night.

"I'll be fine. Promise." Standing on the tips of my toes, I lay a small kiss on his chin. It's the only place I can reach, and I also like the way his nose flares at the act. How he takes in a sharp intake of air while that muscled chest expands with a deep inhale. "Now, get out. I have things to do."

"You do?"

"I do."

"Like what?" he asks, wrapping his arms around me to keep me in place. Theodore's fast, yanking me against his chest before my next blink, and I find myself giggling up at his proud expression.

"What could possibly have you kicking me out instead of being upset that I'll be gone?"

"Paying bills, setting up a meeting with the lawyer you have taking a look at my copyright case, and I need to make a quick trip to the art supply store across town because my usual place is a no go."

"That is a lot on your plate." His lips press in for a quick kiss on my forehead. "Want Tero to come give you a hand? He won't mind."

"No."

"What about his wife, Meera?"

"Don't know her, and again, no." At my refusal his lips part, a rebuttal on the tip of his tongue, and I shake my head, placing a single finger over his mouth. "Trust me, Theo, I have so much to do that I'll be extremely busy for days. I'm already behind as is on the paintings."

"I love it when you call me Theo." My cheeks heat up a bit under his intense stare, the darkening of his irises sexy. "Say it again."

"No." At my refusal, his fingertips dig in a bit, and the playful move right over a ticklish area makes me giggle and his smirk widens. Almost predator-like. "Stop."

"Say it."

"No."

"Final chance." Those same fingertips begin to tap along my skin slowly while growing in intensity before they attack without mercy and I'm left squirming, trying to push away, but his strong hold doesn't allow an inch of separation between his body and mine. "Say it. Say it, and I'll stop."

"Theo!" I yell out, my eyes watering.

"Good girl," he says, chuckling, but then the amusement dies, and his face turns grim. "I'll be back in forty-eight hours, Gabriella." His sad/grumpy expression is cute, and I have this sudden urge to bite him. I don't, but it's there. *I've nicknamed him, and now I'm thinking of sinking my teeth into him. What is he turning me into?*

"Your meeting with the lawyer is set up to coincide with my return. I'll be driving you to and from, so be ready by three."

"Is this a command?"

"More like my way of asking you out on a romantic date."

"How so?" I'm trying to act put off, but the smile on my face is a dead giveaway to the butterflies in my stomach. "First, a meeting with a lawyer is not proper date etiquette. And two, I was never informed of this."

"Consider this your formal invitation and it would be right after the lawyer."

"What if I say no?"

He rolls his eyes at my raised brow. "Then it's a command. Be ready for me."

"I'll have you—" his lips on mine kill the rest of my response. The kiss is quick and passionate, and I'm left panting when he pulls back much too soon, dragging his teeth over my lip before releasing.

"What were you saying?"

"See you in two days."

"Two days, beautiful." Those amber eyes leave my face and travel down my body and up again, pausing at my wrist. "I love your new charm, by the way."

"New charm?"

"Take a look."

Theodore walks down my front porch while I'm busy staring at the jeweled crown on my wrist. It's white gold with black onyx stones surrounding the bottom half with two letters engraved inside. A giant T & G with the numbers 10:04 next to it. It's beautiful and makes me smile and I'm wondering when Theo had a chance to pin it there.

Must've been while I was sleeping. And what does the 10:04 mean?

He's too good to be true.

He's going to ruin me.

BILL.

Bill.

Super-saving flyer from a grocery store.

Another bill.

Some offer for a free manicure if I book a pedi at the new spa.

The fuck? "Why are there black rose petals in here?" My hand pushes aside all the mail I've collected over the last few days, not looking to see what was here before since I know most is trash, but this is out of place. I've never bought nor have I received a black rose before, and this one's dead, completely dry and brittle and as I lift the stem from the bowl, the rest of its petals fall.

Did Elise bring this in? Am I that out of it, I didn't notice the rose?

It was lying on an envelope with my name written across the front in a very neat penmanship, the stark white of the paper casing now stained by the last imprints of its petals. Setting everything else aside, I open the closed flap and pull out a small stack of folded papers.

The company heading is one from the orphanage I grew up in—I'd know the symbol anywhere—and this fills me with trepidation. My heart races and hands clam up, but as I unfold the documents, the first line breaks my heart.

Voluntary Relinquishment of Parental Rights

Voluntary.

Voluntary.

I can't move past that word as it says so much within the confinement of nine letters. The truth is sledgehammering into all my processors—lashing at my nerves with sharp claws, and my chest grows tight. My eyes fill with tears the further down I read, slicing me open as the truth is screamed within each line.

I'm unwanted. Abandoned.

The room feels small and my breaths are coming in sharply, the pain intensifying, but more so when I see their names spelled out above a pair of signatures belonging to the couple who brought me into this world: *Richard and Carla Burgess.*

"I don't even have their last name?" I say out loud while mentally I'm asking who named me. Whose surname was donated to the unwanted child tossed at the system without looking back? Turning to the last two pages, I encounter a bank statement with a large sum deposited days after I was given to the orphanage and a letter of agreement.

My eyes skim each line with watery eyes while stumbling into the nearest wall; I slide down and sit, feeling as though the walls are caving in. Question after question rushes through my mind. About who they were or are. About who really gave me this house.

Was he my biological mother's brother, or my father's?

Then, I ask myself, why now?

Why give me that lump sum along with this property?

With every tick of the clock, my chest tightens. It hurts. Physically and emotionally, I ache in a way I've never encountered before. Can't breathe, and I let the papers fall to the floor. "I need to get out of here."

Jumping up from my position on the floor; I grab my wallet and keys, and rush out the door. I'm in such a rush that I don't remember getting in my car and driving toward Pike's Place. I'm on autopilot and come to when I walk to my favorite artisan stall inside the market.

Everyone looks at me funny as they pass. Staring at the redheaded woman with blotchy skin, tears running down her cheeks, while wearing the equivalent of workout clothes; a sports bra and leggings. I was going to go for a run after handling the bills; I'd wanted to clear my head and work through each beast's placement on the Astor Gallery pieces.

That didn't work out. Nothing will.

My life is a mess of nightmares, lunatic emotions, and now this.

"Are you okay, Miss?" the shop owner, a woman in her mid to late thirties, asks me. No one else is standing near us; they're looking but giving me a wide berth. "Do you need something or for me to call—"

"I'm fine. Just had a rough day."

"Would you like to take a seat? I can bring you a chair." Her hand reaches out for my arm and gives it a squeeze. The action is meant to be comforting, but instead, I'm filled with a sense of longing. How many family members do I have? Do I have a sister or a brother, maybe multiples of each?

"No." Shaking my head, I step back a bit and give her a sad smile. "Thank you for the offer, but right now I just need to walk."

"Are you sure—"

Wiping my eyes with the back of my hand, I give her a smile. "I'm sure. Thank you, though." There are a few more specialty shops in this section and I take my time walking through each, not buying but admiring the artisan pieces made by local artists while staying clear of those shopping. It helps me calm down after a while, calms me to be surrounded by so many one-of-a-kind creations.

My creative soul relaxes. Welcomes the soothing vibes.

However, when I reach the farmers market section of Pike's, I feel someone watching me. Their stare is hard and the footsteps not light in the least, as if they want to be seen, and yet when I turn my head no one makes direct eye contact.

Too many people surround me to pinpoint either.

So I move on, walking down the aisle and only pausing to buy some fresh pears that looked too good to pass up. And when I leave the area, I finally see a man in his late forties with a barrel gut walking closer than I feel comfortable with.

I've never seen him. I have no idea who he is.

But that doesn't stop him from following me for the next fifteen minutes, and after trying to lose him at the Starbucks, I head to my car. Not running, but I take my kitty multi-tool out and slip my fingers through the area below the ears, gripping the metal tight.

Footsteps come closer and I pause, giving myself a second to gather my breaths before whirling around and... nothing.

No man.

No more footsteps.

It's as if I conjured everything and when I look around, taking in the many shoppers and vendors, I'm left questioning my sanity.

Where did he go? "Did I imagine him?"

KING

His screams of pain rend the air, filling the warm summer night with a haunting symphony that makes me smile. His chest is red, the rivulets rising from each cut and flowing down his stomach, disappearing beneath the waistband of his pants.

The man is bound by his hands and feet to the floor of an empty building not far from Gabriella's home and the heart of Seattle. It's an empty space that I own and have soundproofed, dedicated each of its twenty floors to a different kind of torture, reminiscent of my home back in Italy.

I'll bleed him dry here.

Drain him drop by drop until he talks, and still grant no mercy when he does.

This is his fault. Not mine. Not my pretty girl's.

"Speak up, Mr. Hall." His response is more unintelligible gibberish, his bodily functions failing him when the front of his pants become piss stained. *Filthy animal.* "You disgust me."

"Please, I haven't done anything wrong. I was there to—" I cut off his bullshit with a backhand, the force behind the blow to his face breaking the cheekbone and his nose.

"I'm going to ask you again." I snap my fingers and two special creatures slither into the room, watching the man with spiteful eyes. One constricts. One is venomous. "Who sent you?"

"I-I didn't." That's all he manages to get out as the white albino coils at striking distance from his feet. The cobra stands with a regal position, her hood expanded and forked tongue flicking in and out languidly.

I command them both.

The male is mine.

The female is my gift to Miss Moore.

"Last chance." Then, I whistle and the cobra strikes as she knows to do, two puncture wounds on his abdomen that immediately make him tense, a curdling scream escaping his throat. Then again, another dry bite, just because he's pissed me off. Both serpents watch and wait, my hand gestures the only communication we need at the moment. "Are you ready to talk now?"

"Don't kill me."

"You should've thought about that beforehand. No?" I trail a sharp metal nail over the two small punctures at the center and scratch the skin—stretching it while watching it widen. Because the skin's elasticity does give under pressure if the right amount is exerted and right now, I'm slicing up from just below his belly button to his sternum. "Preying on a defenseless woman? Following her around for the past few days?"

His eyes widen, the blood quickly draining from his face. This is a new fear. Nothing to do with the damage already inflicted. "She made me do it."

"She who?" I ask, yet the pieces haven't been hard to put together. The past has a way of finding the present and mixing together in ways that *no one* predicts, but I'm enjoying the idiocy of some. My beast has been caged for too long. My thirst unsatiated.

When he doesn't answer, his limbs shaking, I undo his bindings while the animals watch.

I don't let him fall. I don't hurt him and without exertion carry him to a chair I'd placed where he'd face the night sky. It's an old, ornate chair fit for a king, one that's seen better days and whose stains all reveal a haunting past. Each mark is a drop of my enemies blood, a sign of death.

"I'll tell you everything," David begins the moment I sit him in the chair, tone a little more cooperative. *Idiot.* But then again, that's human nature, to fake complacency until you can lash out and run. It's that fight or flight instinct that pushes one toward survival at all costs; words meant to explain a person's reaction to a certain situation, and yet, all it does is try and hide the truth from a predator weakly. Because fear is a dominating emotion, near crippling, and with enough coercion, any man will crumble. I feed off his dread. Smile down at him. "Just don't kill me."

"That depends on you." Stepping to his left, I crouch down beside him and place a hand on his shoulder. My nails dig in, the skin breaking where the sharp metal tips rip through. Not that I need them to inflict damage, but it entertains me to watch confusion and terror fill my victims' eyes when they see them, a prop given to me years ago by someone I lost as a gag gift. "Tell me who, Mr. Hall. I need a name."

"She goes by Veltross and—" I remove the claws from his shoulder and place the bloody tip over his mouth, smearing his life's essence across his lips. Hall swallows hard, shuddering on a gag he swallows back while with the sharpness of a scalpel, the center of his lips split open. The skin is so fragile there, filets open like a steak would under a butcher's blade, the skin pink and red—tender.

"Thank you for your cooperation."

"Will you let me go?"

I don't answer him, but instead hold up my hand while standing and both animals come near at my silent command. They watch me, heads tilted as if they were twins who shared one soul. There's understanding in each pair of eyes. They're faithful to their master and his chosen.

Always will be.

There's a comforting release when I give in to my nature, the demon that is a part of me and has no remorse. His whimpers once again fill the room, and the heavy scent of blood fills my senses. Death surrounds him, a rotten stench that comes from men like him. Pigs. Pathetic.

A sexual predator.

"You made a grave mistake."

"I didn't do—"

"Silence." My voice thunders throughout the open space. It reverberates as a bolt of lightning flashes across the large windows we face, him in a chair while I take a stand beside him. Not looking. Not talking.

The Seattle sky opens then as the first drops of rain descend, the night turning as black as my heart. Another flash of lightning and the windowpane is assaulted by sharp drops of angry water that batter the glass while no one moves.

I have no idea how long we stay that way. Time has no meaning for me.

Beside me, though, Mr. Hall seems to have calmed down. His bleeding has slowed down a bit, the coagulated drops over the wound providing a barrier.

First rule of survival: never drop your guard.

Second rule: keep your eyes open.

The second those drooping eyes close, I land a blow to the side of his skull that sends him falling, the hard concrete cushioning his head and side. *Did he really think I'd let him walk out of these doors?*

"Why?" Pathetic. Nothing angers me more than a man who can't accept death with some dignity. But worse than that is one who tries to touch someone forbidden and then lies. "It's all that woman. Go find her."

"Are you giving me orders now?" At the tsk, the serpents move slightly closer, a hiss escaping their mouths. "Answer me."

"Never, Mr. King."

"So you know who I am." Not a question, though, and he nods. "You know what I'm capable of?"

"Yes."

"And yet you conspired against me."

"I'm sorry."

"No. You're not." Faster than he can comprehend, two mouths strike and bite, one with venom and the other with sharp teeth that sink in and don't release. They pin him down while I straddle his chest, taking my time while he fights against their hold. More piss escapes his bladder, and I wrinkle my nose in disgust. "Such filth. And you thought to touch what's mine? You wanted to mark her flesh with your dirty hands?"

"I'll go away."

"Agreed." With two fingers, I slide inside his abdominal cavity via an earlier wound. It's just large enough to fit half my hand, and after forcing the tips of four fingers inside—stretching—I rip through and leave behind a six-inch gash that reaches his belly button. The elasticity gives way under pressure and horrified screams fill the air, his blood staining my bare chest and pants.

I pull the red fingers out and find another wound right over his ribs and mimic my actions.

Then another. Three in total, but none deep enough to kill him.

They're meant to hurt. To bathe the floor in his life's essence.

I watch as more blood seeps. As the puddle beneath us grows.

Mr. Hall's eyes roll back but I slap him awake; I'm not done.

"Look at me. Keep those eyes on mine." I'm examining the sharp metal over my fingers, following the small drips that fall from the tip and onto his face. His cries fill every square inch of the space, the sound of a wounded animal dying, but there's one more thing I need before I leave. "You coveted someone who is mine. You tried to touch what is sacred."

His lips open, but no sound comes out as I stab his right eyeball and pull, forcing the orb to detach from the orbital muscles. It pops out, still on my finger, the ripped tissue attached in some places. Then, I do the other after dropping the first on his chest. They stay cushioned in his sternum while two holes are left to remind those who find his body what line to never cross.

Gabriella Moore is untouchable.

No one will harm a single hair on her head.

Only I can break her.

Once I step back, the animals move and begin to bite and tear pieces of flesh from his skin. I'm going to leave him broken, battered, and disfigured for the police to find behind the Astor Gallery.

"The time has come."

Gabriella

It's a little after ten in the morning when I stumble out of bed the next day. My body feels tired, my mind is a bit hazy, and my stomach is in knots. The last twenty-four hours mock me and have been doing so since I read those papers, and I made the mistake of taking one of the new sleeping pills to pass out.

And I did. Shortly after taking the small oblong tablet, I gave in to the effects and slept through without a single dream haunting my rest, but right now the aftereffects aren't worth the nausea and muscle pain throughout my body accompanied by the migraine from hell.

"How did I draw the lucky number to win three side effects at once?" I grumble, a bit uncoordinated as I walk to the bathroom. Inside, I turn on the shower and strip, nearly tripping on my sleep shorts. However, the warm water is worth the almost concussion as it immediately soothes me, my tired body getting a bit of respite while the hot water on my scalp lulls me.

And I let it, standing there until the water turned lukewarm. It's only then that I wash up, quickly lathering my body with my cherry vanilla shower gel. The fragrant scent fills the room and I breathe in deeply, allowing the calming smell to further relax me.

Tiny paws scratch at my door to get my attention and I smile; the little shit has no patience in him. "Almost out, Mr. Pickles." Another scratch and then a bump with his body to the wooden structure. "I'll take you out now. Two minutes."

Not that he understands, but I do hear his grunt and then the sounds of the tinkling bell on his collar as he walks away.

Rinsing off the rest of the suds, I step out and grab a towel, wrapping it around my wet body. I'm a little more alert now, a little less shaky, and take a moment to look at my reflection in the mirror.

The glass is a bit foggy, but I run my hand across the cool glass and stare at my reflection. The girl standing there is sad, but beneath the hurt is a tough heart. She's overcome a lot. Has made a name for herself and even when at the orphanage, she worked toward her dreams relentlessly.

But who left me this home? The money to start out?

"Why would my *uncle* make me his heir if my parents abandoned me?" There are a few possible answers to that question, yet the only one that makes a lick of sense is guilt. "Worrying about this doesn't change anything," I mutter to myself while closing my eyes and taking in a deep breath before letting it out slowly. Being this tense and rushing through possibilities is counterproductive, I know, and I'll talk to Theodore about what I found out. I'm sure he can help me find a private investigator to look them up and get the real story. "For my own peace of mind, I need to find out. To face them if they're still alive and ask them whose last name I'm carrying and why."

Vowing to let this go until I talk to Theo, I hurry and exit the bathroom after brushing my teeth. I'm not going out today, not after yesterday's fiasco, and plan to spend the day inside my studio working on one of the seven paintings.

The beast I choose today is the caiman, this large creature that packs a punch and doesn't hide from his prey. This family member of the gator is aggressive and can reach up to sixteen feet in length, making him a dominant hunter in the many lakes and rivers within the Amazon basin.

"I hope Theo likes it." Not Theodore, but Theo, and I also can't get his reaction to me calling him that out of my mind. He liked it as much as I enjoyed the way it rolled off my tongue as if I've said it a million times with the familiarity of a lover. "He's the only thing that makes sense in my life anymore, and it's also the one that shouldn't. We barely know each other."

I'm going to make myself crazy one day.

Shaking everything off, I focus on getting dressed in a pair of joggers and a tight black T-shirt sans bra before rushing down the stairs, putting my hair in a high ponytail. Mr. Pickles is sitting on the last step when I descend and his eyes are showing mild annoyance, a look I'm all too familiar with when he's hungry or needs to potty.

"Want to go out?" Magical words as these set him off, and I have an excited pupper on my hands rushing toward the kitchen, scratching at the wooden door until I reach him. He seems too impatient today, and I decide to just let him roam the backyard instead of a walk for now. We can do that later. "Sit."

At my command, he does as asked and after a few seconds of eye contact, I open the door and let him out. But fuck me I wish I didn't. I wish that my life was different, and reality wasn't merging with my dreams.

Because thumb-tacked to my door is a picture I'll never forget. Can't unsee.

It's the body of a man, bloodied and without eyes, lying on a concrete floor with the words, *taken care of* written in red sharpie. At least I chose to believe so for my sanity, because the color has a muted tone that looks a bit darker in spots as if it were blood.

The bile that rushes up my throat feels like liquid fire as I bend over, emptying the yellowish substance onto the floor a few steps from where the picture remains. I'm not touching it. I can't see that again, and after the last bit of bile leaves me, the scream comes.

It's loud and I'm shaky and I have no idea how I make it up the stairs to grab my phone, but I do. Mr. Pickles follows me, watching me after seeing my duress, and doesn't leave my side while I grab the detective's card from my nightstand.

I'd placed it there after his visit to the hospital, never thinking I'd have to use it.

With shaky limbs and tears in my eyes, I dial his number and after the third ring, there's the sound of traffic in the background and loud breathing. "Detective Consuelos speaking." My throat feels tight, and I try to speak but nothing comes out. Instead, there's a sob from me and a bark from my dog. "Hello? Hello? Who's calling?"

"Help."

"Who's this?" he asks, the noise level dropping a bit and the sound of a car door closing follows shortly after. "I can't help you if I don't—"

"Gabriella Moore..." I'm choking, chest burning as the sensation of a million ants crawling under my skin takes over "... murder. Please."

"Miss Moore, it seems you're free to go. Someone has come to your rescue," a female cop says hours later, her expression angry and full of disgust. But then again, that's how everyone here's been looking at me. From the prisoners to the officers and anyone else who's in this building and has been in my presence.

They see me and eyes narrow. Whispers begin.

No one has asked me about the photo.

No one has asked the why or whom I think would do such a thing.

No one has looked at my video cameras or asked me if I knew the victim.

Nothing. I'm being made guilty without due process.

Moreover, the moment Detective Consuelos walked up to my door I knew something was very wrong.

The pounding of my front door is loud, the person on the other side inpatient. "This is the Seattle Police Department, open the door." After saying this, the banging didn't cease nor was I given a moment to walk over from the front sitting room. Instead, it was kicked open as four Seattle P.D. officers stormed inside with their guns drawn. I scream and all four turn my way being led by the detective working my case, his service weapon pointing at my head. "Hands up, Gabriella!"

"Detective, what is going on?" I ask, complying with his request. I'm sitting on my couch with both arms up and fingers stretched out, so they see I have nothing in my hand. "Why did you break down my door?"

"Where's the body?" A woman asks me, and I turn my attention to her. Take in the judgement in her icy glare while also noticing she's not wearing a badge.

"I'm the one that called in the photo. I'm the one being harassed."

"Bullshit."

"Stop with the lies," Consuelos and the woman say in unison, the latter backing down but not before sneering in my direction. What's her problem?

"What the hell is going on?" I'm angry and scared and the tears haven't stopped since I found the picture. My body feels beaten and used; my soul heavy while my heart is full of fear. "Detective Consuelos, please answer me."

"I'm sorry, Miss Moore, but I'll need you to stand and turn around."

"What?"

"Please stand and put your hands behind your back, don't make me use force."

"Why are you doing this? I called you for help." As I ask this, the two other males with them leave and start going from room to room,

calling back empty as they stomp around. I can hear things falling and a few glass items meeting their demise on my floor, but what kills me is the yelp of my dog as one of them grabs him. "Detective, I demand an answer."

Said man gives me a look that makes me shrink back. So much coldness. "Gabriella Moore, you're under arrest as an accomplice to murder."

"Who came?" I haven't used my one phone call yet. There's no one to come and help me, and I'd rather sit here for a year than talk to Elise after our last encounter. *Theo?* But he has no way of knowing, especially, since he'll be in L.A. for another day. "There's no one that I—"

"Hurry up, the person is waiting up front."

"Okay." The other women in the holding cell give me wide berth, moving away from the now open metal door. No one moves until I step through and I feel like a monster, so uncomfortable, that I put my head down and follow without another word. I can feel everyone's eyes on me, though. Can feel the judgment and hate but continue walking until we're out and I hear the one voice that makes this nightmare better.

"Oh, sweet girl. What have they done to you?" Theodore's words cause my head to snap up and tears to fall. Moreover, I don't hesitate and throw myself into his arms. He catches me, cradling me against his chest while I let go.

The woman who walked me out scoffs, but then quiets down. Theo's head snaps to the side, his body slightly shaking. "Who the fuck are you? I want your name and badge number."

"Sir, you need to watch your tone. I'm a—"

"It's you who doesn't comprehend the severity of your actions, but I'm sure your boss will be here soon enough to explain."

"That's laughable. Captain Bron wouldn't dignify himself by..." she trails off then and the temperature inside the room seems to drop. I try to lift my head to see what's going on, but Theo's warm hand scratches my scalp lightly while keeping me in place.

Something is happening.

Then steps come closer. Heavy and loud, stopping close but not speaking.

I'm scared. Tired. Angry.

So full of ire for how unjust I've been treated, but more than that, I can't take anymore.

My nervous system has taken a few hard lashes since my birthday, one after another, and mentally I'm cracking. Can feel each open wound grow and morph into hate. Into dark thoughts that I'd never voice out loud.

For the first time in my life, I want retribution. To not be a weak link.

"As your lawyer, I ask that you let me handle this, Theodore. I assure you; they'll feel your wrath."

"Deal with it," Theodore hisses out after a minute, a deep rumble building in his chest with each syllable. His voice is deeper. The command is full of ire. "What they did was—"

"Mr. Astor, can I have a word please?" At the sound of Detective Consuelos's voice, I pull closer to Theo and he responds by tightening his arms around me. I'm not afraid of the detective, but rather the fire that seems to course through my veins at the mere sound of his voice.

I want to hurt him. I want to scream.

But instead, I let Theo be my wall at the moment, a human shield from the bad, and I couldn't be more thankful for meeting this man. He's the only person who's never judged me. Who cares and actually sees me.

"You'll be speaking to my lawyer, Consuelos. And mark my words, this is just the beginning." My brows furrow at Theodore's words. *What does that mean?*

"Sir, the department wants to apologize to you both. We misunderstood the situation and reacted instead of thinking logically as we are trained to do."

"No, you didn't," I say with my head still buried in Theo's chest, but he nudges me back a little and then tips my face to meet his. His eyes are warm and full of so much understanding. Of care.

"Speak up, sweetheart. You have every right to be upset."

"Gabriella, I understand you're angry—"

"It's Miss Moore to you, Detective." Standing up straight, I take in a deep breath and let it out slowly. I give myself a minute to gather the right words because being emotional won't get my point across. "What you did was crucify me without a chance to defend myself, especially from a charge that should've never been attached to my name. I did the right thing, Consuelos. I called you, a detective for the SPD, to come to my aid when that picture was left on *my* door. You never questioned *me*, but instead arrested and then closed the file. No phone call. No court appearance to see a judge for bail. You never upheld my rights to due process, and right now *I'm* disgusted by the sight of you—I see you the same way everyone in there looked at me."

My words caused two reactions from him: anger and shame. His hands clench, the papers in his hold scrunching up. "Miss Moore, it was an honest mistake. After the body was found at the Astor Gallery, we called Mr. Astor and—"

"The body was found where?" *So that's how he found out.*

"At my gallery, along with security footage left behind that showed a man driving an old Toyota Corolla dumping the body."

Man driving a Toyota Corolla. "I don't know anyone that owns that kind of car."

"We know," Consuelos says, his eyes shifting toward the other people I'm now noticing in the room. The woman is still here, yet she's looking at the floor and posture stiff. Then, there's the other two men that I don't know: one in a suit and one in a blue uniform. Both look at me with serious expressions, but not menacing. "Miss Moore, we believe that you have a stalker—"

"What?" Because I couldn't have heard that right. "Please repeat that."

"What the detective is trying to say, Miss Moore..." The man gives his officers a hard look and each takes a respected step back, while I'm busy reading his name tag. This man is the captain, and he looks mad, but then softens his demeanor. "We apologize for the egregious mistake made by this department. We were wrong, and instead of doing our jobs, we arrested someone innocent and who seems to have someone following her." Captain Bron gives me a moment to gather myself after my knees give out and Theo grabs me, pulling me against him with a secure arm around my waist. "I'm sorry, Miss, but these acts of violence are not random but to get your attention. Do you have any ex-boyfriend, or have you dated anyone recently that has shown any level of aggression or unstable behavior?"

"I have no current boyfriend or ex. I'm not someone who dates." The shakiness in my voice is unmistakable and when Theo kisses the crown of my head, a few tears fall. *Why am I being targeted? Why me?* "I'm a recluse most of the time and keep to myself."

THEODORE

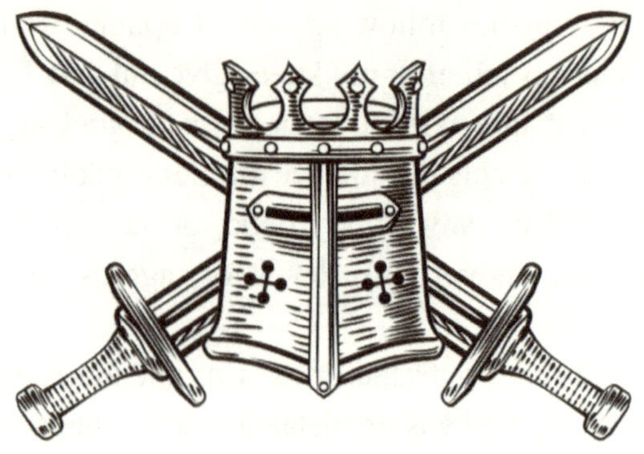

"We're here, Sir," Tero says from the front, pulling into my parking spot while the woman in my arms continues to rest. Gabriella fell asleep a few minutes after we left, her head on my shoulder, and I didn't hesitate to place her on my lap and cuddle her close. She's been through so much in the last eight hours, my little fighter, but I know she'll be okay. She deserves better than the world has given, my perfect girl, and I'll help her every step of the way. "By the way, I've already taken care of her door, and any other damages incurred within the home. I'm missing two knickknacks but have located the replacements on eBay."

She's no longer alone.

I'll be her protector, lover, and friend. Her everything.

"Thank you. Is Meera on the way?" I ask while looking down at my girl's perfect face, from her long lashes to her small nose with a sprinkling of freckles and down to the perfect cupid's bow that I want to bite. She's so beautiful and sweet—too trusting—and it's cost her a lot over the years. Something that ends now that I'm in her life. "Has Gabriella's appointment with my lawyer been moved back? I'll be taking care of that personally now."

No more friends like Elise.

No more men getting close.

No overzealous cops preying on her defenselessness.

"Yes, to both." Tero turns his head, his eyes shifting toward the beauty in my arms. So many emotions flash through his eyes, but the leading one is anger. He's blaming himself for not being in town when I'd given him the day off to spend with his wife for their anniversary. Neither of us could have foreseen this level of idiocy happening. It took me an hour to get everything squared away after finding out, and I have no clue how long she'd already been detained beforehand. *They're going to pay for this.* "She has Miss Moore's dog and is now back to begging for a pet. She's been hinting/demanding that we get a rescue pit-bull."

"And what do you think?" I ask, shifting a little so I can turn my body and get us out without waking her. Not that she realizes as exhaustion hit her hard. "Are you ready for that kind of commitment?"

"I am. We never had kids, and this would be the next best thing."

"Then I am happy for you."

"Thank you, my friend." Tero opens his door and gets out, rushing to mine and doing the same. We don't talk anymore as we head toward the elevator and then ascend, entering my penthouse through the private entrance. I'm not in the mood to talk, and he knows this. I'm trying to control my anger, and right now the only thing that will calm me is laying down with her.

So while Tero waits for his wife to get here with Gabriella's dog, I disappear into the master bedroom and lay her down after kicking the door closed with the back of my foot. And while she quickly settles in, turning to her side while gripping a pillow with her small fingers, I grab a spare blanket and throw it over her.

Seeing her so defenseless today renewed my vow to break her free.

To give her back the power to not let anyone hurt her.

Slipping in beside her, I spoon her body with mine and settle my face against the back of her neck. Her scent surrounds me with that soft vanilla with cherry fragrance that is both soothing and mouthwatering. It envelops me in comfort, and I close my eyes, letting her soft breathing lull me.

"I'm going to make this up to you, Gabriella." I lay a tiny kiss at the base of her neck. "For not being here when you needed me the most."

"I'M REALLY NOT in the mood to go anywhere, Theo. Please take me back home." The silly girl looks at me from the corner of her eye, glaring a bit. It's been this way since she woke up in my bed two days ago after sleeping through the night, screaming at the top of her lungs and scaring everybody in the kitchen.

I rushed to her side at once, finding her huddled against the headboard with wide eyes staring at me. It took her a moment for realization to set in and her nerves to calm, more so when her dog's barking caught her attention. Then, she launched herself out of the bed and ran to Meera, taking her pet back while thanking her.

"You got him for me," she said, voice low and grateful. "Thank you. Thank you so much."

"My pleasure, Miss Moore."

"It's Gabriella..." her eyes went from Meera to Tero and then to mine, so many questions in her jeweled orbs "... and how did you get him? Where was he?"

"He was being held at a local vet's office that attends to the precinct's dogs."

"Christ." Gabriella kisses the furballs head, and he licks her cheek. The smile on her face is enough to bring a dead heart back to

life, but then it drops and her brows furrow. "I'm sorry, but who are you? I know them, but we've never..."

"Never apologize, Gabriella. You've done nothing wrong." Stepping forward, she holds a hand out toward my girl, which Gabriella takes after shifting her hold on the dog. "My name is Meera, and I'm Tero's wife. I'm also the gallery's event coordinator, and we were bound to meet very soon as I need your input for the show."

"No can do, sweetheart. You're kind of stuck with me for a while." Today. Tomorrow. Until the end of time. "Does that bother you?"

"Would you believe me if I said yes?"

"Not when you're smiling like that. No." Tucking a stray piece of hair behind her ear, I lean across the center console and lay a small kiss to the corner of her mouth. "Now, let's get down. There's something I want you to see."

"Maybe another time? I really need to head home and check on—"

"Humor me." Another small kiss, this time to the tip of her nose. "Please."

"You get one hour."

"Sure." I'll let her think that, but she's not going home yet. If ever.

I'm not letting her go.

"Why is it that I don't believe you?"

"No clue." Not giving her a chance to further question me, I turn the car off and get out, rushing to her side. I open her door and hold a hand up—pausing her exit—while quickly opening my glove compartment. She's looking at me funny, a small smile on her lips, but more than that, there's curiosity when I don't show her what I've grabbed.

For now, I tuck it into my pocket and then pull her out, leading us toward the main entrance. It's a little after five now and I had the place closed for us, hoping she'll enjoy the trip more with it being just the two of us.

And I'm right when she gasps after I usher us inside.

"Theo," my name on her lips is a beautiful sigh—so sweet. "When did this go up? Has there been some interest?"

"Before I left for L.A., and yes. A lot, in fact." With my hand on the small of her back, I move us deeper into the reception area where an announcement of the upcoming show has been set up. Her name is the largest of the three artists showing over the next six months, and I'm proud of her. She earned this. Everything good coming her way. "We've already started to build your set as no one else will be using that floor this year."

"No one?"

"No. It's yours." Stepping closer, I use the tips of two fingers to turn her head in my direction. "I've had a special prop delivered for you, too. Meera brought it here today to test its placement."

"What is it?"

"All I can show you is where it'll go?"

"Why?"

"It's a surprise meant for later."

"Okay." And there's the sparkle I've missed over the last few days. This genuine excitement that glows—moves you when she smiles. A real one. When she's content and feels at ease, there's nothing more beautiful to me.

"Then let me show you." I slip my hand into hers and pull her gently behind me toward the elevator, pressing the number three once the doors close. Her fingers play with mine while we wait to reach the top, gently squeezing the tips. However, the moment we reach our floor, I pull her back before the doors open. "Do you trust me?"

"Yes." No hesitation. No doubt. *So perfect.*

"Good girl." Eyes still on hers, I press the hold button so the elevator doesn't leave our floor and then turn her around, pulling the blindfold from my pocket. "Just remember I won't let you fall."

"What are you...*oh*!" She giggles, shaking her head after I put the blindfold in place and checking that she can't peek through. "You came prepared for everything."

"You could say that." With my hand on the small of her back, I walk us into the large open space that will host her exhibit, making sure that the lights are dimmed before stopping at the center of the room. From where I stand, she will be able to see across the room and the covered display. "Ready?"

"As I'll ever be."

"Welcome to a night in the jungle of sin."

"Jungle of sin," she repeats as I pull the blindfold off. I watch as she takes everything in—the dark walls and the greenery being brought in to mimic the Amazon jungle and its foliage. We've put up vines and lighting only in areas meant to host her pieces. Even the flowers brought in to stage the area for her approval add a layer of beauty to the debauchery that will be the final result.

"What do you think?"

"It's stunning." Her eyes are lit up in a way I haven't seen in a while. So much happiness. Excitement. "This is going to look amazing, Theodore."

"Theo."

"I'm sorry?" she asks, and the way her brows scrunch up is quite adorable.

"I'm always just Theo to you, unless you have a sexy nickname for me? Those are always acceptable."

Her blush is instant. "Not yet."

"So there might be in the future?" I hedge, stepping closer. Invading her personal space, I grip the back of her neck while bending low enough that I can press my forehead to hers. "You want there to be one?"

"That's not what I said." Her sweet breath fans across my lips, and it takes everything in me not to kiss her. To taste her. "You're putting words in my mouth."

"I agree, taking your mouth is a tempting offer."

"Theodore Astor!"

"Yes?"

"You're doing a fabulous job at cheering me up," Gabriella whispers suddenly and then presses those beautiful lips to mine in the sweetest kiss. It's short and soft and the literal definition of perfection, but I want more. To own her. To devour. "Now, what's under the large covering?"

"Another surprise."

"Show me." The demanding tone she uses, how she enunciates each word, is sexy and makes my cock throb. The hard son of bitch presses against the zipper of my pants, digging into the teeth in search of a relief we can't have yet. She's not ready for me, for the demonic need only she can incite.

"Not yet." My expression is neutral, while inside I'm a ball of aching fire. Needing. Hungry.

"Why not?" she pouts, and I want to bite her bottom lip.

"One, she's my surprise for another time. And two, because it's feeding time, and someone will be here shortly to do so." I can see the questions brewing at my words, but I shake my head. "Trust me, sweetheart. You'll be meeting her soon enough."

"She?"

"Yes, she." Turning us around, I catch the moment Tero comes in with a box with the animal's meal inside. We pass by each other, him smiling at Gabriella and my little painter curious as ever is trying to look around me, but I don't pause until we're inside the elevator shaft and the door is closed. "I know you have questions and I promise to answer them soon, but that back there is very important. It's more than an opening night surprise. She's my special gift to you."

"That sounds insane."

"Sometimes a little insanity is a blessing, Gabriella. Just like I never expected you, but you've knocked me down and have overtaken my world. Something I will never regret."

Gabriella

I can't get his words out of my head.

Their meaning and the heavy conviction that leads to one word: love.

It's been brewing, growing—consuming my world since we met outside of the cafe a few weeks ago, and while it makes no sense, I'm unable to deny it. To myself. To him. Because there's this undeniable pull that both throws me off my feet while helping me find an inner balance I've been missing.

And all because of him. Theodore Astor.

Being with him—just standing in his presence makes me feel at home, a warmth I've never felt before. Not once. Not with anyone. There's just something about Theo that pulls me in, and I don't fight it—him—the tight binds that both tethers and scares me.

It's also why I'm currently arguing with the man, holding my ground. Arms crossed over my chest; I'm meeting his hard stare with one of my own while his jaw ticks. "Yes."

"No."

"Not up for debate, Mr. Astor."

"You're right." He steps into my personal space, crowding me against the front door of my home. He thinks I'm here to pick up clothes, while I'm here to stay. To get back to work, because I have a show to prepare for and a life that needs to carry on.

I'm not going to hide. I've done nothing wrong.

The police themselves have been patrolling the nearby area the last few nights, and nothing. No snakes. No threats. No bodies. And with the extra officers surrounding the neighborhood, I doubt there will be.

I can't allow myself to think otherwise.

"You're giving in that easily?" He doesn't move back when I give him my best bitch brow; instead, I'm given a smirk. His eyes alight with humor. "What's the catch?"

"Then I'll stay over."

"You want to—"

"I'm going to, sweetheart. Not a question."

"But what about...?" His lips against mine silence me, eradicate any question or concern. It wouldn't be the first time he's slept over or that we wake up in the same bed. And if I'm being honest, the idea of him being here just in case does make my heart flutter.

Theo cares.

Maybe as much as I do.

"Fine," I say just as he nibbles on my bottom lip, dragging his teeth across the kiss-swollen flesh. "But—"

"But nothing, Miss Moore." Another teasing bite. "Open the door for us."

"Okay." Shakily, I turn, rubbing myself against his muscled chest and abs. I don't miss how the area I touch clenches, how he sucks in a hiss through his teeth. It takes me longer than it should to put the key in the lock and turn the handle, but I'm too busy enjoying the feel of him. His harsh breaths. His manly scent. Eventually, I do, though, and step inside with Theodore close behind. "Is there anything you want to do tonight? Have you eaten yet?"

"No and no."

"Are you hungry?" I don't know the fine details of his diet, but I'm sure adjusting won't be hard. I'm not a picky eater. "Can I cook for us?"

"That'd be nice, but I'm perfectly fine with vegging out and ordering in, too."

"Unacceptable, Mr. Astor." He follows me to the staircase's first landing where I turn to face him, using the added height to face him head on. I'm almost nose to nose. Almost. "Let me spoil you a bit. What would make your mouth water tonight?"

"You." No hesitation. There's no stopping nor hiding the way my nipples tighten and thighs clench, the way my chest rises and falls at a faster pace nor the way he takes in each change, his pupils dilating until there's very little of the amber left. He's a beautiful man, and I'm susceptible to his every charm as if God created him for me. "All I will ever want in this life is you."

"I want you too." My own truth.

"But you're not ready yet." Theo takes a step closer, his lips hovering just a mere inch from my own while his arms wrap around my back. I'm held against him, trapped chest to chest and a harsh shiver runs down my body and onto his. "I know you're a virgin, sweetheart, and as much as I want to devour you, I'll wait. We have our whole lives. What's a little more time?"

"You want to wait?" I ask incredulously, because isn't he supposed to jump at the chance to break my hymen? To make me his. There's also no denying my disappointment at this, because while a part of me agrees to wait, that it's the right thing until we get to know each other better, the other wants to spread her legs in offering like a whore.

"Why the surprised face?" he asks, tracing my top lip with his tongue before flicking the bottom one. "I don't need to take the cherry between your legs to own you, because I already do." Theo swallows hard and closes his eyes, nostrils flaring while pulling me impossibly closer. Holding me a little tighter. "No one, not even God himself can break us apart, Gabriella. We are meant to be."

"How can you be so sure?" Even though I feel it too, I have to ask him. Because this has been sudden and my life has been insane lately, but more than that, I can't stop thinking about him. Wanting him close to me or wondering if he thinks of me like I do him. "Why me?"

"Only time can explain those questions, but I'll be next to you as we uncover each answer." Nodding, I try to explain my views when he shakes his head and pecks my lips once. "Why don't you go take a shower and I'll take care of dinner? It's getting late, and I'd rather relax with you for a bit before we head to bed."

"I really wanted to cook for you."

"And you'll have plenty of time to do so, but for tonight I just want to hold you close."

"Okay."

"Good girl." Another gentle sweep of his lips and then I'm settled back on the first step while he moves back. "I'll be here when you finish."

"I'll be back in a bit, then. Order whatever you're in the mood for." I turn to leave, and my right foot is on the second step, when his hand grips my elbow. It surprises me and I look back, scrunching up my face in a confusion that dies off the second our eyes meet again. The look he's giving me is one of a painful hunger, but before I can ask, I'm yanked against his chest.

The contact is blissful and more so is the way he lifts me up with one arm beneath my butt, forcing my legs around his hips. Hips that thrust forward a second later and my eyes roll back, his cock flexing against my core. Right against my clit and a rush of electric heat settles on my bundle of nerves, pulsing, needing more.

"My apologies for leaving you wanting, sweetheart." His voice is gravelly, fingertips digging in as he lowers us slowly onto the stairs. The wood is cold beneath me, a sharp contrast to my heated flesh. It feels good, but nothing can compare to his lips on my neck, littering the tender area with sharp nips and open-mouthed kisses. "You might not be ready for more, not all of me, but that doesn't mean I can't satisfy you. I'm always here to give you what you need."

"Theo, I—"

"Let me take care of you...*please*." His hands unbutton the pants Meera gave me, pulling them down over my hips before tossing them somewhere behind us. Thank God they were a gift with the price tag attached because I'm not wearing panties, a sight that makes him growl—those amber eyes turn darker. I'm bare and slick and swollen. "You've been like this all day? Without underwear?"

"Yes."

"Bad girl." He runs the tips of his fingers from my ankles to knees and back down again. His touch is featherlight, so soft I think I'm imagining it, until the sensation travels to my inner thighs and then I'm arching, lifting my hips in offering. "And so fucking beautiful."

"I need you to touch me."

"No."

"No?" I ask, his answer confusing me until I'm picked up once again while he switches our positions. He stands long enough to unbuckle his pants, pushing them down to his ankles before sitting down while I stand above him. I'm waiting, anxious, but when that first flick of his tongue teases my clit, I moan. It's loud inside my house and I'm thankful my dog stayed the night with Tero and Meera as they try out being dog parents for the day.

I don't want to be interrupted or needed; this is my heaven. Nirvana. A pleasure I chase while undulating my hips over his mouth.

Each stroke gets me closer and closer, my tiny hole clenching every time he dips the tip of his tongue inside, but then I'm moving once again, unable to do anything but let him place me where he wants me. And that's straddling his hips with his cock nestled against my labia while the bulbous tip kisses my throbbing bundle of nerves.

"Just feel me, beautiful. *Motherfuck*, just like that." Theo controls my movements, his strong hands forcing my hips to rub against his length while my juices coat us both. "God, you feel good. Can't wait to fuck you like you deserve, like my goddess and whore."

I clench at those words, not offended in the least.

Nothing this man does would, and I'm loving the filthy promise behind each word.

"So close. So good," I whimper, my fingers finding purchase in his hair and I pull on the strands, needing an anchor when he picks up the pace. Harder. Each roll of my hips envelops his length and I'm dripping, the sensation of his thickness where I need him most has me throbbing, trembling—teetering on the edge.

All I can do is close my eyes while biting my lip and give in.

I have no control. No say.

My body is wound tight while his groans below further push me toward the edge. In Theo's hold I'm a rag doll for his pleasure, and it turns me on. The hissed curses beneath me bring me closer and closer, and just as I'm on the precipice, he bites my neck.

"Oh my God!" Every nerve ending in my body locks down, and it's near painful to move as the first wave of pleasure washes over me. "Theo...I can't...*fuck*!"

"My beautiful girl," he grunts, thrusting harder, slicing through my lips at a faster pace as his come mixes with my own. Each spurt feels like a hot kiss to my clit, marking me as his. Strong hands pull me down so we're chest to chest, his guttural groans reverberating through me and spreading, prolonging my release. "Always mine."

"Yours." Snuggling into him, I close my eyes and breathe him in. The minutes pass like this and he never complains, letting me relax until the last aftershock rocks my frame and I can find my strength. "I'm going to head up now and take that shower."

His chuckle makes me smirk. "My apologies for holding you back."

"Don't worry. This is the best kind of delay."

After taking a quick shower, I come downstairs still feeling light as a feather and calm. My red hair is wet, the tendrils sticking to my back, and I'm wearing a lilac crop top sans bra. I'm dressed to relax and then bed, but what I find at the bottom of the stairs is a tense man who eyes me with hunger.

"Is everything okay?" I ask, stopping on the same step he made me come on.

He notices this, and the harsh look melts into a sly grin. "Yes and no."

"That makes no sense."

"It does to me." He takes the steps between us, stopping when we're almost eye to eye. "Yes, because you're here. Because I can still smell you all around me."

I swallow hard. "And the no?"

"Because unfortunately, I need to leave." Disappointment fills me but I shake it off, keeping my expression neutral. "I'm sorry, love. There's been a family emergency that needs my immediate attention."

Family. *Of course he has one. I just never asked.* He didn't offer either, but what if—

"Are you married?" I blurt out, my chest caving in at the mere thought. How could he? How could I? "Am I…?"

"You're the only," he says, his hands coming up to cup my cheeks. His touch is comforting, gentle and caring. Moreover, there's this exciting spark flowing through his touch. It's pleasant and fills my chest with warmth. I like it. Him. And everything he represents, even though my life isn't in any place where I should pursue a relationship. "That will never change, Gabriella. Please believe me on this."

"I do." Blindly. Stupidly. With him, I find myself following my intuition without caution. "So your family? Are they okay?"

"Just a minor incident that needs to be cleaned up."

"Cleared up, you mean?"

"No." With his eyes on my face, he pulls me to the edge of the steps and against his lips. Once. Twice. His sweeps them back and forth before pausing. "Cleaned up is the right terminology in this instance. Someone has been hurt, and it's up to me to clear their name and forcefully right this wrong."

"Forcefully? Are you going to fight someone?"

"It would never be a fair fight." Dropping his hands, Theo steps back and puts a bit of space between us. "Now, I'll be out of the city limits, but Tero and Meera are only a phone call away. They know to stay vigilant and come right away if anything happens."

"That's not—"

"It's for my peace of mind. Okay?"

"Yes."

"Thank you, beautiful." His eyes travel slowly from my hair to toes and back up again twice, unapologetic in his actions. "I'll be back soon. Staying away isn't an option."

"Then I'll hold you to that." It's a breathy whisper and his hands clench, nose flaring once before he turns to leave. Theo doesn't look back, and I'm left a little achy, needy, and decide to go to sleep instead of watching TV.

The sooner I go to sleep, the sooner he's back.

Gabriella

After locking the front door and checking all the others on this floor, I make myself a cup of tea and head upstairs. The house is quiet. I'm missing the tinkling of Mr. Pickles's collar and small nails on my floor. I'm missing the calm—peace —that being home once brought me.

But now that I'm alone, I see the differences. Take note of the endless quiet. Understand how no one would hear my scream if something were to happen.

It hits me, now that Theo isn't standing as my protector, how much has been taken from me. My security. My mental health. The ability to walk around my home without looking behind me or outside the windows.

"I hate this," I say out loud, my hands trembling a bit. The longer I stand in front of my bedroom door, the more uncomfortable I feel.

My mind flicks through the last few weeks; a sick movie reel flipping through each horrific moment. Tim. The snake. The picture of the dead body and the words attached, and each one has this house as the common link.

I should sell. Get out and don't look back.

But what would that solve?

Am I really being stalked, or is this a fucked-up coincidence? Why aren't the police making a bigger deal out of it?

I'm alone.

"I need to work. Keep busy." Because there's no way I'll go to sleep anytime soon. The what *ifs* will keep me from doing so. "Work. Set up and work."

Turning away from my door, I walk to my studio and turn on the lights. Everything's where I left it, with a painting still on the easel and each color I'll need on the small table next to it. However, my water cups for dirty brushes are empty, and before I fill them, I decide to open the window.

It's warm in here. A bit stuffy, and I don't hesitate to spread the curtains apart and lift the pane. And it's as I do, that I look across the yard and find two glowing sets of eyes.

They watch me. Unblinking.

And the last thing I remember is feeling faint and tripping in my haste to move, hitting my head on something hard.

IT's early morning when I come to and I'm still on the floor, my head pounding. It hurts so bad, and the position I'm in has left me with a sore neck. But it's worse when I stand. *Jesus*, it's so much worse, and my limbs—my entire frame—is jittery and unbalanced. There's also a tender spot near my temporal bone and when I touch it, I find dry blood there with a small gash beneath.

"What the hell happened?" My eyes sweep the room, and I find nothing out of place but the small wooden stepping stool that I use to reach the top of my supply closet. It's not in its usual place and I don't remember leaving it here, but it's obvious that I fell and hit my... "Oh shit!"

Turning, I rush to the still-open window with the sun barely lighting up the early morning sky and search the yard for those two sets of eyes. For anything that proves I'm not crazy. That I haven't lost my mind within the carnival show my life has become.

Nothing. There's nothing.

No animal within the foliage, but I know what I saw and they were not human eyes.

Could it be the snake? An owl, maybe?

"If I call this in, it could blow up in my face." *Like with the picture*. Rubbing my sore forehead, I wince, but it helps alleviate a little of the mounting pressure. This is going to take more than a few ibuprofens to get through the day. "Coffee. Lots of coffee and pain meds."

My reality and dreams and everything in between are a blur of crazy moments that are weighing heavy on me, and I miss Theo. Miss his smile and scent and the ease in which I forget the world around me when he's near.

I close the window and survey the back once again, finding nothing, and I breathe out a sigh of relief. It's easier to chalk this up to *I hit my head and dreamed of eyes* than the alternative. It's probable, not far-fetched, and I'll stick to it unless proven otherwise.

"Sounds good to me." With my plan in place, I head to my room and closet to change. If I leave now, I can be back within the hour and pick up where I never began yesterday: painting. More so because I'm not trying to attract attention and slip into a large pair of overalls with a navy and white striped V-neck underneath.

There's a little cafe near here that I visit every once in a while, with an amazing bagel selection that has my name all over it. That, and I'm going to need a triple shot of everything with a side of more caffeine to get through this headache.

The cut isn't large when I look at myself in the bathroom mirror a few minutes later, dabbing at the area with a wet towel. It's about an inch long and won't require stitches, so small that a Band-Aid does the trick after I arrange my mass of bed-head hair into a bun at the nape of my neck. You can barely see it, the area not as swollen or bruised as I originally thought it'd be, and my fair complexion helps.

"Not bad at all." With one last look after brushing my teeth, I head downstairs and out the door. It's a good and sunny morning for a walk, and I could use a bit of time to clear my head because something inside me knows those eyes were real.

That I'm not crazy.

"That'll be…" I don't hear the rest as I'm paying attention to the person beside me. She smells of too much perfume and looks better than she did the last time we spoke, but still reeks of a bitterness that burns my nostrils. *Is that really coming from her?* The scent is a bit nauseating, but I manage to hand over my debit card to the employee with a smile on my face. "Your order will be ready in a few minutes, Miss. Under what name?"

"Gabriella," Elise answers for me, her body moving a little closer. "Her name is Gabriella."

"I can answer for myself," I say, a fake smile on my face. *Can I please catch a break here?* Moving toward the pickup area, I stop behind an older couple who are too busy looking at some photo on the woman's phone. Grandkids, I think. "Go away."

"We need to talk." There's an urgency to her tone that puts me on edge. She's not looking at me, but up ahead while holding her phone tight in her grip. "Now."

"No."

"This isn't a request, Gabby. I've had enough of your shit."

"Of *my* shit?" Her audacity makes me laugh, a loud sarcastic one that catches the attention of the couple and a few other people around us. "You're still the same self-absorbed bitch you've always been, Elise. It's always someone else's mistake. Always someone else's responsibility for your happiness and worth."

"Don't talk about things you don't understand."

"I just don't care anymore." The couple grabs their order and after giving us another side look, they walk out, leaving me at the front. "Nothing you say will make a difference in how I see you. We're done."

"You stole him from me," she hisses, her hand gripping my forearm. The talons she calls nails dig in and I feel them break skin, but I keep the pleasant smile on my face as the lady with my order comes to the counter.

"Gabriella?"

"That's me," I say while snatching my arm from her grip before stepping up and taking my food and drink. The coffee is piping hot, and the bagels smell amazing; I can't wait to get home and eat. Elise hasn't moved, eyeing me, but I wave as I walk by her. "Have a nice life."

The sun feels good on my skin as I step outside the busy cafe toward home, but before I can make it to the crosswalk, I'm pulled back by a hand on my arm. I almost stumble at the force they use, dropping my bagels, but somehow saving the coffee. The food is in a sealed box, and I yank my arm free once again, bending to grab it before looking at Elise.

Her perfume is unmistakable. She really stinks.

"You have two minutes before—"

"You're going to drop the lawsuits, Gabby. Drop them, and disappear from Seattle, or I'll be forced to remove you."

"No." I'm not sure which lawsuit she's talking about since I've let Theo handle the copyright issue; we can't do more than present my rightful ownership and wait for a judge to decide. Denying her, however, is bringing a smile to my face. I've had enough of her pushing me around. No more. "Don't make this worse for yourself,

Elise. You did this—" My words are cut off by a hard smack to the face, my head whipping to the side while I taste a bit of blood in my mouth. She caught me by surprise and my grip on my breakfast is tight enough not to drop them, but my coffee is done for. The squished cup has spilled, and my skin is red—hurts.

"You will do as you're told, or that will feel like a gentle pat compared to what I'm capable of." Before I can stop her, she has my chin in her grasp and is tilting my face to inspect the damage. "Ruining your pretty face would be a pleasure, a motherfucking aphrodisiac, but I can't afford to have attention on me right now." Her face lowers to mine, her lips teasing my own. "Someday, though, I will."

"Promise or threat?" I ask through squished lips.

Elise throws her head back and laughs. She's deranged. "I'm going to miss your idiocy the most."

"And I'm going to enjoy this." Before she can ask, I throw my arm back and snap it forward, landing a punch square to her stomach with the mangled to-go cup—I make sure to spill the rest of my coffee on her. Elise doubles over, releasing my face, and clutches her midsection. And while she groans, I drop what's left of my food on the ground with a longing look before bringing my knee up, landing the next blow to her face. "That looks painful," I taunt, giggling a bit just to annoy her.

"You bitch," she seethes, moving out of the way before I can kick her again. "I'm going to kill you, Gabriella. Mark my words, I'm going to—"

"What seems to be the problem here?" a female voice comes from behind me and Elise pales, stepping further back away from me while I look over quickly. Meera's eyes meet mine and she winks before a stoic expression overtakes her pretty features. "I asked you a question, Miss Scott."

"Nothing." Her reply comes quickly—too obvious, and I snort. Elise's hands clench at that, her posture almost coiling into herself.

She's afraid of Meera. "I tripped and my friend was helping me." She looks away from Tero's wife, and her eyes turn icy. "Nice to see you, Gabby, and thank you for the help."

I don't glare at her. Instead, my smile is saccharine sweet. "You're welcome, and I'll be ready when you are."

My ex-best friend opens her mouth to say something, the nasty retort sitting on her tongue, but Meera pulls out her phone and takes a picture. "Mr. Astor will be hearing all about this friendly encounter, Miss Scott."

"That's unnecessary." Elise coughs at that, a nervous gesture. Her eyes are also wide and alarmed. "I'm sure he has better things to do than worry about girlfriends catching up."

"He doesn't when it comes to her, Miss *Scott.*" *Why did she emphasize her last name?* "Have a nice day, and don't make a habit out of tripping into people because there are loyal guards out there willing to return every favor tenfold."

Their exchange is weirder than mine with Elise, and when my former friend hurries away as if Hades himself was after her, I look at Meera. "I need more than a vacation at this point."

"I'd say you do," she says, looking at my face where Elise hit me. Her eyes narrow and expression hardens, but she doesn't ask. "But better times are coming, sweetheart. Trust me on this."

"I'll try." I shrug. At the moment, it's the best I can do. "But now, I'm going to double my coffee and bagel order so I can pig out when I get home. Are you interested in joining me?"

"Can't. Tero's waiting on me with Mr. Pickles at the park for a walk."

"Ahhh, little guy must be loving that. What time are you dropping him off?"

"He is and later this evening. Is that okay?"

"That's fine."

Her concern is written all over her face, but I'm thankful she doesn't question me. I have no doubt that her boss will do enough of that at some point. "My car is here, though. How about a ride instead before I meet the boys?"

"You don't need to do that. This is a ten-minute walk—"

"I wasn't asking, sweetheart. Go get your food."

I laugh at that. "So bossy."

"More like I'm loyal."

KING

I take in a deep breath and hold it as her scent infiltrates my senses. It owns me. Tortures me, and I'm here to return the favor.

I'm done waiting.

It's time for my queen to rise while our enemy falls.

Pushing off the wall of her room, I stop at the edge of her bed and place a knee on the mattress. It dips, accommodating my weight as I crawl a little closer, stopping just beside her unconscious body.

My pretty girl passed out an hour ago, due to exhaustion or maybe the sleeping pill she took out of desperation, I don't know. Don't care either. Not when I can lay beside her and touch, sliding a hand up her bare thigh while she's uncovered.

But that's a Gabriella thing. Every night without fail, she bundles up and then kicks the oversized comforter off a few hours later. It's a trait I find sweet. Alluring.

Like her soft skin and scent. Like her intoxicating smile and green eyes, always so curious and fierce, but I know the demon that resides within—see her lurking behind that expressive stare—and I vow to bring her out. To bring her home.

Her small bikini panties are a lovely shade of pink tonight with just enough fabric to cover her sweet little clit while her labia peeks out. They look petal soft as I part her legs, and my mouth waters at the debauched sight of a tiny wet spot at the center.

"Motherfuck," I hiss through clenched teeth, pulling the panties aside while enjoying the slow parting of those lips and the little hole I plan to break, worship, and pray to for the rest of my existence. "Mine." The one word rumbles up my chest, shaking the bed slightly. "Always mine."

My face lowers to her neck, and I place a small kiss there and then over the bruised skin from her altercation with her so-called friend. *My poor beauty, so much pain and so much betrayal surrounds you.* I trail my nose down her chest and the flat of her stomach, keeping my weight off her body. I'm barely touching her, keeping it featherlight until I stop just above her mound where I keep her underwear pushed aside. *Many will bleed in your name; I promise you this.*

My face is inches from her pussy. My nostrils flare, pulling her scent deep into my lungs as every muscle in my body aches with the need to sink into the pink flesh.

I want to fuck her.

I want to mark her.

And I will.

But there's someone I need to visit first. Someone who forgot her place.

"I'll be back for you." With my nail, I lightly carve out the word *soon* on her thigh. The cuts are very shallow, just a drop or two of blood seeping through, and I lick them before pulling back. *Christ,* she tastes of ambrosia. "My sweet, pretty girl."

With one final glance, I leave a sharp paring knife as a prop beside her on the bed before walking to her closet. My gift is right where I left it and I grab it, taking it with me as I walk out of the room and toward her studio.

The room is a bit messy when I enter and her dog looks up sharply when he sees me, watching me, but a lot less nervous than before. We have an understanding, he and I.

He behaves, I reward.

"Relax," I say, and his head immediately goes back to lying on his paws. His big eyes watch me walk over to the old dresser she keeps in here as secondary storage, not a single grunt from him, while I rummage through her things. The unit stores paints inside and tools used to achieve different finishes, but what I need is the hidden compartment that slides out from underneath the middle shelf.

This is where she keeps a gold locket that was supposed to be her mother's and was given to her by the group home when she aged out. It's something she holds dear for some reason, some of which I will never understand, but I know she'll come looking when she finds the drawer pulled out.

"It's time to remember, pretty girl."

I'VE BEEN SITTING in her living room for the past hour. Thinking. Planning. Making necessary arrangements since the woman I came to see is an idiot. Someone who fancies herself of my social standing, and yet I view her as no better than the dirt beneath my shoes.

Unprepared. Unable to make a single move in a world where I reign—wouldn't know about a few seconds after. I have eyes and ears everywhere.

An army at my disposal who is loyal.

Trained to kill on command.

But then again, that's her fucking cross to bear—not mine—because idiocy leads to bad decisions on the way down the road toward death. And I'm here to deliver the final notice; my patience runs thin.

The apartment is small and disorganized; a cluster of journals, details of her goals, and the one atop the coffee table still open has a vivid and incorrect detailing of each interaction we've had.

"Motherfucking delusional." I'm disgusted by the mere thought of her. It's a little past four in the morning when the door bangs open, revealing the angry woman in question. She storms inside with a male. He's young, impressionable, and is dead before the door closes with a bullet to the head.

"What the fuck?" she screams, wiping her face where the blood splattered.

"Good morning, Elise."

At my voice, she stiffens, her eyes snapping toward mine. "Your—"

"Silence." Standing from the oversized bubblegum-pink chair, I stride across the room and pause a few steps from her. She trembles in fear, her chest heaving while her body betrays her and thighs clench. I arouse her. I scare her. "You made a mistake, Elise. A costly one."

"Please, let's talk about this."

"We've talked in the past, and yet you don't listen." Another step forward, and she takes one back. "I've given you chance after chance to accept your fate with dignity until she doles out your punishment."

"She's not one—" Her scream is cut off by my hand wrapping around her throat, squeezing until bruises begin to appear and her face becomes a nice cherry red. "Please." The word is low, muted by my tight hold, but I hear her loud and clear.

"My patience with your acts of grandeur have reached their end, Elise." My fingers tighten, the flesh giving way beneath the pressure. "You will stop, and you will bend. Do you understand? Nod if you do." Her nod is barely perceptible, but enough for me. "You will wait for her decision with grace. Again, nod." She does—frantically, with tears streaming down her cheeks. "Attempt something again and it will be my wrath you'll face. I hold no qualms in holding a public execution, Miss *Scott*. Be afraid, because I am watching."

With that, I release her and she drops to the ground, cupping her neck as she tries to regulate her breathing. Her choking sounds are pathetic. Show who she truly is.

Bending to her level, I gingerly push a few strands of hair behind her ear, an action she automatically leans into while my lip curls in disgust. "You have no shame. No self-pride." With two fingers, I trace the shell of her ear, causing a shiver to run through her. "But then again, you're the daughter of a traitor. One I took great joy in dismembering while still alive, and who then took his final breath as the flames rose, disintegrating his limbs."

"Stop."

"Why should I?"

"I'm the right one, and you know it."

"Do I?"

"Yes." Her voice betrays her—her fear is palpable, and I revel in it. Smile down at the pathetic woman on the floor. "There's still time to make the right decision."

"She will always be the right choice. The only fucking choice." Then, before her next inhale, I hold her earlobe in my hand while she screams. Blood pours from the wound. The hole looks nasty—painful, but I hold no remorse. "This is my last warning, Elise. The next time, it'll be your throat I hold in my hand instead of your ear."

Leaving her where she lays crying, I walk out the door without looking back while pocketing the cartilage. She'll strike. She'll come for my pretty girl. Her problem is that she thinks her puppet-master act will continue to work, unaware that she's dangling from my strings.

I move her.

I force her hand.

And the next time we see each other, my queen will have risen.

Gabriella

I've been awake for days now, watching the shadows on the walls.

I'm not okay.

I'm scared.

I'm still tracing the letters on my thigh, fighting the instinct to run because where do I go? Who will believe me when everything points to this being my own doing?

Someone had to be in my home. There's no other plausible explanation.

And the knife beside me? How do I explain that?

What the SPD Captain claimed could be true, and yet, either way I don't feel comfortable going to the police. Not after the last time; I was arrested for being scared out of my mind. *Call Theo. He'll help...I know he will.*

But that brings in another set of problems. My association with him is the cause of the fading bruise on my face and the loss of my best friend. Shitty or not, she was all I had. For so long, it was the two of us, and now I'm alone. Mentally breaking every second of the day, and I'm afraid of what will be left behind the moment I shatter into a million pieces.

Will I recognize myself? Will I want to remember anything?

"Breathe in. Breathe out." I've been surviving on food deliveries dropped outside my door and coffee—lots of coffee. Unhealthy and probably making it worse, but the terror is forcing my actions. Reality or possibilities—I don't know which is worse. "I'll get through this like always. Focus on work."

My cell phone pings with a message and I look at the screen, placing my paintbrush in the water cup. It's him. As if he knows I need him.

> Why are you avoiding me, sweetheart? ~Theo

Another message before I'm done reading the first.

> What's going on? Are you sick? ~Theo

The guilt that hits me at his show of concern nearly bowls me over. My chest feels tight, and my body shakes as tears brim my eyes. The fight between my head and heart are making me doubt him, wondering if he'd abandon me too if I became one of those clingy women who carry too much baggage.

Swallowing back a sob, I type out a short reply.

> All is bueno. I'm just working in the studio as I have a deadline fast approaching, and the owner of the gallery is a real tyrant. First two are done, BTW! ~Gabriella

Three small dots appear on the screen signaling he's typing.

> Are you lying to me? ~Theo

No. Of course not ~Gabriella

For a while he doesn't respond, and the bothersome sensation that I'm betraying him doesn't abate, especially when the next message comes in. Instead, it feels ten times worse—my chest squeezes painfully tight, and I have to walk out of the room and to the bathroom, splashing cold water on my face, on the back of my neck—anything to calm my beating heart and churning stomach.

I'll wait for you. Come talk to me when you're ready to be honest. ~Theo

"Maybe I should set up another appointment with my therapist?" I have a few probabilities—theories floating around in my head since the mail incident with my birth parents' information. I could be a sleepwalker. I could be someone with multiple personalities and I wouldn't know this, because there's never been any testing done.

It might be me. It might be someone stalking me.

The problem is that I have no proof either way, and it's driving me insane. I can't sleep, eat, or breathe without wondering about the what ifs…

And the dead bodies. There's no making sense of that because the large snake in my backyard was real. The video of a man dumping the body of who I now know was Elise's lawyer in the fraud copyright case is real.

Coincidence? Maybe.

They, too, had a grudge against him? Could be.

Either way, the uncertainty is eating me alive, and I don't know how much more I can take. I'm jittery, panic rising at every turn.

"Lord help me." My doorbell rings then, and I pause my internal rambling. I'm not expecting anything today. The person rings again and I rush back to grab my phone, opening the Ring app and waiting for the live feed. It takes a few seconds, but an older man comes onto the screen wearing a mail uniform and holding a manila envelope. I press the speaker icon. "How can I help you?"

"Hi, good afternoon. I have certified mail for Gabriella Moore. Is she available?"

"Can you leave it there for me?"

"I'm sorry, I need a signature on this one."

"Give me a minute." Putting the phone down, I dry my face with a towel then send Theo a response.

> I just need a few days. We can talk then.
> ~Gabriella.

His response is just as quick, and it makes my heart flutter this time.

> I'll always be here waiting. ~Theo

> Thank you. ~Gabriella

My phone chimes with another message and it's Elise's name that flashes across the screen. I click to see what she wants, but it's nothing but more bull crap. More demands. More fake concern for a friendship she trampled on.

> Gabriella, we need to talk. Enough is enough.
> Please think of our friendship…stop hurting me.
> ~Elise.

"Why can't she leave me alone," I mutter, closing her message and typing another one for Theo. *Maybe if I ignore her, she'll go away*. Not likely, but here's to hoping.

> I'm about to receive certified mail at my front door.
> Don't know what it's about. ~Gabriella

> Go ahead. It's from my lawyer and the Hall
> firm. ~Theo

That makes me feel better; knowing he's aware brings a little peace to my chaotic mind. The man is patient and kind, never pushy or rude. I wish he was here.

> Thank you. ~Gabriella

> And I miss you. ~Gabriella

I don't wait for his reply and rush downstairs where the man is still waiting. He's patient. I can make out his form typing something on his phone from the windows on either side of the door.

He then pockets the device seconds before I unlock the door and open it, meeting his eyes. "Sorry for the delay. I was in the middle of something important."

"It's okay, Miss. Just sign here for me." The older gentleman hands over a clipboard and pen and after I sign my name, we switch, and I get my envelope. "Have a nice day."

"You too," I call out to his retreating form, but I don't think he hears me. Stepping back in, I close and lock the door before tearing off the flap sealing the documents. The first thing I make out is the letterhead from Hall & Associates. Just one Hall, not two as it had been before in the paperwork Theo showed me. Then, I see the contents and I am floored. Literally left standing upright while I smile—breathe—for the first time in a while without choking on my pain. "*Christ*, he withdrew everything. She won't own anything."

Tears fill my eyes as I scan through the rest.

This is from the younger brother, the remaining Hall, and it's more than I ever thought to receive back. There's an apology and so much more, line after line of willing help.

We will file the right copyright free of charge.

We will pay for any fees you will incur and fight on your behalf, legally, against those who sought to hurt you through this fraudulent claim.

We are sorry for what a member of our family has done to you, your name, and your property/business. Please let us make amends on the actions of my deceased brother. He was wrong, so wrong, and my family and I vow to make reparations to those hurt by him as more of his illicit activities come to light.

I can feel their pain through each line, and my heart hurts for them. None of this is their fault, and this goes beyond what they are liable for. Because money is one thing, but to truly want to help and follow through with your time and dedication means a lot.

It also makes Elise's sudden panic clearer. Her words the other day that I withdraw the case.

And yet, I can't help but feel that there's something I'm missing. A part of the puzzle that hasn't revealed itself.

A yawn escapes me then and I close my eyes, head thrown back as I stretch. Days without sleep are hard, especially without the hour cat nap to help. My body goes through lethargic moments and others of manic energy; the yo-yoing effect causing me to stumble toward my TV room in the back of the house where my comfy couch awaits with my favorite afghan.

The news and the revelations continue to mount and for some reason, I feel struck with a whip and need to take a breather. The papers fall from my grip and onto the couch cushion beside me.

"Just for a second." That's all I need before making my fourth cup of coffee today. "Ten minutes at the most..."

His hand is on the small of my back as we follow the hostess to our table. The young woman in front of us sways her hips, tries to garner the attention of every man in the room, and yet fails miserably. Pathetically.

I'm embarrassed for her. *I giggle through our mind link—our sacred bond—and he chuckles, amused by my candor. But then again, I'm always nothing but honest, that breath of fresh air in his frozen lungs.*

His dead heart beats for me.

His darkness surrounds me in warmth.

Moreover, it's been that way since I broke into the vampiric kingdom one late autumn evening and sat atop the king's bed waiting for him. His bed.

The plan was to ask for a truce. To demand the vampire patriarch back off my family's territory and end his kingdom's raids—the search for the daughters of the dead high priestess and their warlock king.

My sister is clairvoyant.

I control death magic.

Princess twins with more power than our parents, and while seeing the future can come in handy, it's me he truly seeks. Isabella has seen this, and she went to make an alliance with the werewolves just in case. To ensure the safety of our people because the vampire king has detailed plans for me and the gift I've carried since the night of our birth.

I can take a life and give it, moving pieces as I see fit to the prosperity of my people. I can talk to those that have passed and everything breathing, no matter the species.

Their king wants me, to possess that kind of power at all costs, and has killed many in his search.

And yet, the moment our eyes met, a sharp strike froze my veins and held me captive. Every molecular cell in my body came alive with the force of a thousand suns—scorched my very being, and I could see it in his eyes that he felt the same. We couldn't deny each other, and yet, it was his knees that dropped to the ground with his sword at my feet while pledging his life to me.

To the brave witch with red hair and green eyes who barely reached his chest and who weighed less than a hundred and twenty pounds soaking wet. And while I watched the handsome man with dark hair and smoldering eyes crumble before me, I gave him my soul on a golden platter.

Because mates are sacred, holy in our world, and my life began the moment I glared at him.

"Humans are disrespectful by nature." My voice is low, but he nods. His face holds a bit of disgust. He hates to be around mortals, but came for me. To celebrate a human holiday because I find the idea of Valentine's Day quite adorable. That, and he loves his macabre gift of a steel blade he can attach to the end of his finger like a claw. It's silly, totally unnecessary for a vampire, but it inspired him to make a reservation for this romantic dinner.

"They hold no qualms in trying to bed a taken male or female, my love. No honor. No code."

"That they are," I say as he pulls me a little closer, his arm wrapping around my midsection. His need to feel skin on skin rivals mine, and I sigh when he places a chaste kiss on the nape of my neck.

The hostess leads us to a table set for two near the back with the dark night sky as our backdrop. The windows are open, and the moon is high—the stars light up the dark abyss above while I sit in the chair he pulls out for me. We ignore the hostess and her idiocy. The placement of my husband's menu across the table and away from me is not lost on either of us.

Nor is her scent. The differences that let her fit in amongst those in the city.

"Is this table to your liking, Sir?" the woman asks, moving closer to his side, but before she can place a hand on my mate's arm, he has her wrist in his hold. Had we been anywhere else, he wouldn't hesitate to rip it off, but for now I'm satisfied by the subtle crunch of bones and her yelp. "Sir, you're—"

"Never touch me," my husband hisses out, the command of a king, eyes flashing red while she begins to shake. His fangs descend for a second, piercing the gums while she watches in fear. "Disrespect my wife again, and I'll have your head on a spike outside the palace walls. Now, go back to the front and don't come back."

"My apologies."

"Not accepted, hybrid."

"How?" the hostess asks me while holding her wrist against her chest, voice trembling. She knew who we were. "No one here—"

"Silence." Her immediate compliance to my demand is false, belittled by her earlier behavior. Stupid and idiotic; I study her for a few minutes, stretching out the silence while she shifts nervously, a whimper escaping her. "Name."

"Elise."

"Elise what?" my husband asks, even though I have an idea of who her father is. Even though half human, her essence is reminiscent of his. Earthy, but mixed with roses to enhance her femininity.

"Veltross. My name is Elise Veltross."

"The daughter of one of my generals. One who would be embarrassed by your behavior and punish you just as swiftly." Coincidence, or…? *my mate asks through our link, tilting his head while studying her.* Have you spoken to Isabella?

"Yes." Eyes on the ground, she takes a step back. "I'm very sorry."

We're to meet tomorrow afternoon. *"You let your human side overpower and disgrace our very nature and laws, Miss Veltross."* Eyes narrowed, I watch her through slits while clutching the napkin in my hand. I'm not buying her sudden contrite act, nor do we trust her father. He's a good general but thinks too highly of himself and his position. *"How dare you try and touch my mate and your king."*

"I was being—"

"You speak when spoken to. Understood?"

"Yes, My Queen."

"Do not step a single foot out of line, Elise. This is my only warning."

"Yes, My Queen."

"Leave."

"Thank you, My Queen." Elise scurries off and doesn't look back, hiding up front while I am served dinner by an older gentleman and my husband watches me eat. It's something he enjoys, to sit and quietly observe while I return the favor when he hunts. When he lets nature take its rightful place and he momentarily satiates the never-ending thirst.

My king has great control over his impulses. He only kills to eat, as any hunter would do.

It's his nature to kill and drink. It's sexy to watch him overpower his prey.

Like the man from last night, a drunk imbecile who thought it prudent to grab my wrist and yank me back, but before I could slam my elbow in his face, my husband had him by the neck with his feet dangling above the ground.

No mercy. No hesitation as he ran a metal nail—a humorous gift I had made for him—from one side of the man's neck as if he were a chicken at a slaughterhouse. His eyes were an angry ruby red as the demon within him took control. Absolutely glorious to watch, a true aphrodisiac as he buried his fangs deep into the man's neck and drained him of every drop of blood within his dead veins.

It was messy and angry, and my thighs clenched then as they do now with the memory, an action my husband catches. His nostrils flare and eyes become darker—hooded and hungry. A little feral, and I lick the last bite of my dessert sensually from the spoon.

A move he follows with a different unrestrained hunger.

"Two minutes, Gabriella."

"Two minutes?" I ask, feigning an ignorance that makes him flash those sharp fangs at me. He's yet to turn me at my request; my sister and I are bound by loyalty to our people after the death of our parents, but the time to crown a new ruler has come and our baby

brother is now of age. He'll be fair. He'll do right by the throne while my sister and I follow two different paths.

One with a werewolf.

One with a vampire.

"Run, pretty girl."

"I'm not afraid of you," I taunt, leaning over to nip his jaw. "Now close your eyes and count to sixty. Come find me if you can."

"Are you challenging your king?"

"Always, love. Always."

Gabriella

I wake up panicked, a scream caught in my throat while a bit disoriented. There's someone pounding on both the front door and back, multiple voices yelling, and then the wood splinters as they're kicked open.

"What the fuck?" As I say this, my home becomes crowded by officers aiming their guns at my head, shouting orders that I don't understand. It all feels like gibberish, like a Peanuts cartoon until I'm yanked up and thrown to the ground by a man twice my weight and pinned, hands pulled behind my back at an awkward angle.

It hurts. My head is fuzzy.

I'm lost between that dream, how real it felt compared to this, and I can't make heads or tails of anything. Was that real and this is the dream? Why am I being arrested?

"Get off me," I manage to squeak after a minute, lifting my head enough to take in the scene around me. They are trashing my house. The pictures on the walls are being torn down while the furniture is kicked over by a man and woman who I'm starting to loathe.

Her I don't know, but Consuelos has become a familiar face.

"What are you doing to my house, Detective?" My voice rings out clear through the chaos, and all movements cease. "What right do you have to do this?"

Consuelos stops what he's doing and walks over, pausing two steps from me. "You're under investigation for the disappearance of Elise Scott, Miss Moore. We are placing you under—"

"Where's the signed warrant from a judge?" I interrupt, knowing my rights. This is the third attempt to trample on them. "Why haven't my rights been read, or the paperwork shown?"

"People like you don't get those privileges." The woman sneers, and it's then I notice she's out of uniform, dressed all in black and the name *Diana* is spelled across the small breast pocket of her cotton shirt. "She told you to back off."

"She who?"

"We have some blood on a tree near the back of the lot!" someone shouts from the kitchen area, prompting another two men to exit in a rush. No one speaks for a few minutes, but the tensions mount between those left inside. I'm left with Diana, Consuelos, and the man pinning me down. "I need someone to call in the forensics team."

Nobody takes out their phones, though. Instead, the two standing look down at me with condescending smirks on their faces. "So where did you hide the body?" Diana starts the questioning, squatting down to where I'm being held, my body crushed against the floor. "Do you hate your best friend so much to have killed her? You stole her husband, and now this?"

"What body? What husband?"

"Theodore Astor has been married to her…"

I drown out the rest. That makes no sense.

It has to be a lie. I asked him, and he told me he wasn't.

That I was all he wanted.

"That's a lie."

"Is it?" Diana pulls something out of her back pocket, a folded note with some writing on it that looks too new to be real. "Here's their marriage certificate. Believe me now?"

The paper in question is dropped right in front of my face. Moreover, it's a marriage license, dated and stamped by the courts ten years ago, and yet, the ink is dark blue, something that no government agency uses. It's all black. End of. Second, what stands out is Elise's signature, yet Theo's is off.

That's not the one I saw in my contract.

"So they're married?" I ask, my voice low and sad. I'll play along until I manage to get Theo on the phone. "Why didn't she tell me? Where is she?"

"Why don't you tell us? Is that her blood on the tree?" Consuelos looks around nervously, meeting Diana's gaze before shifting to the man on the ground and nodding. "Stop resisting, Gabriella! We only want to help you."

"Hands where we can see them. Hands where we can see them!" This came from Diana, and dread fills my chest. *Lord, please help me.* Something is very wrong here.

"I'm not resisting—" Pain explodes behind my eyes, the side of my skull feeling as though they've cracked it, and the last thing I remember as I'm thrown over a man's shoulder and rushed into the back of a dark green car is the white snake.

It's coiled along the large tree in my front yard, watching while the door is closed and my eyes roll back. And yet, I manage to open them once more and meet its eyes, milky blue and unafraid, and right before something is pressed to my nose and mouth, it nods.

My body aches when I come to. My head feels as though it's been split open by a jackhammer, and yet it's the least of my problems. I don't know where I am or why, but I'm inside of an all-white room with padded walls and a single window up high. Out of reach.

It's there to let me know the sky is dark out, and it's a rainy night at that.

The water pelts against the closed panes and I look up, catching a shadow looking in. Two beady eyes.

"That's it. I'm certifiable." The animal head-butts the glass hard. Once. Twice. Three times before it shatters and the pieces rain down on the ground. "I wonder what did me in? Did I snap like those people on all the crime shows I watched? Will they make one about me?" I mutter under my breath, sitting up with my back against the wall.

My mattress is on the floor with only a thin blanket and pillow atop of it. I will say I'm thankful to still be in my clothes, the paint splatters from earlier today now dry and caked on my skin.

The animal starts to descend into the room headfirst, but pulls back when the *clack, clack, clack* of heels comes near. They stop at my door for a second, the feminine voice saying something to whoever is with her before turning the handle.

"Nice to see you're up." Elise walks in and stops a few feet from me. "Not that you'll be around much longer."

"What are you doing here? Weren't you missing?"

"To the world, I am missing." She takes another step closer, and there's something in her hand that looks like a syringe. "Just like you'll be soon."

I'm wobbly when I stand, stumbling a bit, but I manage to pull myself up against the wall just below the window where I know it's hiding. "Stay away from me."

I don't know who's worse; the snake or her.

"Or what?"

"Elise, this isn't funny. You're going too far."

"He will never know what it's like to rule with you by his side." Her eyes hold so much evil. So much hate. "Long live the queen, Miss Moore."

Her hand snaps back and forward quickly, and I only manage to catch the glint of metal before it's coming toward me. I'm paralyzed, stunned she'd do this, but then it falls to the ground somewhere to my left.

The python slithers down the wall, its large body falling slowly to the ground before taking its place in front of me. Like a protector would. It coils, but its head remains off the ground while staring her down. For each move she makes the snake follows it.

I don't scream. I don't cry.

I watch and wait.

Surprised when Elise attempts to walk back out slowly, the fear I felt now reflected in her eyes. "He's coming."

The serpent doesn't move, but flicks it tongue out almost lazily. Almost taunting.

"Fucking shit!" Screams come from the corridor then, a mass frenzy of terror, and I slide down the wall behind the albino guard. He's either here to kill me or protect me, and right now, either sounds fine. "This isn't over. Tell him this isn't over!"

Then she turns and runs, yelling at someone to get her out before they are caught and killed.

And through it all, as doors slam and people's screams begin to fade, I remain where I am.

It could be minutes or hours, who knows, but my rational mind comes to when a cold head lies atop my hand on the floor. Its skin is smooth, it's presence a bit comforting, and I smile down at the creature.

"If you're here to kill me, go ahead. At this point, it might be better this way." An angry hiss is the response I get, and I nearly laugh at the sound. *I'm hanging with a snake. I'm touching a snake.* The animal takes his eyes off me, taking in my reactions, and after a few minutes rubs his head against my skin the same way that Mr. Pickles does. "Are you wanting me to pet you?"

Not that I expect a response, but when I get this small little nod, I laugh. Loud and near hysterics, but I do. I run my fingers over the head and down the neck in slow passes while looking toward the room's entrance. I can still hear some commotion outside this room—try to ignore the shrill screams of agony—until it all dies down.

Then there's nothing.

A stillness that is eerie.

But through it all, my companion stays by my side and poised to strike, if it comes to that.

That is, until footsteps come close. Closer.

They stop just outside my door and a sharp whistle rends the air, a sound my new friend follows. No looking back. No goodbyes.

Who knows what fate has in store, and I close my eyes for a second. I'm accepting. It is what it is until a throat clears, and a scent I'd know anywhere greets my senses.

I don't need to open my eyes to know it's Theo.

"Look at me," he commands, voice deeper. Rougher than I've ever heard, and I follow the order without pause, nearly screaming when I see his bloodied clothes, his features hardened with eyes glinting red, and the two white fangs protruding from his gums.

"Hello, pretty girl."

Vampire King
THEODORE ASTOR

"What did you just call me?" Gabriella's shaking, her hand in her hair and fisting the lovely red locks I adore. "This can't be. No. No. NOOOOOO!"

"Relax, sweetheart. Just breathe, and I will explain."

"What the hell is there to explain? It's just a coincidence and—"

"You're busy making excuses when we both know I'm real." I take a step closer but she scrambles up, pushing against the wall as if it would move for her. "When you visit me each night in your dream, pretty girl. When you taunt me every moment of the day while awake."

"It's a dream. Just a dream." Her head shakes from side to side, and her breathing becomes choppy. My beautiful little artist is panicking, but I'm not going to stop. I've waited so long for her. For this moment. "This is just a figment of my imagination…I'm probably on heavy medication and seeing shit."

"Then why do your legs still clench at the sight of me?" My nostrils flare, and her sweet scent seeps—infiltrates my senses.

Watching her simply breathe is arousing to me, but scenting her desire is a weakness; always has been. "Why does your pussy clench in need? Why do you still want me no matter how many men I killed outside this room?"

"I don't." Yet I catch the flash of fire in her eyes. My bride is there. Trapped. "Besides, this isn't real. None of it is."

"Are you sure?"

"I am."

"Okay." Theo makes a whistling sound, and a second later the albino python slithers inside once more, stopping at a safe distance from her. He turns his head toward me, asking for permission, and I nod while watching my beauty break and crumble. Her mind is shutting down, while her body wants to flee and never stop running. Silly girl.

"What's happening? Why is…" she trails off, freezing, as her serpent guard becomes Tero who watches her through caring eyes. He's known her just as long as I have, a century of missing his queen, and his loyalty is unbreakable. She saved his sister, the only family he had left.

"My Queen." He bows, looking toward the ground, but Gabriella makes a tsking sound—one she's made a thousand times in our past, and a small smirk curls at my lips. Her human mind might not process like we do, but a part of her remembers.

At my smile, she tilts her head to the side while I simply raise a brow. "What about now?"

"I need a minute."

"That's understandable."

"Alone," she clarifies while I scratch my jaw, the drying blood on my hands making her shake. "Just a few minutes is all I ask, and then we can talk."

Liar. "Go ahead and run, Gabriella," I croon my mate's name, and I revel in the pleasurable shiver that runs through her at the sound. The way her nipples pebble beneath the thin shirt she wears, her bra nearly nonexistent. She's still attracted to me even while trying to make heads or tails of what's real and what's not.

I've played dirty with her.

I've hurt her.

"You'd chase me?"

"To the ends of the earth without hesitation."

"Would you let me go if I asked?"

"Never." At my honest answer she closes her eyes, breathing in deeply before letting it out slowly. "Tero, please head out and deliver the package."

"Consider it done, Your Majesty."

"Thank you, old friend." He exits after giving Gabriella a bow, leaving us alone. Then, I walk deeper into the room and calmly survey her—take in any bruise she may have—and I see red when I smell blood coming from her head. Lost in her arousal and discovery, I didn't smell the older blood, but now it's a pungent calling that I don't ignore. I have her in my arms before her next intake of breath, my lips at the cut. "Who did this to you?"

"How did you move so fast?"

"Who hurt you?" Each word leaves me on a growl, my anger palpable, and she pales. Her fear is as delicious as her arousal, and I take a moment to inhale deeply and hold her essence in my cold, dead lungs. Every part of her is a heady distraction; always has been. "You're bleeding, pretty girl, and I don't like it."

"It was a cop. Never seen him before," she says, tone breathy as I skim my lips over the area. Tasting her. "He was a little older and heavy set."

"Did they touch you anywhere else?" I lick the small head wound, cleaning her up. The cut closes a second later. She'll have a tiny scar, but it won't hurt.

"No. I'm okay." There's also no missing the way she leans into me. Subconsciously, she misses my touch even though there's a hint of fear lingering in her scent, that vanilla with cherries that drives me wild. "But I would like that minute alone."

"I won't stop you, pretty girl." My lips skim down to her cheek and then her ear, nuzzling her a bit. "But please know that there's nothing more pleasurable to a vampire than the chase." Her nod is barely perceptible, the salt of her tears sweet on my lips. "You have five minutes. Use them wisely."

Then I leave, walk out while she stands in the middle of the room, confused and without direction.

Is it fair of me to prey on her weakness? No.

Do I care? Not in the least, when the end game will always be her. In my arms. Back where she's always belonged.

And if this makes me a deplorable son of a bitch, I'll proudly wear the badge because this life came with a heavy price I'll be lifting tonight. They bound my beauty—her powers hidden and suffocated by the greed of the Veltross family for over a century. Her soul survived in limbo, unable to inhabit a body until the day of the sacred moon twenty-one years ago tonight. Her real birthday.

Something Elise knew and tried to prevent, but failed. At every turn. At every lie.

And while the sacrifice made to bring her back bound my hands, I never stopped watching from a distance. Protecting her without being seen. Gabriella never knew the danger her life has been since birth, and I made sure it stayed that way.

Until tonight.

No more lying. No more pretending to be what we're not.

She is mine, and I will always be hers.

At the two-minute mark she exits the room, her cautious step still loud inside the room, but more so are the gasps and choked sobs that escape her small frame when she comes face to face with the carnage I left behind.

The employees at this facility were vampires, all of them, and tonight, they had two rooms occupied. One with Gabriella. The second was a woman with similar looks to Elise and had been dead for hours; her neck is snapped, and body drained of every last bit of blood by those who worked here.

The four men and two women are members of the Veltross family: one bastard son who continued the bloodline years ago with his offspring. They blame my girl for the end of their patriarch, hate me for tearing him limb from limb, while I could give two fucks.

Their low screams—a crying whistle infiltrates every square inch of this floor while they burn. One body part at a time, I left them in a pile and lit a match for Elise to see. Because she's here—hidden—and I'm going to enjoy the day she's caught.

Not today, though. Today is for my bride.

"My King, we have Consuelos and Diana at the warehouse. Should I proceed?" Captain Bron asks from beside me. He's a retired general I placed here to protect Gabriella after she was born. "Everyone is waiting on your orders."

"Not yet." Taking in a deep breath, I let her enthralling scent dominate my senses. It prickles, excitement flooding through my system. She's running. "First, I need to pick up my bride."

He nods in understanding, a smile on his face. "We've all missed her."

"I know."

Gabriella

I'm running.

Scared out of my mind and running toward God knows where with no destination in sight. I can't stop, either. Not when nightmares are real and the man I'd fallen in love with is the devil incarnate.

He'd never hurt me.

My subconscious knows this, but I can't control this fear. Can't stop questioning every interaction and every touch and the soft look in his eyes whenever I laughed. The anger when I cried.

I saw all those emotions. They weren't pretend or fake; Theo cares but he's also—

The dead bodies. The snake. The dream.

"Why did you do this to me?" I ask out loud, a small minuscule part of me hoping for an answer, but there isn't one. To be honest, I'm surprised he hasn't found me yet with all the noise I'm making, but I also don't hesitate to toss a chair behind me when it's in my way after making it to the lobby. There's fire and smoke and this pungent scent that's a bit sickly sweet. "Need to get out."

Where is the exit? The smoke is dense, but after taking a right turn, I find the main entrance door. It's open and pulling some of the smoke out which I follow, nearly dropping to my knees when I can breathe in clean air again.

The entrance has cars blocking the area, some pointing toward the door with others staggered about, their doors half opened. And I find one still turned on, it's lights blazing through the night sky.

I run toward it.

Run because the devil himself is behind me, but as I grow near, my attention is pulled to the side.

"How can this be real?" Two heads snap up and look over. One black and one white. A cobra and a python. They're choking the life out of the guard who nearly cracked my skull during my arrest; his face is nearly blue, and blood dribbles from his mouth.

His expression is one of horror, of helplessness, and I don't feel an ounce of sympathy for him.

Not after what they did to me.

The python tightens his grip around the officer's neck and something breaks, the light in the man's eyes vanishing. They don't stop, though. If anything, they're even madder, hissing and biting, and when I finally meet the eyes of the cobra, my world stops.

"Marcia, your brother is going to kill you. Get down from that tree."

"But, Gabriella," she whines, using a tone that makes me cringe from her perch on a low branch. She's one of the few people I've forbidden from using my title.

I see her family as my own.

"Don't 'Gabriella' me." My brow arches and Marcia looks down, a bit contrite. "You have a date tonight with those lessons, and there's no getting out of it."

"But shape-shifting is hard."

"Life is hard, kid."

At that she scoffs, her jet-black hair rustled by the wind. "Tero doesn't struggle like I do, Gabby. And by the way, you're only three years older than me."

My response is a roll of my eyes and a tap to my watch. "That's because he studies and takes his lessons seriously."

"You're not letting me off the hook...are you?"

"Not on your life, my friend. Not on your life."

Reality slams back into me when the man is tossed aside and hits another car, the alarm going off. What I saw, what I felt looking at that girl, was friendship. Affection, and my hands clench as the need to reach out and touch the cobra becomes nearly unbearable.

What the fuck?

I take a step forward. My feet carry me without my permission.

"Pretty girl, this isn't considered running away." My head whips back, and I find Theodore standing against a pillar near the entrance watching me. "Or are you done fighting something your heart is secretly yearning for? We are your home, Gabriella. We are your family."

"Please let me go," I beg, his words hitting harder than the memory.

"I've waited a century for you." His sad expression strikes me in the chest, and I get a pang—this pain that comes every once in a while—that nearly doubles me over. "You have sixty seconds left, Gabriella. Make them count, because once I have my hands on you...I'll never let you go."

"I'm not who you think I am." *You are.* A voice whispers in my head. My eyes snap to the cobra, and I know it's a her. She's speaking to me. *I've missed you so much, Gabby. We've all needed you.* "Make it stop. Make it all stop."

"Be specific, sweetheart."

My eyes flick to his, the tears in my eyes making him a bit blurry. I try to wipe them away, but more fall. "The voices. These thoughts."

"I can't control your subconscious, Gabriella. This is all you."

Remember me. Remember your family.

"I'm nothing but an orphan who paints and—"

"You are and will always be a queen. *My Queen.*"

We were walking through the castle's corridor; Tero was to my left and Marcia to my right, much like they've done since I came to live here, my ever-present shadows, and I know Theodore cares for them too. He wouldn't trust them to be around me otherwise. He wouldn't have brought them to live here under his protection when their parents died when they were mere kids.

They've been arguing all day, complaining about some guard who asked his sister out on a walk around the garden, when various voices begin to shout.

I can't make out what they're saying, but a second later it doesn't matter as the ground shakes and a wall to my left crumbles. The sound is loud, hurts my ears, but I'm being pushed aside before a large boulder can crush my left side.

"What the hell?" Tero yells, his voice frantic as I sit up and try to gather my bearings. I'm trying to take inventory of the situation, my hands shaking and chest feeling so heavy for some reason. It feels as though— "No. No. No!"

The gut-wrenching pain in his voice makes me look over, and the sight that greets me breaks my heart. My beautiful, sweet friend is on the ground with a large portion of her body buried beneath the rubble.

She's not breathing, a large gash on her forehead.

"Marcia! Sister." Tero's body shakes, his voice cracking. "Please open your eyes. Please."

"Tero, move." He doesn't hear me, trying to push the wall off himself. "Tero, move!" Those sharp light-blue eyes snap to mine at my pleas, so much like his animal, and in them I find so much sorrow. So much need. "I can't help her if you don't get out of my way." His head tilts. He's not the one here with me anymore, but rather his snake, and I'm thankful that the beast took the forefront.

I'll need its strength. "Help me move the rubble and then go and get Theo. Please. Can you do this for me, my friend?"

His head bobs while his human body begins to remove the heavy rocks one by one, only stopping once to glare at those responsible. Three men and they all look worried, scared. I'll question them later. Right now, I need access to her full body.

For a few minutes, no one speaks. No one moves.

But I feel the energy all around me, the shift in temperature, and it begins to drop as I center myself. I can't call upon her spirit if I'm not in control or I will lose myself, something that I'll never allow to happen. Theo needs me.

"Done. My Queen." Tero hisses and steps back, his muscles coiled and ready to attack if anyone comes near me.

Nodding at him, I get down on my knees and place my hands above her chest. Her energy is missing, but there's a tether still lingering in the earth, fighting to stay, and I focus on it. My hands begin to shake as I give some of my life's force to it, feeding it my essence.

There's another commotion near us and the skies above rumble, lightning striking a few feet from me. I know the voice but choose to ignore it and continue to nurture the energy—make her a part of me. And as I do, it grows stronger. It becomes stable. "Resurgemus, Marcia," I breathe into her mouth, and her chest expands but her limbs do not move. She's hurt, her scream of pain filling the now silent space. If she doesn't shift, she'll die. "Shift."

I'm feeling faint, my nose bleeding, and Theodore rushes to my side. He tries to pull me back, to stop me, but I'm not done.

"Pretty girl, I need you to stop. She's back."

But I'm shaking my head before he's done talking. "If Marcia doesn't shift, she'll die for good and I'm too weak to help her. I can't finish until I recoup. I gave her too much."

"Tero, coach her to shift. Get her—"

Her body convulses, blood pouring from her mouth and I drop to my knees, pushing my husband's hands away. Crawling until I'm hovering over her, I press my forehead to hers and exhale, a breath she inhales and clings to. "Shift now, Marcia. Now!"

Oh God.

Oh God.

I'm shaking as I move back, and tears continue to pour from my eyes while they watch on with sadness. What I saw can't be real. This must be a figment of my fucked-up imagination, and I take off running before anyone utters a single word.

I don't know what I'm doing or where I'll go, but I jump into the still-running car and slam the door closed. "Come on, focus. Put the car in drive and—" I'm cut off by the ripping of the car's door off its hinges. The screech of metal is loud, and I cover my ears, trembling as it's tossed aside, and a hand grips the steering wheel. The plastic crumbles as if it were a cookie and I scramble to the other side, fighting with the lock until it gives way and I fall out.

My palms sting under the asphalt, and my knees shake when I get up, taking off into the night without looking back. I'm afraid of what I'll find. Of what he'll do if I do.

He won't hurt us.

"He has."

Only to bring us back.

"And now I'm talking to myself." Not knowing where I am doesn't help, but I just keep running in a straight direction, heading toward a bunch of buildings up ahead. I pray that one of them is residential and I can run inside, calling the cops— "Can't call them. Consuelos is after me too."

My chest burns from exertion, and I feel the prickles of eyes watching me. The sensation mocks me—it also warms me, and the contradicting emotions are wrecking my mental state.

Do I stop and listen to him? Do I hide for the rest of my life?

The sound of an aluminum can being kicked causes me to stumble, my body lurching forward, but before I hit the ground two strong arms catch me. His chest rumbles against my back, the noise soothing, and I lose all the fight I have left.

"No more getting hurt, pretty girl. I don't like it."

Vampire King
THEODORE ASTOR

I carry her bridal style into the warehouse where our people wait. They're quiet, standing straight and with smiles on their faces when they see her, our beloved queen. And my girl looks at them too, taking in the familiar faces and the few that have never had the pleasure of being in her presence before.

They drop to one knee as we pass.

Their right hand pounds where their cold hearts once beat.

"Rise." My voice rings loud and clear inside the large, enclosed space. The two bodies chained and on their knees tense at the sound: the man is a bit bloodied, while the woman remains untouched.

Meera and Marcia will deal with her.

Every member of our kingdom in attendance stands side by side, creating a large circle surrounding the center of the room. And at the helm, I place Gabriella in a chair she recognizes from her dream.

"How the hell…?" she whispers, but to the room it's as if the words are being shouted.

"This has always been your chair."

Someone scoffs at that, and I snap my eyes to the woman in question: Diana Veltross.

She's the daughter of Elise Veltross with a human.

She's the sister of Tim Roy, who she shares a father with, and who also had a sick obsession with Gabriella.

And lastly, she's married to Detective Consuelos who she's dragged down into a predator's trap.

"Something on your mind, Diana?"

"There is." Her tone is a bit snooty, and her body language is of someone of importance. Who thinks they're untouchable. So much like her grandfather. When I don't question her, she lifts her head and glares at Gabriella. "How could you choose this whore over my mother? She's your wife. Your…fuck!"

Marcia's tail smacks Diana across the face, cutting her off and knocking out a few front teeth in the process.

"Does that answer your question?" Bending a bit at the waist, I drop a kiss to my pretty girl's head and pull back, walking to where Elise's daughter kneels. Dropping to my haunches, I stare down at the girl and wait for her to look up. She's young compared to me and the rest of the men and women in the room, and even though a bit of vampiric blood runs through her veins, she's not worthy. A human with the privilege of having a bit of our lineage and nothing more because she'll never be changed.

She's a useless toy her mother used, corrupted, and will now be responsible for her death. "Because I wouldn't touch your mother with someone else's cock."

"How could you!"

"Please don't hit her," Diana and her husband say in unison. His lip is split open, a large bruise adorns his upper chest, and the bindings are cutting deep into his wrist. The man is a mess, too easy of a kill for me, and I find myself having a bit of pity for him. He loves her, while she takes advantage of that.

"You beg me, and yet I wonder if she'd do the same for you."

"My loyalty is to my mother." Diana answers my question, and I could see his heart break. He does love her.

"Why did you do it?" I ask the man, his eyes bloodshot while his skin has grown a bit pallid. He's scared, and should be. There is no getting out of this alive. "Why did you harm an innocent woman? Why did you pay off the cops who died tonight—tell them to bring Gabriella to a mental asylum with the promise to also use her at their free will?"

"I didn't."

"Number one." That one costs him his hand as I rip it clear off and toss it at his wife's feet. "For every lie you tell, I'll take something from you. Now, tell the truth."

"Elise asked me to." His voice is shaky, blood pouring out of the wound, and my mouth waters. I've been careful with my feeding since Gabriella was born into this human form. I'd never touch someone who's innocent, but tonight I'll give in and she'll see me as I've always been.

"To what end?"

"Don't answer," Diana grits out, yet her body shakes. Their combined pheromones create a heady scent in the room. Many begin to shake. Some let their fangs drop.

"I'd be quiet if I were you," I croon. "There are plenty of hungry vampires in here ready for their pound of flesh. Conspiring against the queen is punishable by death in our world." Turning my eyes back to her husband, I shake my head. Pathetic. "Carry on. I want the full story."

"I'm sorry."

"You truly are, Consuelos. I'm not arguing that. But finish the story."

"We were told that Elise is your mate and Gabriella was a witch who cast a spell on you. That she turned you against your wife, and I believed her. This was over a hundred years ago. I had no way to verify, and chose to trust those I call family." His chest heaves, a sob catching in his throat. "At first, it was supposed to be Tim that took care of her after the brunch meeting—make Gabriella disappear while Elise grieved by your side. Reconnected with Miss Moore out of the picture, and with her son's infatuation at her disposal, Elise used that to her advantage by enticing him to kidnap her and then keep her as a pet. Her only goal was to make you forget her."

The room erupts in angry hisses. Many shout curses and demand for me to shed his blood.

"Silence." All noises cease. "Continue, Detective. Gabriella deserves the truth."

At that, she makes a small, distressed sound, as if she doesn't want to hear any more.

I'm sorry, my love.

"But when you killed Tim, plans changed, and I was brought in. My wife signed my death certificate when she begged me to help her frame, kidnap, and then sell Miss Moore to the highest bidder in an overseas auction." Said wife doesn't look at him, not an ounce of shame or affection on her face. "I know I'll die because of this, but please, spare her. Send Diana away from her mother's influence—"

He's silenced by my hand around his throat, squeezing hard enough to cut off his air supply but not snap his neck.

"Theo!" Gabriella calls out and I turn to face her, the choking man in my grip now off the ground and his neck exposed to me. "You—"

"They were going to rape, sell, and eventually kill you," I growl, voice thundering throughout the room, and the vampires within all bow their heads. Even Meera, Tero, and Marcia, who are from a line of witches and shapeshifters, show their respect and kneel. My anger can't be abated. Not by killing him or his cunt wife. Nothing can take away the anger but my wife, and she's the one who's carried the brunt of injustice at every turn. "His sentence is death."

"Is there any other way?" Her timid voice and the fear in her eyes hurts, but I harden my features instead. She'll remember soon enough.

"No." And then I sink my teeth into his neck, lip curled up as my body vibrates with ire. Each drop of blood that flows down my throat brings my beast further out, my need for vengeance overriding my senses.

What they almost did to her…

I rip his arm clean off his body and toss it at his wife. Her screams rend the air, causing the others in the room to begin stomping their feet. Next, I send her his right leg and then left while pulling in the last few mouthfuls of his blood, what's left of him is limp in my arms.

Diana is crying, trying to move away from the parts of his body near her, but what's in her eyes isn't love or remorse. No. It's disgust and anger; like her mother, she's bitter and shrewd.

When I'm done with him, I toss what's left with the other body parts. "Go ahead and put your toy back together again. Or better yet, let's see if your mother comes to save you."

Gabriella

"Why?" is all I can think to ask, my mind trying to make sense of the incomprehensible—a nightmare come to life. Diana's chained in front of me and wearing her husband's blood after a confession that rocked me to my core. What have I ever done to these people? Her clothes are in tatters while the crowd begins to chant around us, their feet stomping the concrete ground.

Then, there's Tero, his wife, and the cobra that lies closest to me in her coiled form, creating a barrier between me and the crowd. She's attuned to my every move. Her head is low to the ground in a non-threatening way, and it reminds me of Mr. Pickles—

"My dog," I say suddenly, and the room goes quiet. They all look at me with affection. With the need to help me, but don't know how.

"We have him," Meera says, stepping toward me with both hands up. "Tero called me when they took you and I brought him home; he's asleep next to our rescue puppy. See?" She's holding up her phone, and on the screen is a live feed of both dogs asleep and cuddled up next to each other. "I wouldn't let anything happen to him, Gabriella. He's safe."

"Thank you." There's an audible sigh of relief from the others in the room, but Theo has yet to say a word, although it's better this way because seeing him handle Consuelos like a ragdoll gave me an adverse reaction to what I should consider normal. He was a beast, and while it scared me, a small, hidden part of me liked it. Enjoyed seeing a man—the killer beneath the façade of a handsome man gives into his baser need.

For revenge.

For death.

To protect me.

The latter of which I'm still choosing to ignore because anything otherwise means I'm giving in. That I believe all this is real and not part of a broken mind's hallucinations.

And yet, I've seen Theo's bloodied fangs. I watched him drain the now mangled body of Detective Consuelos, tossing him aside as if he were trash. *This is real. Accept it.*

"…finish the story your husband began, Miss Veltross," Theo snarls suddenly from beside me and I yelp, his bloody lips curling over his fangs. However, my brows scrunch up for a different reason. I pause because of that name. Why does it sound familiar? Why does the blood within my veins sing with a burning ire each time he mentions it? "Tell Gabriella why she died in my arms over a century ago after your grandfather slashed her chest."

My hand instinctively goes to my chest while my mind revisits that dream. I remember vividly how the man in the dream took me, made my body sing with pleasure, and then the words that followed.

"They did this to us," I whisper and his head snaps to mine, the softest look overtaking his features. "That was really you in my dream, wasn't it? It was you I visited?"

"Yes."

"How?" How the hell is any of this possible? "How did I see you…how did—"

"With the help of Meera and your sister, I was able to dream walk."

"Dream walk? My sister?" I sputter, not knowing which one to dissect first. "Please help me understand, Theodore. I feel like I'm losing my mind."

"Once the truth is out, it can't be undone. Don't turn your back on my mother again," Diana begs, drops of bloody spittle staining the dirty clothes she's wearing. Her hair is matted to her forehead, her stench reaching me where I sit on a throne made for a king—solid gold with a crest embedded into the velvet cloth covering the seat. "Gabriella isn't one of us. She's never belonged in our world."

Theo shakes his head, a cruel smile on his face. "Why don't I tell you a few things you didn't know, Miss Veltross."

"This woman isn't your mate. She can't be."

"Did you know your mother thought herself so smart, her plan so solid, that she never once questioned who Gabriella's benefactor/uncle was all this time?" A gasp escapes me at his words, but Theodore doesn't look at me. Instead, he lightly squeezes my shoulder in a show of comfort.

"It was you," I say on a shaky whimper, my heart breaking all over again. "So I really had no family, not a single person that wanted me?"

"I'm sorry, love. But I've been protecting you since the day of your rebirth." His revelation doesn't shock me. Being honest, it gives me a bit of relief to know someone cared. "But it was when your painting of a warrior's death crossed my desk, you were about eight at the time, that I had the proof I've been waiting for all along."

"How? Why is...Christ, this makes no sense."

"And yet deep down you know it's true." I do. Every cell in my body is begging me to accept him, while my fight or flight is demanding I run. "The original of that painting sits in our home back in—"

"Italy," I answer for him, and he nods.

"Italy."

"How did I know that?"

"Because it is who you are. Our life." The small smile on his gorgeous face falls, and I'm once again greeted by the monster in him. His expression is hard and his muscles coil, his anger palpable as he turns to look at Diana. "You have sixty seconds before I rip your head off and feed your blood to the vampires standing guard."

"Theodore, please," Diana cries out, her desperation mounting. She fights against her bindings, the metal digging into her wrists, and rivulets of blood fall down each arm, creating a puddle on the ground. Is that the human side of her? "She will never be good enough for you. For our kingdom."

"There has never been an 'our,' Miss Veltross."

"Don't do this."

"Do what?" I ask.

"You're willing to end a pure bloodline for her? A priestess?"

"Yes." Walking behind me, Theodore grips my ponytail and wraps the long strands around his fist. He gives one sharp pull to the side and I'm left exposed, at his mercy. "I'm sorry, my love." With the tip of his nose, he skims the length of my neck before placing a chaste kiss over the juncture before exhaling roughly. "I've missed you and can't live another day like this. In a world where you don't walk beside me."

"You're scaring me," I say, my eyes closing to avoid meeting anyone's eyes. Too many are witnessing my death, and the joy on their faces breaks my already fragile mind. "Please don't kill me."

At those words, an animalistic snarl leaves him, the sound pained and angry. "Out."

The people in the room don't hesitate and run out; they too are afraid of his wrath. And when the last person exits, he releases his hold and comes back to my front, squatting down to meet my tear-filled eyes.

I look away.

"Please don't. Not you, Gabriella." His emotions are my own. I feel him in that moment, and the anguish nearly makes me fold into myself. The depths—the yearning causes me to shiver and cry out, teeth chattering as a painful iciness seeps into my bones. "In this world, you are the only person who is safe from me. The only person with the power to kill me, and I'd let you. No questions asked, my wife. If it's my life you want, I'd die with honor knowing it made you smile."

"Don't," I say without hesitation. The mere thought of him not standing in front of me brings on a different level of pain—of anguish—and while I don't understand it's meaning; the other choice is unacceptable to me. "Don't say that."

"It's my truth."

"But not one I can accept." Tears fall, running down my cheeks while his hand cups my jaw. He's trying to comfort me, to soothe me with his touch, but fear is a dominating emotion, and right now it's clashing with its direct counterpart. Theo is my comfort, while King is a killer.

He's my Dr. Jekyll and Mr. Hyde, and one doesn't exist without the other.

"I've loved you for over a century, Gabriella Moore. It has always been and will always be you for me."

"What will happen to me?"

At my concern, Diana scoffs, her chest vibrating, and the look on her face is one of disgust as her dark orbs meet mine. "You were weak then too, you know. Even with all the power you held, the curse your kind looked upon as a gift, you were a disappointment."

"And yet, I sit where your mother—you—wish to be?" I ask, but there's a tinge of taunt in my tone. Some malice. I'm not weak. I've just been thrown into a world I don't understand. "Tell me, Diana. What did I ever do to you?"

"You existed." The chains around her wrist rattle, the scent of burning skin heavy in the air around us. Whatever they did to those bindings are slowly melting her skin off, imprisoning her. "You took the throne from my mother, my grandfather, and now me. And even if it takes my mother another hundred years, My Queen..." she spits out the word with malice, so much hatred "...the Veltross family will kill you."

"*A glorified necromancer as the bride of the vampire king. I never thought I'd see the day the monarchy stooped so low,*" a male voice I'm familiar with says, entering the library where I'm relaxing. I've had a busy morning so far, dealt with a problem back home, and all I've wanted since opening my eyes is some peace and quiet. Nothing else.

"*What can I do for you, General Veltross?*" My tone is bored, and facial expression holds annoyance. I tolerate him as much as he likes me. "*As you can see, I'm busy.*"

"*You don't belong here. Your kind is an abomination I'd have eradicated if—*"

"*You'll never sit on that throne no matter how much you whine about it.*"

"*And he'll never change you. I'll make sure of it.*"

"*I'm sure you'll try.*" Standing from my seat on the couch, I take the steps between us and stand toe to toe. I will never be intimidated by this man who reeks of narcissism and greed. "*But keep in mind that I'm a firm believer in an eye for an eye. And while you have fangs and sharp nails, I can take a life with a few simple words and the touch of my hand. Do not threaten me.*"

"*Those things won't work once you're dead.*"

"*They will when I come back. And I will,*" I say with a saccharine-sweet tone. "*My deal with the devil is sealed in my enemies' blood, and I deliver on my promises. Never threaten me again.*"

"My love," Theo says, and I'm snapped back to the present. Each of these feels like memories fighting to break through. Like missing pieces of a story I've forgotten.

"That's where you're wrong." Turning my head slightly, I meet Theo's eyes and even though I don't understand what she's claiming, I'm willing to accept my fate. There's a reason I am here and feel what I do the second we touch—the electrifying current that ripples up my arm and squeezes my chest while causing my core to throb.

There has to be a reason that explains why I know my life would lose all meaning if he walked away. "Bite me."

Each memory uncovers a stolen moment in time that shows the life we've been robbed of.

Each time he touches me, I find myself wanting to be closer.

I need to know the truth.

"Are you—"

"Bite me, Theo." Mimicking his actions, I cup his chin and then lean my forehead to his. I stare into his eyes and let him see me. All of me, with every fear and pain filling my heart, but the knowledge deep down that this is right. We are right, no matter how much I want to fight it. "I need this."

"Thank you." Then his lips are on mine, a reverent kiss that steals the very breath from my lungs while feeding my soul. Slanting his mouth over mine, Theo moves his hand from my chin and places it over my neck, fingers spread out. His hold is a little tight while controlling the kiss, dominating my senses with sweeps of his tongue over mine before embedding his teeth into my bottom lip.

Then he's dragging them down my chin and the column of my throat, leaving behind tiny nips of pleasure that make me wet. Embarrassingly so.

"I am darkness. I am sin," he says against my skin, his tone gravelly. I tilt my head a little more to give him better access, and I'm rewarded by a hum of approval. "I'm the devil incarnate and everything you shouldn't want, but I am yours, Gabriella. Today. Tomorrow. Always."

"Always yours." My answer slips past my lips before I can question the words, but the smile on his face tells me I've done something right.

"Always yours." Then he bites down, breaking my skin and coating his mouth with my essence. At once, blinding pain overtakes my senses and I gasp, clutching his arm, but he only digs deeper. His snarls become louder, and just when my body becomes faint—my eyes roll back and consciousness begins to evade me—a euphoric feeling I've never experienced before rocks me to the core.

It slams into me with the weight of a freight train, robbing me of every one of my senses while pleasure pulses from every cell in my body. I come. I lose myself as wave after wave of bliss pours into me before everything goes black.

Vampire King THEODORE ASTOR

I'd been out most of the day, meeting with a small coven of vampires that lives in New Mexico. They'd been asking for support on a small problem with a nomadic trespasser in their territory, and I'd conceded to send three of my men to scan the area and deliver a message.

Control your body count, or I'll take that as a personal disrespect to me.

"That took longer than expected," Tero says from beside me, keeping up with my pace as he writes a few notes down. He's been working longer hours for the past week, trying to repay us for Gabriella saving Marcia's life, something that isn't necessary. My wife loves them both as if they were her siblings. Feels a connection that ties them together spiritually.

"It did. Do you know where—" I don't finish as my chest

suddenly explodes with pain. This near crumbling pressure knocks the air out of me, and I lean on the wall for support.

"My King!" Tero yells, grabbing my arm to keep me upright. The throbbing is nearly unbearable. "What's wrong? Why are you grabbing your chest?"

"I don't know." The alarm sounds then, coming from the southern tower, and the heavy footfalls of guards rushing follow. There's screaming, the sound of women crying, and I take off running—I'm a blur through the courtyard.

I make it to where they've gathered. So many voices yelling.

"Murderer."

"You will pay for this."

"I command you to let me go." It's my general, the head of my army whose voice rises above the others. He's thrashing, and I can see his arms flailing while a group of women and Marcia in her cobra form hover in a protective stance. "I did this for the crown!"

"What the fuck is going on here?" I say, the booming tone causing everyone to drop and kneel. Even my general whose arms are pulled out to his side by two soldiers, is forced to his knees.

The women, though, stay around a body who I now recognize as mine. My wife.

There's blood on the ground. Her blood, and my legs feel weak. My stomach rolls.

Every muscle in my body seizes and the world shifts, shaking beneath my frozen form.

"Who?" This doesn't come from me; I'm already looking at the culprit. Tero's animal is coming forth, pushing against its owner, and the skin of his python begins to rise on his arms and face. He walks toward Veltross. "What the hell happened here?"

"Stop." He does at my command, changing his course toward Gabriella. He kneels beside her; his body shudders and I steel myself for the worst. "Bring him to me." The guards stand and drag a kicking, screaming Veltross to me. They toss him at my feet and step back.

"My King, I—"

"Stand up, General."

"Please, listen to me." When I don't reply, he shifts a bit, looking for an out. To his bad luck, he's being blocked by the same men he's trained and led into battle. They are an impenetrable wall. "I did what I did for you. Our people deserve—"

He's cut off by my hand on this throat, lifting him off the ground. He thrashes, tries to remove my hand, but I walk us to where Gabriella lies, her back supported by Tero. And my wife, she's pale and her chest is red, a large gash crossing from side to side. It's deep. She's lost too much blood for me to seal the wound. *He bled her.* "I will never marry your daughter."

"She's better—"

"You and your offspring will die by my hand, no matter how long it takes." My hand squeezes, and for each staggered breath my wife takes, I tighten my hold. With my other, though, I puncture his abdomen with the use of my nails, tearing out chunks at a time. His side. His dead organs. His bones.

I don't stop until the bottom half of his body is on the floor, and his chest with the head attached is all that's left.

"Dad!" Elise screams suddenly, rushing to where we are, but Meera flings her back and across the yard. She lands awkwardly and is knocked unconscious, yet no one checks on her. I also didn't realize Meera's set up to work. She has herbs and crystals surrounding Gabriella.

Did Tero call her?

Or Gabriella?

"We need to bind her soul, Theo," Meera says from beside me, her hand on my shoulder. "We don't have a lot of time. End him now, and I'll do everything in my power to bring her back."

Her pleading gives me breath, but the pain I'm experiencing intensifies when her eyes close. My wife's chest still rises and falls, but those gems I love no longer have the energy to meet mine.

"You will never be a part of the royal family," I snarl, holding him at eye level.

"Please stop. You will be so much—"

"Your children will never amount to anything, Veltross. Nothing but be outcasts in my kingdom." With that, I rip his head off and toss it aside, leaving it for the guards to clean while I rush to my wife. Her body's shaking as I pull her gently against my chest, tears running down from closed lids, and I've never felt more useless in my life.

I'm the king, and yet I can't save the one person in this world I breathe for.

Meera whispers something in her ear, and the only sign of life is the small squeeze of my hand that's barely perceptible. And I hold on to that moment, close my eyes, and control my body as a sob rocks me, my body covering hers as the last breath leaves her small frame.

Those around me weep. The sorrowful cries of every vampire can be heard for miles as they feel her connection wane, and then nothing. She's gone. My love is not here.

Throwing my head back, I let out a deafening roar that shakes the ground we stand on. A few windows shatter, and those around me whimper and cower in fear while I crumble as her man.

"Is there anything we can do?" I ask Meera, the sound of my voice sounding foreign. Lifeless.

"I can bind her here; she showed me how to in the past."

"But..." I pull Gabriella a little tighter against me, my face buried against my mark on her neck. Kissing it with reverence because she'll always be my gift. Mine.

"I can't predict when she'd be back. Her soul will belong to this world, but not her body until death decides otherwise." I can smell Meera's tears, and if I could, I'd be bawling like a child myself. My heart feels broken, although it doesn't beat. My soul feels ruptured, and existing in a world where she no longer exists isn't something I can do. We either walk side by side, or leave together. My life has been in her pretty little hands since the day we met. "I'm so sorry, My King. Only she can take and give life."

My face snaps to hers, my chest heaving harshly as the beast within rattles the cage and thirst for vengeance. To kill. "Do it." Standing from the ground, I lay my beauty down and then place a tiny kiss across the cupid's bow of her lips. "Do whatever you must. No matter the cost."

"We don't know when she'll be back and in what form, Theodore. The payment will be steep."

She's not trying to put me off, I know, but I react and grab her by the throat. "Do it, Meera. Fuck the consequences."

"Yes, My King." She doesn't fight me, and her husband watches calmly. They know I won't hurt her—that if alive, Gabriella would kill me if I did. Moreover, it's someone else I'm aiming for. The blonde cunt that took off like the roach she is—like father, like daughter. "This is the one thing Gabriella taught me before she brought me here as her assistant. Before I met my Tero."

"Go on." I can barely get the words out. My chest is tight, and limbs feel heavy: dead.

"The price is something you both coveted. Something personal."

"I'll pay with my life if it brings her back." *I can live without offspring, but not without her.* "She's all I need."

"We all want her back."

"I know." Gently, I let Meera go and then kiss her forehead. It's the most I can offer as an apology right now. "And I don't care what it takes. I'd wait a lifetime for her."

Vampire King
THEODORE ASTOR

Her eyes flutter open five hours later.

Five agonizing hours after I reclaimed her and she fell into a peaceful sleep, her body frozen—unmoving—while I brought her home. To the house I bought for her when she aged out of the system and had nowhere to go. Those years waiting for her were hell. The memory of watching her grow and struggle still eats me alive because my hands were tied.

To bring her back, I couldn't interfere.

Meera couldn't adopt her.

I couldn't mess with her fate until the night of her twenty-first birthday: a condition signed in her blood and my name to satisfy the God of Death amongst his other requests. I gave up something we both wanted. I would've given everything to be with her.

"Open those eyes for me, pretty girl."

The last word hasn't passed my lips when her eyes snap open, meeting mine. They're a bit darker than her natural green eyes, the outside of the iris a blood red, and I've never seen a more beautiful thing.

My pretty girl is now a vampire.

Mine.

"Theo." My name on her lips is a soft caress. So lovely. So sweet. "My King."

"Happy real birthday, pretty girl." That spark I've missed is in her eyes, the one she got every time I used my name for her. Because she will always be that: my pretty girl. "I've missed you."

"And I love you." She's in front of me in an instant, a little surprised by her speed, yet I'm her focus. Her hand comes to my cheek, cupping the side of my face. "Thank you."

"I'd do anything for you. Even if it means breaking you, to bring you back to me."

They stripped her of everything. Her emotions. Her memories. My pretty girl was left naked and vulnerable which others took advantage of, while my hands were bound by blood to not interfere. Because doing so could mean losing her all over again.

This was her journey—her fight back to me—and I had to hurt her to bring those repressed feelings to the surface. Gabriella's emotions and powers go hand in hand.

"I know." Her nostrils flare a bit, scenting me. I'll smell a little different to her. My scent is stronger than her witch senses remember. "I'd never be angry over what you did to bring me back. Never judge you, because I'd do worse if it meant being in your arms again." Gabriella's eyes leave mine for a second to survey the room. She's still as adorable as ever. Still as nosy. "Why are we here, though?"

"Because I've hidden two gifts in this house."

"Two gifts?" Her lips curl into a smirk, her left hand—her ring finger twitching. "Is one of them the heartbeat, I hear?"

"Possibly, but not until after."

"After...?"

At that moment, everything hits me. Slams into her. The years apart. The loneliness.

Our needs explode. It's violent, a palpable volcanic rush that consumes and breaks and when my arms encircle her back, I breathe for the very first time in a hundred years.

My lungs expand, and she's all I see.

All I hear. All I feel.

I'm home.

Our mouths clash, the taste of her lips making me growl as I pull her against me. My hunger is demonic, and I don't hold back, slamming her against the wall where the painting of our bedroom in Italy hangs, her sweet little tongue caressing mine. Moreover, she's just as desperate.

Just as needy, clinging to me as though afraid I'll disappear.

"Fuck, I've missed you. Hungered for you." My words incense her, those lithe thighs encircling my waist and she grinds, desperate to feel me. Her body was made for me. She's a gift I'll always treasure. "Tell me what you want, needy girl, and it's yours."

"You. Always you."

"Then have me." I croon against her lips, tasting the natural sweetness that's always been a weakness. Embedding my fingers in her hair, I tilt her head back and rake my teeth down her lips and chin, not pausing until I reach the hollow of her throat. My mark is on the right; the imprint of my teeth forever brands her as mine.

Scraps of her shirt fall to the floor; the lace of her bra is next, and her heaving chest beacons me. To taste. To worship. "Motherfuck, beautiful."

An intricate tattoo similar to the one on my back, but on a smaller scale, now adorns her flesh. It's the mark of the royal family and appears on its own; a pair of dark wings stretched out—open— with beads of crystals and pearls. There's a longer strand, though, that I can't see because it disappears under her bottoms.

"Let me see you, too," she pleads. Her eyes roll back when I cup her tit, pinching the tight little tip between two fingers. "Please, Theo. I need my King."

"You want me, Mia Regina?"

"To worship every solid inch." God, I've missed her mouth. The way she's always spoken her mind, never holding back her emotions.

Her love. Her anger. Her wrath.

Slanting my mouth over hers, I take it in a quick yet brutal kiss. I'm re-familiarizing myself with her plump mouth and eager tongue —hearing her moan in pleasure as I nibble and then lick her lips. And it's like the first time all over again.

"I love you so much, Gabriella." My tongue intertwines with hers, fighting for a dominance she succumbs to and then lets me take. To possess her like she owns me. "I've needed you so much all these years."

"I love you, too," she says, her fangs descending. And fuck me if the sight of her like this isn't delicious. My beautiful little demon. I also do something I've dreamed of for over a hundred years, licking each between harsh nips of her bottom lip. "Fuck me."

"I will." Another bite, this time to her jaw. "You have ten minutes to do your worst, pretty girl. Anything you please."

"Just ten?"

"Ten. Not a second more." Placing her back on the ground, I tear her bottoms and panties off with one hand while tracing a finger from her right nipple to the left, leaving the sting behind of a smack to each hard tip. "I'm counting."

She's bare before me, standing like a goddess with a curvaceous figure and perky breasts. Her thick hips and the wet juncture of her thighs makes my mouth water, but I stand firm.

I'll give her this. Just these next minutes, because when I take her again—fuck my wife—she won't get a second to think or do or feel anything but my cock stretching her wide.

Gabriella takes the two steps between us, stopping when our bare chests meet again; she rises onto the tips of her small toes. It's sexy how she can't reach me even like this.

So tiny. So delicate. So mine.

"I'm sorry," she whispers against my throat, sweeping her lips back and forth while her hands wander down my chest. Her touch is gentle, with reverence, and I hiss out in pain. My cock throbs while my chest expands with a rough breath.

I haven't felt the touch of a woman since her death. I'd never cheat on her. Never so much as look, because there's no comparing and lowering my standards was a crime against her memory.

Our union.

"I've never blamed you, pretty girl. Not once."

Her head shakes, and a tender kiss is placed where my heart once beat. "Please forgive me for taking so long to come back. For leaving you alone." Another kiss, this one on my stomach just above my belly button. "For forgetting who I am." Her knees meet the ground, and her sharp nail rips the jeans I'm wearing from waistband to ankle on each side, the denim material falling to the ground. "But more than anything, I forgot who we are to each other, and I'll never be able to forgive myself for that."

I swallow hard, cock throbbing. "The moment you took your first breath, nothing else mattered to me." A bead of come pearls at the tip, and the little she-devil watches it. Licks her lips as it slides down the engorged head and toward the underside.

She stops the drop with her hand, gripping me tight. "You took care of me." She pumps me once, twisting her hand on the upward stroke. "You killed for me."

"No one will ever hurt you again," I groan. Her lips are wrapped around the head, tongue flicking the slit. "Not even me."

"I know, and I forgive you. You broke my mind but set me free." Then she's taking me in her mouth, not stopping until her lips kiss the base. She swallows, hollowing those cheeks while her tongue licks the underside.

"Motherfuck," I snarl, almost angry at how easily she pulls me to the edge with a few flicks of her tongue. My hands caress her head before gripping the long tresses, holding her there while those hungry eyes watch me. "I'm going to fuck that pretty little mouth before I destroy your pussy, Gabriella. And I'm one lucky son of a bitch because you'll let me. Won't you, pretty girl?"

Her lips stretch into a grin around my girth; the sight is obscene. Filthy. *So beautiful.*

"That's not ten minutes."

"I know." Then I pull out just enough to leave the head sitting on her tongue, rubbing it, before slamming back into the hilt. Her throat expands with each thrust, and had my wife still been human, she would've been dead.

My strokes are punishing, almost a blur, yet I pet her hair reverently.

And with each swallow around me, she says *I love you* in return.

I take my pleasure from her and she lets me, sucking a little harder while I throw my head back and revel in the warmth of her mouth. With the way her nimble fingers tug on my balls, causing a deep rumble to build in my chest and shake the windows around us.

I don't care who hears me.

I'd gladly expose my kind for the honor to fuck her mouth.

Pleasure licks up my spine; a fiery trail spreads through every nerve ending. I'm shaking, my balls so fucking heavy, but before I come, I pull out. A string of her saliva connects us, her pouty lips so shiny with it and I hate to break the connection, but I do.

"I'm not coming in your mouth."

Her tongue traces her bottom lip, catching the drop of spit and my pre-come combined. "I want it."

"You'll have an eternity to taste me…" I yank her to her feet and into my chest, my hands encircling her waist "…but I need to feel you wrapped around me. I need to feel your walls clench—squeeze me until I bathe you in my come."

"Please." It's a moan. A desperate plea.

Before she can beg again, I have us on her bed with her thighs cradling my hips. My cock, still wet from her mouth, is at her entrance while her small hole flutters against the head. It's trying to pull me in deeper; the sensation fucking drives me insane.

"I love you," I say against her mouth, my body covering hers—skin on skin. "Always and forever."

"Always and forever." Our vows. The same words we said the day we married in front of her people and mine, uniting two species through our bond. "Thank you for giving me my life back. For coming back for me."

My response to those perfect words is to snap my hips forward, burying myself to the hilt. And then, I'm home. The one place in the universe that's solely mine. My resting place.

I don't pause for her to adjust. I stole her innocence once before, but this is more.

My chest rumbles, the beast inside me satiated for the first time in a hundred years, and I fuck her like the animal I am. My hands skim her sides from hip to chest and then find their anchor on her shoulders, using them to keep her in place while I drive in and out, riding her hard.

"Theo!" she screams out, her fingernails digging into my back. It stings a bit, but that hint of pain heightens the pleasure. Her hips meet mine through every thrust, wanting more, begging me with each rush of wetness and the purring in her chest to break her. I'll give her that and so much more.

"What do you need, love? Tell me and it's yours."

"Mount me." No hesitation. No shyness.

"So perfect," I whisper, licking my mark on her neck before flipping her onto her front. She wants my beast; he's hers. "Rise up and arms out. Show me what's mine."

And she does, lifting onto all fours with her head low and both holes on display.

In one fluid motion, I'm back inside and she clenches hard. Her walls clamp down at the intrusion while her juices run down my cock and balls. And she's arching, back bowing deep while a scream rends the air, her nails destroying the sheets.

"My King. My love," she moans, pushing back against me. Her asscheeks bounce, the supple flesh so perky and round. *Smack.* The sound is loud in the room, but her scream will be heard down the street. Another. And another. She can take it, and by the way she clamps down, I know she loves it.

"You feel so good, pretty girl. Your cunt was made for me." Another punishing stroke and her body shakes, walls fluttering around me. "Again. Tighten like that again."

"Please." Her wail makes me grin, reminds me of all the times I fucked her while people walked the halls outside of my office back in Italy, the castle's staff trying to make the least noise possible so as to not embarrass her. "I'm so close. I need—"

"Me." I slam in three times in rapid succession and pause, ignoring her desperate yell. "Tell me you need me."

"You're all I'll ever need. Just you."

Those words hit me in the chest, my dead heart coming to life and beating for her. For the treasure I've been given, have killed for, and I would do it again if we always end here. In each other's arms. Breathing in the other's exhale because it's what gives us life.

"I will never love another. You are the beginning of life and where it ends." Then, I'm fucking her like she asked, giving us both the relief we need. My pace is near animalistic, every thrust harder than the last, and her cries are lullabies for me.

Moreover, I'm the man lucky enough to spend the rest of his life worshipping her. Listening to those cries again and again.

Slipping a hand to her front, I cup her neck with my fingers, touching her mark. The simple contact makes her tremble, her body shaking beneath me, and when her walls clamp down on me as she comes, I can't stop myself from letting go.

Her come and mine mix, the heady scent permeating the air while I continue to stroke in and out, loving how she still meets each thrust. How she tightens and claws at the bed, losing herself to the pleasure only I can give.

But just as soon as one need is satiated, another arises, and I'm prepared for it.

I cannot wait to watch her feed.

Gabriella

There's a burning sensation in my throat, this uncomfortable flame that seems to grow hotter and hotter with each passing second. I've gone from remembering my life to loving Theo and to now this need—hunger—I've never encountered before.

That I don't know how to address or respond to.

My hand claws at the front of my neck, rubbing at the area, but it's Theodore's eyes I'm fighting to focus on. There's a bit of amusement in them, yet so much understanding. So much love.

"The thirst is always the worst in the first month," he says calmly, lying down beside me in all his naked glory, his release and mine still drying on his cock. "You need to feed, pretty girl. Once you do, it'll abate. Not disappear, but it'll be manageable."

"Is it always this way?" I ask, taking in the subtle changes from over the last century. He looks tired. Like someone that carried the weight of world on his shoulders and is just now taking a breather. My poor love.

"It is." For a few seconds he doesn't say anything, as if he were waiting for something, and then I know why. There are two things in this house that are calling my attention; one is down the hall, while the other is downstairs and frightened, her mumblings getting on my nerves. "Are you ready to hunt?"

"You brought me food already."

"That's just the appetizer. Her mother is the main course." My eyes turn to slits and I sit up, throwing my legs over the bed. "I'll take that as a yes."

"You'll take that as the cue to clean up and meet me downstairs. I need to stop at my studio first."

"Why first."

"Because I'm not spending another second without your ring on my finger."

"Good girl."

"Always," I say, and then lean over the bed to peck his lips before pulling back. "I imagine you have clothes here?"

"A suitcase full."

"Of course, you do." A giggle escapes me, and my eyes roll. "How often did you stand guard outside this house?"

"Never."

"Never?" That's shocking. "So out of character with the man I know."

"It shouldn't surprise you that I never left, pretty girl. My post was that wall next to the window each night."

I LEAVE him in the room after getting dressed and head straight for my studio. It's calling to me, his scent meshing with that of metal, and they pull me toward a semi-open cabinet. The same cabinet that I once used to store the woman I thought to be my mother's, a piece of crap locket that holds no true value.

Not anymore.

My real parents died so long ago, leaving my sister and I behind to face the hunting of my kind and the needs of our people. Because those with magic and powers are coveted like prizes and sought to control.

Isabella not as much as me.

Our younger brother isn't as strong, but he holds himself with the same morals as our father.

I miss them.

Shaking myself out of those emotions, I vow to look for them after. Much after.

"Elise and her kin all need to die first."

Striding to the furniture, I smile to myself when I find the half-opened drawer with a small leather pouch inside. It's familiar to me. The same one I used to carry the earrings my real mother gave to me a few months before her death.

I pick it up with a shaky hand and open it before pouring the content into my hand.

My ring is inside. The same one from when we said *I do* with the large ruby stone in the middle of a gold band surrounded by black diamonds.

The heart that no longer beats inside my chest gives a hard thump, almost restarting again as I slip it on my ring finger where it'll never leave again. I also catch the light of the charm he placed there, and the date engraved holding a special meaning; the day we wed. *He was always trying to make me remember. He truly never gave up.* Tears brim my eyes but don't fall, my chest expands on a shuddering breath that I don't release as so many emotions hit me at once.

I died.

I suffered.

But he brought me back. He's always been there. Here.

And I've never felt more loved in my life as I do now.

Rushing down the stairs, I pause next to Diana and snap her neck, not giving a single fuck about her. Her wants or what she has to say hold no bearing on me. She's as insignificant as her mother, more so as a human who's been fed bullshit all her life and bought into a reality that was never part of her destiny.

Her hate for me was clear back at Theo's warehouse. Nothing had changed from now to then.

Their plan failed, and I'm here with my King and that's all that matters to me.

"That was your meal."

"I know." Placing my hand wearing his gift over his chest, I grip his shirt and pull him down. Those amber eyes I love darken at seeing his ring there. "But first, I need a kiss."

"Just one. You need to eat."

"No."

"No?"

"I have time to drain her, but nothing will ever come before my need for you." And then he's kissing me, groaning into my mouth while destroying my clothes that lay in tatters on the floor while my legs are wrapped around his waist.

***

OUR FEET CROSS into the Alaskan wilderness twenty-four hours later after my first feeding. Her daughter wasn't fulfilling in the least, and Theo procured a donation from the hospital to satiate his thirst and mine.

But now we're in the territory where my brother-in-law reigns as Alpha of Alphas with Tero, Meera, and Marcia, who's back to normal. For years she suffered because I couldn't finish the words needed to bind her spirit to her human form, leaving the animal as her only choice of survival. A whisper, my hand over her chest, and Marcia walked on two legs again.

"Ready?" I ask Marcia, my knees on the ground beside her body. We're in my backyard and everyone is ready to leave, but I refuse to do

so without doing something a century too late. "Give me a nod, and I'll say the words." The movement is subtle, a small tear spilling from her eyes as I place my hand on her body and mouth against hers. "I'm sorry it took so long, sweet friend. Ligatus ad vescendum carnes."

At once, her form slightly trembles as she retakes her human form. There are hisses from her that turn into screams, her shiny scales receding into human flesh while she gives into the pain. I know it hurts. Bounding her and then freeing her soul took a lot from me, too, but I continue to feed her my energy until I look into a set of eyes I haven't seen since my death.

"Gabby," she whispers, voice rough from disuse while I simply hug her. Cover her slim body with a blanket I'd brought out with me. "Please tell me my lessons are done?"

At that, I laugh, head thrown back as my frame shakes. I've missed her sass. "In my opinion, you've graduated and surpassed Tero, Marcia. I'm proud of you."

"And I've missed you, My Queen."

Cupping her cheek with my hand, I place my forehead to hers. "Not queen, Marcia. We're sisters."

"Are you ready?" Theo asks from beside me.

"I am." He knows I'm a bit sad, but I also understand. They're not here—my sister and her mate—having left to deal with a problem on the East Coast with a pack, but he left his Beta, Cain, to help us.

At one point, werewolves and vampires didn't mix. However, hurting your mate is a sin, something you don't do at any costs, and both races understand that. I'm a Queen. My sister is the Luna Supreme.

Two women whose destiny changed the supernatural world.

"Beta Cain," I say, extending a hand out in greeting, which he takes. He's gawking at me a bit, not in lust but surprise, and beside me Theo growls. "Stop it."

"He's staring."

"You look so much alike. Not identical, but the resemblance is shocking when—"

"I know." And I did. My death hurt more than Theodore and those of our kingdom, but my sister and brother—the races they oversee. "But it'll wear off the more you see of me. I miss my sister."

"And she's lived in hell without you," a soft voice calls from behind the Beta, and the warriors standing behind him move out of the way, letting the owner pass. At my first sight of her, a sob gets caught in my throat, tears that don't fall gathering at my eyes before her warm body slams into mine. Isabella is stronger than before, the mark on her neck altering her slightly.

"Sister," is all I can manage to choke out, holding her to me while she cries into my neck, hugging me back just as tight. "How? I thought—"

Pulling back, her blotchy face smiles at me. "If you thought I wouldn't be here for this moment, you've become stupid in the last hundred years. Nothing could keep me from you."

"Things change."

"I don't." Raising my hand, she intertwined our fingers the same way we've done since we learned about our powers. She fed from me and I from her, exchanging our feelings and energies through touch. And right now, her aura is glowing with love and excitement, an exact mirror of my own. "By blood and by pact."

"We are one."

"We are one," she repeats and then gets a devious look in her eyes that has gotten me in trouble many times in the past. "Now—we have someone to kill. Any preference, or are we going in there, guns blazing like the wonder twins we are?"

"Christ, I forgot how cheesy you can be?" I snort, which causes her to laugh. "That was bad."

"Oh hush, just because I'm older doesn't mean I'm out of touch with the youth here."

Another presence makes itself known a moment later, and I'm

not surprised as one never moved without the other before. "Alpha Xadiel, how have you been?"

"Her joy matches my own, Gabriella. We are all happy to have you back."

The sincerity in his eyes brings tears to my eyes that will never fall. "Thank you, brother."

"Okay…" Isabella claps her hands, winking at her mate and mouthing the words *I love you*. "First, did you push the meeting back?"

"I did," my sister's husband answers without pause.

"God, I love you."

My eyes shift to Theo, who shakes his head. *We are not that bad, pretty girl. It's the part dog thing that makes them cheesy.* I'm not going to respond to his mind link, choosing instead to turn back into the conversation my sister is leading. "And two?" I ask.

"Two, I know where she is. No one steps onto our land without us knowing."

———

THE SMALL COTTAGE Elise ran to is deep in the Alaskan wilderness and right near the border of Xadiel's land. It's far enough to not draw too much attention, while still being within the territory. It blends into the scenery, a little dilapidated, but enough for one person to hide.

I can hear her heartbeat from where I stand.

She knows we're here, too.

The moment she sensed our presence, she panicked, the cadence of each heartbeat rising, and her breathing followed. Funny. For someone who's the daughter of a proud general, she sure tucked tail and ran. She never did the dirty work, but involved her own offspring, lying to each to manipulate her narrative.

I also wouldn't be surprised if she'd procreated with a human, knowing they'd be weaker—easier to manipulate than that of a full-fledged vampire/hybrid union.

"And she says I'm the weak one," I say loud enough for her to hear and those around us laugh. "Come out, Elise. Don't make me go after you."

Nothing. Not a peep.

However, I do notice the small shift in the front window curtain and the two eyes that peep through. So sad. So pathetic.

"I won't ask you again." I'm positioned in front of the door, the only in and out the place has, except for a window in the rear that Cain is currently watching. To leave, she has to exit from here. "You have a minute before I enter."

"You won," Elise yells out from behind the door, and that pisses me off. Is this the kind of ire that Theodore feels when I'm wronged? When he's disrespected? "You took everything from me and won…congratulations."

"Thirty."

"What more can you take? Let me live my life in peace here!"

"Nineteen." My feet carry me closer, every step toward the cottage's entrance making me shake. In anger. In disgust. "Ten."

"I don't want to fight anymore."

"One." Her steps retreat into the house, reminding me of a frightened rodent without an out. And I'm the cat in this scenario, kicking down the door with enough force that the wood shatters—the splinters flying across the room and one piece in particular embedding in her back.

She won't die, but it does hurt.

"No…please. I'll disappear."

"You will," I say, stepping over the threshold while the others stay outside. Not even Theo can be in the room, as we agreed. He wasn't happy with it, but understood I needed to unleash my anger without distractions, and he is a very potent one. They also know to not interfere, no matter the circumstance. "I want you to regret your birth. To hate your father."

Anger flashes in her eyes at the mention of him. "Don't."

"Don't what? Call him out for being a piece of shit who treated women as commodities, trophies to own and use at his discretion?" Her features harden, lip curling over her much smaller fangs. "Does that hurt? Having it shoved in your face that he didn't love you, or is it that he used you as a way to further his own agenda?"

"Shut. Up," she seethes, her claws extending. "He loved us. He took care of us."

My tinkling laugh fills the small cottage. "He wanted to sell you to the highest bidder. The problem was that who he wanted had no interest in you. Theo always saw you as weak and superficial, Elise. Just another social-climbing whore who tried and failed to take what's mine."

"I'm going to kill you."

"Like I snapped your daughter's neck or how Theo murdered your son?"

"You bitch!" she lunges, going for my head, but I sidestep her. I'm faster. Stronger. Her body flies past me and hits the wall where the fireplace is, shattering the mantle.

"Is that the best you have?"

"You're dead."

I don't bother to answer, because technically, I already am. Instead, I crouch and take notice of her foot placement. Elise leans heavily on the right, and when she jumps to tackle me, I kick out her leg, forcing her to fall into a split. Then, I'm on her and use a trick I picked up from watching Theodore dismember Detective Consuelos.

Digging my new claws in, I tear through her flesh and twist, breaking the bone and tossing her leg behind me. "Ouch. That does look painful." Her whimper is a sweet little melody that I want more of, and I tear the other in the same manner. "Do you remember that day outside the café when you backhanded me, threatening to do more than that?"

"Please stop. You won."

"I'm going to return the favor." At my words, she tries to crawl away, but I reaffirm my position, dodging her hands as they come for my face. However, she's not as fast and I have a chunk of her face in my hand before she can scream.

Her right cheek and half her lips are gone and blood seeps from the wounds: the same area she hit when I was defenseless.

Then again on her chest, exposing the muscles and ligaments below.

She might be a hybrid, but her human side is stronger in this instance than her vampire.

She'll die like one.

Elise lays limp beneath me now, no fight left as the puddle beneath her grows.

"You once told me I was weak. Not worthy." My fingers crawl over her exposed flesh toward her neck. Slowly. Meticulously, while also hoping she'd fight back. Elise doesn't though. Instead, she shows me the scared girl she's always been. "You could've had a beautiful life alongside your family. Watched them grow, have kids of their own, and now there will be no legacy left behind. Your name will be erased, and the last name Veltross dies with you."

With that, I sink my nails in and tear out her throat, watching as the last of her life's essence stains the ground and her breathing becomes shallow. Her heart stops beating. Her eyes are now lifeless, and I finally breathe out with peace settling into my bones.

Her death means a new beginning.

No more fighting. No more threats.

"Mortem," I whisper low, my bloody hands touching the ground as I push the last tendrils of her energy toward death. She will no longer be of this world. She can no longer return.

I have no idea how long I sit here, lost in thought, when two strong hands lift me into a warm embrace. He will always be the right temperature to me. "Are you okay, pretty girl?"

His eyes are so warm. They hold so much love, and I cup his cheek with my blood-drenched hand and pull his mouth down to mine, kissing him with every bit of the love I hold for this wonderful man.

"I am." And it's the truth. I have my family back.

He may be a killer, but so am I.

He may be obsessed with me, but my need to possess might surpass his.

"And now?"

"And now…" another peck, a small bite to his bottom lip "…now we celebrate. I have over a hundred years of catching up to do, but tonight…tonight is for us."

"For us?"

"Yes." At my words, his eyes become hooded and the tips of his fangs poke through his upper lip. "I have a king to spoil and a cock to ride."

"Good girl."

QUEEN
Gabriella

Every person inside the room stops the moment we step through the gallery's doors. They're watching. They're murmuring amongst themselves about my coming out, and it's hard to keep the smile from my blood-red lips.

Theodore's hand on the small of my back tenses a bit, his muscles coiling as one man in particular looks me up and down, lingering on the low neckline of my Venetian-style dress with a dip in the front that stops at my belly button.

It's sexy while classy. White to symbolize the innocence he adored about my humanity in this life.

It also shows off my tattoo; a similar piece to that of my king's that encompasses from sternum to just above my mound. The dark wings of an angel stretch—are open in all their glory while adorned with beads of crystals and pearls. Yet, the focal point is a large red ruby which hangs from the longest necklace and stops a few inches from my clit.

The only color on my pale skin.

Just like Theo's tattoo appeared when he took the throne, mine came the day he bit me. The day my mate gave me back my life.

"Down, love. The show first..." I trail off while turning toward him, my hand skimming down the front of his black dress shirt with the top two buttons undone. I flick each onyx stud on my way to the waistband of his slacks, then finger his Cartier belt with the gold buckle. "But after, you can do as you please while I help Tero and Marcia after my parents' visit."

"Such a lovely couple," he remarks, knowing my punishment will outweigh his. A public death in the name of art. They fought me on this, cried and begged for their lives, but my heart held no empathy for two people who used a defenseless child for monetary gain. "Aren't you glad I had your birth certificate tampered with when they gave you up? You could've been Hilary Burgess."

"That they are, and yes. That name doesn't suit me one bit." The bold red carpet we walk through has security on both sides, preventing the press from coming closer. Each of them wears the emblem of the vampire monarchy, a golden pin across the right lapel of their all-black tuxes. Both male and female, they stand straight while looking ahead with serious postures and a bit of hunger on their faces.

They won't attack, though.

Not tonight. Never in a public event.

The clear path leads to a set of wide, white marble stairs that leads to the upper floors, and no one moves until we reach the very last step and into my exhibit. Every square inch is bathed in black, the few light sources coming from the glass dome ceilings and the strategically placed soft white lighting above each piece.

The perfect mixture of innocence and sin.

Light and the dark.

The two marry together in a way that sends chills down the

spines of those who have seen the final product. Because I'm not hiding who I am anymore.

He embraces me as is, and I do the same.

Every piece, the paintings I did while human of an unknown man, fills the different areas side by side with its sinful counterpart in animal form.

My king's reign.

Tero's deadly poise.

Marcia's strike.

Meera's knowledge.

Elise's greed.

Isabella's sight.

My touch.

We are the seven deadly sins, and I've embraced my truth. Hold it close to my heart because it is a part of me. I won't deny it. Us.

What home will always mean.

A round of applause rings throughout the room as those with V.I.P. access watch us walk toward the main stage. They're looking at me, then Theo, sensing something's off but they can't put their fingers on it. Instead, they celebrate my interpretations while behind two glass enclosures a familial set of predators awaits.

Marcia, my beautiful girl, has been given a treat along with her brother. A meal. Their favorite kind.

Their individual sizes vary, with Tero being the largest, making the choice easy.

Theodore steps toward the mic and the room grows quiet; if a pin dropped, it would be heard.

"Thank you all for coming out tonight in support of my talented wife." Applauses grow louder, the confirmation of our relationship I'm sure will make the front-page news of some magazine in the next few hours, but I could care less. "Please enjoy the show with an open mind. Her interpretations of the seven deadly sins are incredible, and I hope you imbibe in a bit of the macabre with us tonight."

The covers are removed from the glasses and the audience gasps at the brutal scene.

Two beasts.

My favorite snakes are in rare form, letting go and feeding. It reminds me of the yellow anaconda display that Theo took me to where I watched the beautiful animal feed. They've already broken down their victims.

Marcia was given my human mother.

Tero, my father.

They've already killed each, one by suffocation and the other by envenomation before the crowd could fully see what they'd be digesting. I might have a disturbing mind, but I won't expose my kind to the idiocy of humanity.

A part of me admires them after living amongst them.

Tero's jaws are unlocked, his bloodied cage a mess as he swallows my father head first, the carnage left behind from the kill making his body unrecognizable. Too much blood mixed with the low lighting only let the audience see what we want them to.

Marcia's cage is much the same. My mother was already swallowed, leaving behind the giant bloat on my special girl's stomach where her meal is.

The applause that thunders in the room is deafening, the ground shaking, and I smile toward the crowd. They love what they see. They have no idea that they've just witnessed the murder of two of their own, and yet, I'd bet money that some wouldn't care either way.

After a bit, when both snakes lay in contented bliss, the crowd disperses to walk the rest of the room. The murmur of people inquiring about purchasing a few doesn't surprise me, but the sight of Xadiel standing in the middle of the room, his face etched with worry, freezes me in place.

"Xadiel," I call out, voice too low for the humans, but everyone else hears and are on alert. "You guys didn't let us know you were coming?" His features tighten at the word *them*. Him and my sister. "Where is she? I don't smell her?"

"Gabriella, she's…I don't—"

"Where. Is. She?" Dread fills my veins, and Theo beside me tenses.

"She's gone."

"Gone?" Theo pulls me down the stage, not stopping until I'm standing in front of a man whose suffering is palpable. "Xadiel, what's going on. Whatever it is, we'll help—"

"She's gone, Gabby. Isabella disappeared, and I can't find her."

Outtake
THEODORE ASTOR

There's a change in me the moment I step inside the castle, an overwhelming hunger that pulls a deep rumble from my chest as an intoxicating scent infiltrates my senses. It's sweet—so fucking alluring—and I follow it to my private wing.

Every vampire in the palace has made themselves scarce; I can still hear the whimpers of many as they ran from me, and the low warning growls escaping the back of my throat. And they're completely right in doing so because the volatile emotions rushing through me will blind me.

My mate is here, and jealousy is an unpredictable emotion. I will kill without remorse if anyone were to come near her.

Every muscle in my body—every single molecule in my vampiric DNA accepts her—and I don't pause until I'm outside my bedroom door.

It's then I make out her heartbeat. This *thump, thump, thump* that lulls me into a state of serenity I've never experienced before. That I don't know how to feel about. It's confusing yet intriguing and I'm hungry for a taste of the woman responsible.

"Motherfuck," I hiss out, rubbing a hand over my thick cock—pressing down hard enough to alleviate the uncontrollable need to mount her, but it only serves to make it worse. So much fucking worse when I hear her take in a deep breath of her own, pulling me into her small lungs and letting out a breathy sigh.

Such a sweet little sound. So perfect.

Then, there's the shift in my mattress, the small rustling of sheets I can clearly hear, and I'm barging in without a second thought. The door slams against the wall, her plump mouth lets out a squeak, and her head turns toward me.

The second I see her face I'm done for.

Nothing fucking matters.

I'll live and breathe for my pretty girl.

* * *

GABRIELLA

"Pompous, arrogant jerk," I grumble, stealthily walking the hall toward the vampire king's bedroom. "Like I don't have better things to do than come and kick his butt."

The palace seems empty today, and I'm wondering what poor kingdom is feeling the wrath of his search. He's been looking for me. Plowing through small covens in search of mine, although we're in plain sight.

That alone lets me know that he's trying to catch me off guard. That if caught, I'd be taken against my will, and I won't let others suffer for his greed.

His room is closed when I reach it and I don't hesitate to step inside, closing the large wooden door behind me. The first thing I notice is his scent; it permeates the room and calms my nerves, settling at the core of me, and I find myself liking it.

Then, it's the size of the room and the bland décor.

Not a single trace of femininity anywhere.

"What makes you tick, Theodore Astor?" I ask myself, taking a seat on his bed while nearly sinking into the plush bedding. "What would it take for you to—"

The bedroom door is slammed open and a large man steps inside, his warning snarl loud. The walls shake, and I let out a whimper. Not in fear, but for some reason, it makes my skin prickle with excitement.

"Who are you?" Theodore asks, his voice low and tone a bit gravelly. It licks at my skin, an illicit caress while the blade of his sword glints in the low light. "Why are you in my bedroom?"

"You've been looking for me," I state simply, my hand slowly moving toward the small holster at my side where my knife hides. "So here I am."

"Have I?" he asks, not fully stepping into the light. He's in shadow, but those amber eyes glow and his strong build is mouthwatering. "What's your name, pretty girl."

"Come a little closer and I'll tell you." There's no mistaking my breathy tone nor the way I cross my legs, the skirt of my dress parting at the split revealing the side of my thigh and lower. Moreover, he follows the move with hunger, his chest expanding as he takes in a deep breath. "This conversation needs to be face to face."

In a flash, he's kneeling at my feet, his hands on the bed trapping me while my knife is at his throat. If he's surprised, he doesn't show it nor does he try to disarm me. "Can you tell me now, my queen? I need to know my mate's name."

"Mate?" I ask, the blade digging a little deeper, an action that hurts me. "You're mine?"

Is that why my heart is beating fast?

Is this why my palms are sweaty?

Is this why I find his dark, black hair and amber eyes so sexy and the thought of hurting him makes me feel sick?

Mates are a special thing, a gift, and there's no denying the need you feel. It's all consuming and sudden and unforgiving as you give yourself without pause or consequence. A few words and your world changes, an instant love that gives your life true meaning.

"I'm yours." His smile is beautiful and the look in his eyes so soft, a complete contradiction to the man who's been pillaging in his search for me. Threatening covens under my family's protection, terrorizing them into telling him where I am while failing at every turn.

They're loyal to us. They'd never sell me.

But how can he—this vampire—be my mate?

"And you've been looking for me." At my words, spoken low and a bit sultry, his eyes snap from my lips to my eyes, widening as they sink in.

"Gabriella?"

"Theodore."

The minutes pass and neither of us speak, lost in our thoughts. However, it's his hand on my cheek that calms me just when I think it's better that I run. It's the feel of his lips on my neck and the arms around my waist that anchor me as the knife slips from my fingertips, clanging on the floor.

So simple each touch, but from your mate—the one person made for you—it gives your soul purpose.

"I'm sorry," he says it so low I almost don't hear it, but I do, and a shuddering breath escapes me. This is the last thing I expect from the proud king, but right now he's humbling himself while the sword he held moments ago is now astride my lap. An offering. "You are the lesson I needed to learn, Gabriella Moore. My life is yours."

"Theo, I—"

"Say it again." His purr-like rumble tickles, creates a vibration through me that makes me laugh. "Please."

"Since when does a king beg?" I ask, and this flirtatious side of me is new. And so is the way I clench at the sight of his harsh swallow—the delicious way his throat bobs with the action.

He pulls back so I can meet his eyes. See the sincerity in them. "Since the moment I laid eyes on you."

A blush spreads across my cheeks, and I bite my bottom lip. "Does this mean you'll stop hurting innocent people?"

"This means my life is yours to command, pretty girl."

"That's a hard offer to deny, Mr. Astor…"

"Then don't." He lifts me with ease, tucking me against his chest while seating me on his lap. We're on the floor, his body cradling mine, while those lips kiss from the crown of my head to temple. "Let me love you. Let me be the one you lean on."

"You've hurt my people."

"And I will make the reparations necessary." With the tip of two fingers, he nudges my head so we're eye to eye. His lips hover, and I can taste him there. His natural sweetness is a tease to my senses. "Let me spend an eternity making you happy."

"What will it cost me?"

"Your heart, and in return, I'll give you all of me."

THE END FOR NOW. . .

SERIES ORDER:
LITTLE LIES
LITTLE MATE
HALF TRUTHS: THEN
HALF TRUTHS: NOW
OMISSION PART ONE
OMISSION PART TWO

SPIN-OFFS:
COME TO ME
THE HUNT

The Beautiful Sinner Series are all interconnected standalones full of suspense and romance and an OTT alpha willing to burn the world to the ground for the woman he loves! It's sexy and has an edge of darkness that will leave you breathless! #MAFIAROMANCE

Now Live!
SIN #1
COVET #2
MINE #3
YOURS #4
RISQUE #5
OWN #6

Beautiful Sinner Spin-Off:
CORRUPT
MY SINFUL VALENTINE
SAVAGE KISS
ONE RULE

ABOUT THE AUTHOR

Elena M. Reyes is the epitome of a Floridian and if she could live in her beloved flip-flops, she would.

As a small child, she was always intrigued by all forms of art: whether it was dancing to island rhythms, or painting with any medium she could get her hands on. Her passion for reading over the years has amassed her with hours of pleasure, but it wasn't until she stumbled upon fanfiction that her thirst to write overtook her world.

She's a short and sassy Latina with an adorable pup, a kiddo that keeps her on her toes, and a husband who claims she'll cause him to go bald prematurely. Lol

Want to keep up to date with Elena's crazy book life?